EASY MONEY

Habent Sua Fata Libelli

Manhanset House
Shelter Island Hts., New York 11965-0342
bricktower@aol.com • NewPulpPress.com

The New Pulp Press colophon is a trademark of
J. T. Colby & Company, Inc.

Library of Congress Cataloging-in-Publication Data
White, Robert
Easy Money
p. cm.
      1. FICTION / Mystery & Detective / Hard-Boiled.
      2. FICTION / Thrillers / Suspense.
      3. FICTION / Noir.
      Fiction, I. Title.
ISBN: 978-1-955036-51-1 Trade Paper
Copyright © 2025 by Robert T. White
Electronic compilation/ paperback edition
copyright © 2025 by New Pulp Press

October 2025

EASY MONEY

Robert White

Also by Robert White

Thomas Haftmann, Private Eye
Thomas Haftmann (#1)

Nocturne For Madness
Thomas Haftmann (#2)

Saraband For A Runaway
Thomas Haftmann (#3)

Doggerel for Dead Whores, A Thomas Haftmann Novel
Thomas Haftmann (#4)

Haftmann's Rules
Thomas Haftmann (#5)

Thomas Haftmann, P.I. —The Dearborn Terrorist
Thomas Haftmann (#6)

Burning Girl
2nd Place Winner, Whodunit competition

Available from
NewPulpPress.com

For Shirrell Rhodes

Table of Contents

Part 1

"The most dangerous dog is a wounded dog."

—proverbial saying

Chapter 1
Northtown, Ohio

I was washing off the mud when I got fired. My ankles were sore inside my work boots from slipping into ruts gouged by the crane's tractor treads all week. The rain made everything worse, and I was feeling ragged from another bout of insomnia, a self-inflicted curse from doing time a few years ago. Some cons learn to sleep twenty hours a day. I thought I could leave that habit behind when I moved north, but it came up with me. Like the past. It's a beat-up suitcase you never leave it behind. Thing is, you leave nothing behind.

That morning, Gerald, our tall, black supervisor, crooked a finger at me as soon as I punched in. He told me I was working with Angelo again out back in the scrapyard.

"C'mon, Gerald. Stick somebody else with that guy. He's a crane cowboy. He nearly dropped a refrigerator on me two days ago when you were off."

Gerald's dialysis kept him shuttling between the hospital and the auto salvage. He never complained, never lost his temper.

"I heard about that, Wade. Angelo says you was the one at fault on that."

"The guy in the crane has the responsibility, Gerald. I'm not a monkey. I can't be climbing on a mountain of junk cars and watching him, too."

"I know, I know. Just see if you can get along with him one more day. I'll put somebody else on with him tomorrow."

He wanted me to remove a truck transmission from an '89 Western Star lying midway in a stack of junked cars. Donnie Perdue was walking by at the time and he had his big ears out, listening to Gerald. Miming my stutter, Donnie said, "G-Good luck with Z-Zorro."

Angelo's other nickname; he was the owner's nephew, too, which made matters worse. On Halloween, Angelo had dressed up as the masked figure in black outfit with cape and sword. He rented a white stallion and galloped down Lake Avenue waving his sword. Traffic was jammed at the light, people stopped in the middle of the road to watch the spectacle, and the horse got spooked. It flipped Zorro onto the street on his back. Anyone else would have been in a wheelchair with a spinal cord injury, or at least traction for months, not Angelo.

He operated the crane, a privilege he reserved for himself despite the fact he was no more qualified to be in that cab than a balloon-blowing goat. A former football star in high school and a stud in his own mind, though married, he thought the world owed him constant adulation and a good living to boot. The man I replaced was killed in an accident when a car rolled over on top of him. No surprise, Ange was operating the claw the day when it happened. He had no more respect for that machine than a kid with an arcade claw. Once the cops finished their investigation, and declared it an accident instead of involuntary manslaughter, he could breathe easily again. He cracked jokes about it in the yard with Donnie, who, like me, was a ridge runner except his folks had been here longer.

Donnie liked to show off for Ange, act the tough guy. He was no different from the cons who tittie-bumped new fish in the yard to see what they'd do about it. My cousin Kenny did time in a max-con prison. Me, I was lucky. Denmar Correctional was a soft joint for first-time felons. Many of the inmates were college-educated, bagged up for white-collar crimes like check kiting and corruption. After two weeks on the job, I told him to knock it off when I heard him mocking me.

"W-what you g-gonna do about it, h-hillbilly?"

"I'll knock your t-teeth down your throat, and then Angelo can get some good f-fuckin' in."

That wouldn't pass for much of a threat at Denmar Correctional, with or without the stutter, which was where I first heard it, but you'd still have to scrap. It did the trick with Donnie, even though he liked to push his luck by imitating my stutter whenever he could clown for the boss' nephew.

Getting into my coveralls, I overheard Perdue saying something to Benny Rodriguez that made him laugh as they headed for the pallet trucks. Moving pallets filled with cubes of crushed aluminum and steel against the warehouse walls usually went to Don or Benny "by seniority" despite the fact we were all hired on as laborers and the place wasn't unionized. No union or union rules. Rules of any kind were scarce as fleas on eels unless Angelo, Benny, or Donnie wanted something. Pick-a-Part Salvage, as far as I could see, was a family-run business and the Bucci family made up its own rules to suit themselves and their favorite lackeys.

The salvage business was booming now that metal prices had gone up; the other part of the business was unofficial yet done out in the open because half the town was either in on it or knew about it. Tony Bucci, the boss, was a bookie who wrote down the bets coming into the shop on the pad next to the landline phone. I asked Gerald why Tony didn't use a burner like any decent lawbreaker.

"No need to. Cops'll come tell him to lie low if somebody loses big and wants to complain to the gaming commission."

West Virginia jumped into betting years ago with horse racing and casino gambling. Ohio was catching up by making sports betting legal that year. It seemed old-fashioned to call a bookie when you could go online and find a national sports book to lay down a bet. Gerald told me that Tony's book catered to degenerate gamblers he let build up a tab.

"He like a trapdoor spider, Wade," he said to me. "He watches and watches, and when the time is right, he jumps out and gobbles 'em up." If they had to sell their house instead of leaving it to their kids, too bad.

"Lots of husbands don't want their wives to know how much of their paycheck they're laying down. Tony likes to say he provides a needed service for guys that got their online accounts blocked."

I hadn't been there that long but at least once a week some stranger would pull up to the office and ask for Tony.

"They call in bets, but they come through the door," Gerald said, meaning Tony's office, "they're looking for a more time to pay off their gambling debt."

"Nice guy, Tony, huh."

Gerald's laugh sounded like a horse's nicker.

"That Tony, *shee-yit*, he just pumps up the vigorish. "It's like rich countries and poor countries. You own the debt, you own *them*."

Strutting past us, Angelo barked orders, as if he owned the place: "*Mafunculo*, Cardell. Quit fuckin' the dog, God damn it. We're not paying you two to shoot the shit."

Gerald stopped in mid-sentence; he was telling me in precise detail the best way to get that transmission. He always wore gray coveralls with his name stitched above the word *Supervisor*. He was the only one qualified on forklifts and other heavy equipment, not that he'd ever get that magnet crane away from Angelo. I liked him for two reasons: he didn't make fun of my stutter or my speech, which Angelo and others in Northtown called "hillbilly talking." And he gave me some good advice on staying safe in the yard— especially when working with "the junkyard prince" because of the way Ange lorded it over everyone. Perdue and Rodriguez called him "Mr. Big Shot" and "college boy" behind his back. Gerald never cracked a smile around Angelo; the mere sight of Angelo would set his lips in a tight grin. Angelo had gone one year to the local community college before bombing out, mainly to play basketball and baseball, and score with girls.

The day he came into the breakroom waving his letter of dismissal around, cursing the instructors, and blaming everyone but himself, Gerald snatched a peek at the letter and saw the grades— all F's and one D.

"Looks like you been concentratin' too hard on one subject, Angelo."

From that day on, Gerald landed on Angelo's shit list and remained there. I was the second one to earn a permanent slot on it, but from time to time, we'd be joined by others who had temporarily earned Ange's wrath. Rodriguez wound up on that list when Ange heard him refer to him as "Einstein." He had a sister in Puerto Rico studying to be a lawyer and knew something about earning good grades. It took Rodriguez weeks of diligent ass-licking to get his name removed.

Gerald told me Rodriguez's tongue was as tough as shoe leather by the time Ange came around and started giving him the easier tasks around the place. It sickened me to watch my fellow employees compete like trustees in a prison for the cushier jobs, as though masking a beer run for the boss' nephew was something to be proud of.

I grabbed my goggles, hard hat, and heavy gloves and ran to catch up with Angelo, who was already climbing into the cab of the crane.

Angelo didn't speak to me unless it was to give me an order. The yard had a knuckle-boom crane that was better for that job, but Angelo insisted on the magnet crane every chance he got because he could throw cars around like some kid smashing his toys. My first week on the job Perdue and Rodriguez were in the two Bobcats shoving smaller scrap into piles for crushing. I was designated "paint monkey," the one who scaled the metal piles to tag appliances with Day-Glo orange. Angelo worked behind us in the crane, which had the claw attached instead of the magnet plate.

I'd just marked a freezer when a car smashed into the top of the pile I was working on and rolled over the top of me, missing my head by inches. I kept the high-and-tight buzzcut from prison just to remind myself I never wanted to go back. I had just enough time to duck, and still, it left a slight friction burn from the force of the metal box passing over me. Then the whole stack began shifting. Next thing I know, I'm going down in an avalanche of metal junk. I made a wild, leg-swinging leap to the ground and rolled free of the refrigerators, washing machines, and stoves thundering to the ground all around me. A washing machine bounced end-over-end past my head as I lay in the dirt panting like a dog, sick to my stomach from the adrenalin jolt, spewing up a string of caramel-colored bile from the coffee I'd drunk that morning.

Angelo came down from the cab and stood over me, bellowing curses, calling me a "stupid hillbilly fuck." Donnie and Benny both had to hold him back from kicking me.

I sat up and another surge of bile came up my esophagus. I leaned over to gag and spit as much out as I could.

"You—d-did—that—on—pur-pur-purpose . . ."

I managed to get the words out; my anger made speech more difficult than normal.

By the time I'd washed up and got to the boss' office, Angelo was already inside explaining what happened. I heard "dumb hillbilly" and "asshole" several times. As I knocked, Angelo pleaded with his uncle to fire me.

"He wasn't supposed to be working on that pile," Angelo explained, eyeing me, his face suddenly expressionless, lying with convict sincerity, a thing I knew something about.

"No way could I see him from that position on the pile, Tony."

Angelo always called him "Tony," never "Uncle Tony."

"Is that right, Cardell?"

"He knew d-damn well which pile I was working."

"You stuttering, white-trash motherfucker." He repeated it in Italian, "*figlio di puttana*—"

"Ange, *Marronn'*, Jesus, Mary, shut the fuck up!"

"All I'm saying—"

"I said shut yer fuckin' mouth, Ange!"

Tony wasn't a bad boss, all in all. I could see it in his eyes. He had twin purple bags under them that always looked darker whenever his nephew caused him grief. He was grossly overweight, and from his eating habits in his office, I figured he had a heart the size of a canned ham to go with his truck-driver's ass.

Tony swiveled in his chair to glare at me, mumbled in Italian, and said, "Wade, you know better. You keep that operator aware of your position at all times under the crane . . ."

Angelo sprinkled his speech with Italian, mostly cussing, like his uncle: *facia de merda* and *bafangu chooch*. I used to wonder why it was only my language they made fun of.

"Angie, *ritardato*, shut the fuck up, will ya, for Chrissake."

The two of them gabbled at each other in a mix of broken English, Italian cuss words. Angelo looked fierce at me, until I turned around and walked out. My heart hammered in my chest and my hands shook. If I lost this job, I'd be back in the hills and mixed up in the same criminal shit that got me sent away for two years.

It took all morning to free the transmission. I don't know how many tons of metal I had poised on top of me the whole time I was on my back. My coveralls were ripped from jagged edges snagging my coveralls every time I shifted position. I kept a sharp eye out on Angelo the whole time. Finally, we used a harness to pull it free and lower it to the truck bed.

I was washing up when Tony came in to tell me I was done. I looked at him behind me in the cracked, pockmarked mirror—a stubby man with a pot belly and those unhealthy purple halfmoons under his eyes. Perdue said Tony's "mad face" was the same color as the head of his cock when he made his "German soldier" march.

"I'm sorry about this, Wade, you know, but I got no choice," Tony said. "I really don't. The business just ain't been good lately. I can't carry this many full-time workers."

"What about Angelo?" I asked him, not expecting anything. "He's pure dead weight but you carry him."

He shifted nervously from one foot to the other, getting angry.

"Family, Cardell," he said. "You know that. You're last hired, first fired."

Those magical union rules that appeared whenever Tony r Ange wanted them. When people go to stick it to you, they're going to find some lame-ass saying to give *them* comfort, never mind how you might feel.

I could have said more, but it would have come to the same thing. Truth was, he treated me fair, paid me on time, even if the money was diddly squat, as we say back home. Tony was on a shorter leash than me. He puffed and wheezed all day long, sometimes twelve hours, around the yard or at the scales. He never missed a call or failed to show at the scales every time some "pop can pirate" staggered through the doors with 50 cents' worth of cans in a garbage bag or some transient from the high-rises downtown clutching some copper tubing, Venetian blinds, or a strips of aluminum siding he'd just ripped off from an abandoned house. Tony Bucci wasn't going to be around long. I pitied him his short leash. The Grim Reaper would harvest him someday soon, and I knew I wouldn't get a day's work in after the funeral once Zorro took charge.

He plunked down my last wages on the edge of the sink in grimy bills. He walked away muttering and making his usual noises. Like a tired old bull worn down by life. He didn't wish me luck, not that I had any to spare; it wouldn't have made me feel better if he had.

Gerald stepped up to me as I left the office. He shook my hand and wished me good luck.

"Don't let this get you down none, Wade. You'll be fine."

Donnie and Benny were sitting outside on the stone wall taking their lunch break when I came out. I had my extra coveralls, spare socks, and tee-shirts in a garbage bag full of rips from cans some veteran scrapper had left behind when he sold off his cans.

"Ha, man, I hear you just got shit-canned," Perdue said.

"You have anything to say about that, Donnie?"

"Nope. That Angelo's a fuckhead."

"How 'bout you, Benny?"

"Ange, he did you, man. He did you good."

Benny jumped up to mime a man energetically fornicating doggie-style.

"Tony got a call from his sister yesterday. She screamin' at him, like, O man, you could hear it down the street! Her baby boy Ange. I was outside the office when she called."

It didn't surprise me Tony got the work out of me before he fired me.

"Where's Zorro at, by the way?"

"Where the hell you think? He's riding his favorite toy. Handles that machine like it's his bitch. . . . Hey, hey, where you goin'?"

Something told me not to keep going that way for my own good. I should have listened to Gerald's calming advice. Trouble is, I had too many years behind me of avoiding what that voice said. I made a beeline for the back where a junk car was being hoisted aloft in the grabber's hooks like a stunned rat in an owl's talons. The boom swung, the car hovered over a small hill of other junk cars, and then dropped as the claws opened.

"Hey, Angelo!"

He couldn't hear me but he saw me approach. . . . Then: *That same shitty-grinnin' smirk.*

I could tell even through the safety glass he was pleased for getting me canned.

Spotting loose rebar in a nearby pile of concrete chunks, I came up with it in my hand and in one motion heaved it at the cab. Angelo flinched as the steel bar clanged off the top of the cab, cracking the glass of the cage, and ricocheting off.

Hard to see through the windshield glare, but I could tell I'd stunned him. Then he turned angry. He recovered, grabbed two levers, and jerked the big claw into motion. The boom and attached cage swiveled around toward me, the massive claw swung back and forth like a pendulum. His jerky movements in the cab made him lose control. The crane lurched forward, its steel treads pulverizing the ground, mud spewing everywhere from the sprockets for traction.

By then, I'd grabbed a couple more rods and circled away from the swinging claw.

David versus Goliath—

I wasn't feeling as cocky now. My footing in the churned-up mud slowed me as I tried to gauge distance. I wasn't wearing my work boots and the mud was so thick I was afraid it would suck the shoes off my feet.

The crane's hydraulic engine screamed, big plumes of blue exhaust rose up behind the cab. Angelo swiveled to track me and then he jerked the claw up high. I'd be smashed into the filth when he released it.

He's going to kill me for throwing that bar . . .

I lost my footing whirling to get out of the way and did a face plant. Turning my head, I saw the claw's fingers open directly above me. I rolled, terrified. The claw hit the ground and shook the earth feet from where I'd stopped rolling. Angelo disengaged the holding brake—it acted like a wheel chock to prevent the claw from dropping randomly. That second's worth of hesitation saved my life. I rolled as far from those massive steel fingers as I could before he recovered control. Just swinging the sheer tonnage of the claw's weight at me could crush me like a bug.

Jumping to my feet on firmer ground, I caught a glimpse of Angelo's face. I was surprised to discover I was still gripping a rod in my hand. I reared back and threw it from no more than ten feet. It spun through the air, whistling end over end, and speared a hole into the glass like a bullet hole.

Right where his head was.

My cousin Kenny, a streetfighter, taught me some things in brawls. I had his voice in my head: *Don't stand there looking at him once you get him on the ground* . . . I looked around for another bar to fling. Then a high-pitched scream like a fox in a leghold trap split the air above the din of the crane's motor.

Angelo lurched out of the cab, walking in a stumbling, herky-jerky motion, like a cartoon figure goose-stepping off a cliff in midair. He dropped straight down, did a belly flop into the muck beside the tractor treads. Scrabbling to his feet, clawing mud between his fingers, he stood finally, wobbling like a toddler, his face streamed blood from his forehead. It poured off his chin. For a long, crazy second, I thought he was going to charge me, as dumb as that sounds. I didn't realize how badly injured he was at the moment. A soft moan turned into a wail like some cop cruiser's Doppler effect. Then Angelo took an uncertain step forward, tilted backward, and dropped straight down to the muddy earth.

I stood frozen, watching, unable to think what to do. Part of me wanted to run, part wanted to help him. Then he started to paddle in the mud with his hands, slapping at it blindly, slithering—but making no progress forward. All my anger and fear dissolved as I watched his weird dog paddle in the slop go nowhere fast.

When he made it to hard ground again, he rose, dripping blood and mud; then he staggered to the back doors of the warehouse. Mud the color of baby shit was stuck to his body from his hair to his boots. He looked back once. Maybe he saw me, maybe not. He groped at the door, flung it open, and stumbled inside.

I never saw him again.

How long I stood there like some hypnotized dummy, I don't recall. I heard a commotion behind me, turned around to see Perdue running and shouting. From that distance, his face wasn't clear, so I looked around for more rebar. Maybe I had to fight him, too. I thought: *He wants to play hero for Tony Bucci.* Donnie was older, forty pounds heavier. Like me, he was from hill country—only Tennessee. Our friendship was brief; it cooled soon after I was hired because I wasn't willing to act like his stooge, lend him money, cover him when he was too drunk to go in to work. I needed most of my money to send home to my mother who was sick from cancer.

Coming closer, seeing the steel rod hanging from my hand, although whether I would have used it was another matter, he slowed down to a trot. Walking up, both hands up, palms out, his face suddenly widened in a grin. I remember that I stared at a missing incisor, that dog tooth he lost in a bar fight at Jefferson-on-the-Lake last summer. The bug-eyed Rodriguez trailed just behind.

"Better run for it, bro," Donnie said. "I'll tell Tony you went off in the other direction."

I dropped the rebar and ran.

In a way, I haven't stopped yet.

* * *

Chapter 2

The apartment I rented at the Imperial Arms on Lake Avenue was flanked by a BP gas station and a pizza parlor, a known haven for Northtown's drug addicts and dealers.

Every other car that passed me trotting down the sidewalk had a gander at my appearance—smeared in filth, not as badly as Angelo stumbling into the back of the warehouse but a spectacle at any time of day. I walked fast, sprinted across the street until I was breathless, wheezing like Tony hoisting himself from his chair. My stomach in knots, I didn't know if Angelo dropped dead inside the warehouse or stumbled to Tony's office and called the police. Before I was hallway back, I heard a siren screaming north on Lake. That meant little because Northtown's only hospital was a half-dozen blocks from the salvage yard.

Getting inside my apartment without being spotted wasn't easy because of the time of day. Few residents worked, most were welfare on SSI disability. Single mothers predominated, most with biracial children and boyfriends they had to hide from caseworkers making unscheduled visits. My next-door neighbor was a 30-year-old single male receiving $770 every month from the government; he spent most of it on dope. He said he didn't work because he was bipolar. I told him he was "bipolar lazy."

Had it been nightfall, the parking lot and most of the apartments near mine would be full of noise from people coming and going—babies crying inside, unattended children wandering the halls, teens hanging out vaping in the parking lot. The resident druggies always slept late, their dealers, however, were early risers prowling the lot like pigeons looking for scraps. I had some insight into how it all worked from dealing back home with my cousin. West Virginia, to quote a preacher I heard on the radio was a state "besotted with opioid addicts," he said to his listening audience. I'd relocated addresses to a new state, hoping for a new start after my incarceration, but I hadn't improved my lot in life.

I stripped as though my clothes were on fire, headed straight to my chest of drawers, and grabbed everything I needed for traveling and sleeping rough. My Levi's were still damp. I had no other clean pants except for work and those were grease-spotted and torn from climbing around rusty junk. I stuffed all of it, including the shoebox containing the cash I'd saved from my last three months' wages, into the duffel bag I brought north.

I used to switch burner phones like someone changing socks. I couldn't afford a cell phone on my wages. The last resident of my apartment, angered about his bail revocation, damaged the place on his way out the door; he even removed the flush plate from the wall and snipped the wires where the landline phone went. With my earthly goods stuffed into the duffel bag and a backpack, I hit the refrigerator for a quart of milk and half an orange. Casting a final look around, I remembered my bible next to some used handbooks on mechanics and electricity, two paperbacks on resume writing and computers, both with *FOR DUMMIES* on the front covers.

Tossing the apartment keys on the kitchen counter, I bolted for the back stairs and the outer door to the parking lot. A police cruiser wheeled into the lot from Lake Avenue. That wasn't unusual. The Northtown paper claimed cops made a couple hundred calls to the place every year.

Hard to say why now, knowing what happened from that moment to this. I experienced a rush in my chest, a feeling of exhilaration. My revenge and the escape reminded me of those past thrills of easy money and close calls back in Clarksburg running with my cousin Kenny. Living on the edge was something I thought

I'd put behind me. The second I picked up that rebar, I knew I hadn't straightened out. My past was two inches from my forehead. I didn't linger once those two cops buzzed their way inside.

Thoughts tumbled in my head as I hoofed it from the apartment toward Ohio Avenue behind the building. I had no plan in mind, no place to run to. I knew few people in Northtown beyond the ones I saw every day at work or passed in the street. I don't make friends easily because of my stutter; it made people uneasy. Going back home was my first instinct, but Clarksburg might as well have been on the Moon from where I was at the time. With little money in my pants, no clear direction other than to put distance between me and the cops, I was walking fast right into the maw of those random forces that possess you when you lose control.

I turned onto 13th Street, cars passed coming and going from Lake Avenue, a major street in Northtown harbor. Pedestrians didn't stand out. No more sirens since that one. I kept going west, head down. Single males with backpacks on foot or bike, even packing folded tents, wasn't that abnormal a sight now. The same drugs that blighted life back home had crept north and you saw it in the transients, the vacant stares and twitches of people walking aimlessly around town, hanging out in public parks, and libraries.

In a curious way, I felt at peace. I'm not violent by nature like my cousin Kenny. His daddy got tired of my aunt's neglectful ways and tried his hand at bank robbing in Chattanooga. He wound up doing twenty-five to life in Brushy Mountain. Last I heard from family back home, he had words with an Aryan Brotherhood member in his pod and wound up with his head caved in by a Brand enforcer with a pipe. The men on my father's side were coal miners until the mines closed down; they either drank themselves to death or died in accidents that weren't always accidents. One of my cousins was doing life-without-parole for shot-gunning her husband while he slept.

I kept walking, confused, thinking about my family and the black cloud that descended over us. We were expendable people. Farmers and factory workers, miners, and loggers, cannon fodder when there were wars to fight. It seemed you couldn't walk fast enough or far enough to get away from fate—whatever the pinheads who write the books call it. My cellmate at Denmar had college degrees. He didn't want to talk to me at first but he had no choice. He said there's no such thing as luck; he said it's a message in your DNA that spells out your whole life's destiny.

I was thinking of the blood pouring down Angelo's face when I reached the community college parking lot a mile up 13th. Figuring I was close to their age and didn't look all that much different from the students arriving or leaving the campus with their books and backpacks. They walked out the main doors in singles and groups, talking and laughing. Maybe some test they'd all taken together. Maybe about their plans for lunch or for their lives ahead in good careers. I envied them. Cars started up, music blared from speakers here and there. None of it country-western.

Why not? I figured. I was tired from the fats walk, confused and worried. As good a place as any to wait it out until either the cops found me or I came up with a plan to get out of this.

As I walked through the glass doors, I thought again of stooping low to pick up that rebar. One split-second's decision turned my life upside-down.

* * *

The hallway corridor flooring was composed of yellow, red, and green tiles the size of a thumbnail. I followed them to the tee that split the hallway into two more corridors. I turned right and walked down the hall to a set of double doors with a small brass plate above them etched with the word *Commons,* which puzzled me. I peeked through the glass slats the size of the food trays in my former cell; we called it a bean chute. A dozen students sat around tables talking, eating cafeteria food, reading textbooks, or studying alone. A couple tables at the front sold pastries for a student association or a club.

I walked in. No one noticed me. I chose a table near a wall that looked out onto a courtyard with an empty fountain and iron all-weather tables and chairs. No water in the fountain or umbrellas in the tables. Spring was barely underway and this far north with an open lake between America and Canada, winter wasn't giving up yet.

The plaque on the wall said it was dedicated to a former dean whose face in profile was etched into the brass. I was holding my breath in, worried a campus cop or authority figure would mistake me for the transient I resembled more than these students.

I shoved my duffel bag beneath the table and placed my bookbag on the chair beside me. Around me, a dozen bookbags rested on tables while students ate or talked among themselves. That relaxed the tension.

I'm not religious despite the fact my mother insisted I study the bible at home when I wasn't outside running around in the woods. I hated my grade school and all my teachers. She couldn't make me read the bible when I was in high school, but phrases popped into my head, especially when I got into a jam with some teacher or some student who wanted to fight me after school.

I must have spoken aloud what I thought: ". . . Moses named him Gershom, saying, 'I have become a foreigner in a foreign land.'"

"Huh? What did you say?"

She was young, nineteen or twenty, slender, a pretty face. Two bright spots in the center of each cheek probably from coming inside from the cold; her blonde curls stuck out from a woolen knit cap. I thought of a kewpie doll. I assumed she was mocking me. I was used to it from childhood.

"I was reciting something . . . from class," I lied.

"Do you always do that? Talk to yourself in public?"

Heat rose to my face. Only the tips of her hair were blonde. When she pulled off the cap, a head full of curly chestnut hair sprung loose.

A heavy-set girl with butter-blonde approached us, grabbed her by the elbow and shook it like a playful puppy.

"Come on, Niya," she said. "We have a table over there."

Niya smiled at me, shrugged her shoulders. Standing , she let the chubby girl lead her away to another table where some students had gathered. I had a grandmother, nearly blind, who hated people grabbing her by the triceps.

My heart jumped into my throat from her speaking to me. I half-expected to be confronted by a cop or a security guard with a badge, not by a pretty girl. The heavy one leading her off, looked back at me. I read her lips: "Who's the weirdo?"

Maybe not such a good idea comin inside, I thought. Tired from the walk and the adrenalin jolt, my body seemed drained of that burst of energy that got me here. The room was warm though spacious. I wanted to put my head down on the table and nod off like a couple of students here and there were doing. The salvage yard belonged to another time and place.

Resisting the urge to sleep, I got up and headed to the cafeteria counter and ordered a large black coffee.

"You pour it," a short woman at the counter said; "right there, hon. Just pour it yourself."

She nodded her head at the stacks of Styrofoam cups beside a pair of coffee pots on the counter.

I paid and returned to my table. A glance at the other table showed me I was being watched by the two girls. I concentrated on my hands to keep them encircled on the coffee cup and made a point of sipping my coffee as though I belonged there, had a test coming up I was thinking about. I turned my chair sideways to look out the reading court windows at the darkening sky. Ragged clouds scudded overhead.

Two boys came over to their table and sat down. Both sported head and facial hair. I wanted to hear what they said. I didn't know some of the big words and concepts they used but some of it sounded familiar from my conversations with my educated cellmate.

I was used to the obscenities and grunts of the salvage yard. Niya was the centerpiece of her table, the one your eyes naturally drifted to. She wanted to talk about what a professor said in class about "Maslow and self-actualizing."

"We have a test Monday, you know," she said.

The others didn't seem much interested. Four people at a table nearby all checked their cell phones at intervals. Their heads lowered to their smartphones at intervals to check emails or google like cowbirds billing to show which is the bigger bird. The two males swiped the screens, ignoring Niya's attempt to engage them with her concerns about the upcoming test.

I remembered one conversation with Harold about psychology. He told me about Jung's archetypes and Freud's theories of infant sexuality. He said I was most likely I was frustrated by my lack of formal education but as often as not, I amused Harold, my cellmate, with my ignorance. He explained infantile sexuality, the oral and anal fixations, and infantile amnesia. How a child is taught love by its mother who shapes the child's own sexuality with feelings derived from her own sexuality. It occurred to me in my eavesdropping that Maslow was pretty simple-minded compared to Freud.

The light out the windows was going grayer by the minute. Late March this far north was tricky. You could get a sunny day in the sixties followed by ice-cold winds blowing across Canada to barrel down Lake Erie from the northwest. Lake effect snow squalls, whiteouts weren't uncommon. I didn't want to leave a warm place for a hike to nowhere in the cold. The skin around my waistline was chafed from the still-damp Levi's. The longer I sat there pretending to be a student, the less I felt like one. Doing two years with a mix of white-collar criminals and first-time felons was bad enough. Going to a state penitentiary for assault with a deadly weapon was a whole other bag of worms.

I watched their table, waiting until they were about leave. I had a plan—of sorts. All at once, as if a signal had been given, they began gathering their books and putting away cell phones. I rooted around in my duffel bag for a flannel shirt to go over my tee-shirt. I'd thought about what I was going to say for the past couple of minutes. As soon as Niya lifted her face to look at me as I approached, I lost what I'd mentally practiced and began my familiar stuttering.

"Hel-lo, again. M-mind if I ask you'ns a question?"

Shit, fuck—meant to say 'you' there . . . my hillbilly talk could undo me—

"Sure," Niya said. "What is it?"

They were all aware of the slip. The heavy-set girl elbowed the boy next to her, snickered, *"You'ns*—what is that?"

The boys exchanged a look with her.

"Lynne, be nice."

"My friend's in class r-right n-now," I stammered, feeling the flush creeping up my neck. "H-he's sup-supposed to d-drive me. I need to leave right now. I heard you say you—you—you were heading that way."

Lynne giggled some more, mimicked me with a *you-you-you* at the same boy. She cursed like a man and used words I never heard before. Inwardly I writhed, but I had the discipline to ignore it. My home in West Virginia might be a short drive away but people my age up here seemed crude, disrespectful, and full of contempt for anything they didn't find online or explained in *Wikipedia*. I had nothing to lose.

"Do you mind if I b-b-bum a ride that way?"

Lynne covered her mouth in an exaggerated attempt to stifle laughter. The boys were more discreet; one looked away. I was close enough to them now that my size intimidated. One boy had a glyph tattoo on his neck.

"We don't know you," Lynne said. "You could be a serial killer for all we know."

"I'm sorry," Niya said.

"I promise youns—you, I'm not a serial killer."

"She didn't mean that," Niya apologized.

"Who are you? I've never seen you around here."

That from the boy, with the neck tattoo. He confronted me the way boys used to on the playground. Cowbirds billing. I remembered my cellmate's fondness for theology and philosophy. The flyer on a table I'd passed announcing a room change for that class.

"My friend, he's taking a sociology class on religion."

I checked my watch. "See, I have a job interview coming up. I need to get ready for it soon."

"We look like Uber drivers," Lynne snapped.

"Lynne, My God, do you have to be so snarky?"

Cuntish was the word I had in mind for her.

"I'm really sorry but I—"

Fuck this shit, I have got to do something fast—

Reaching into my pocket, I pulled out some bills, fanned out two twenties, and placed them on the table in front of Lynne.

"Maybe you could help me out by being an Uber driver just this one time."

"C'mon, Lynne," Glyph Boy said, "You aren't a serial killer, are you, dude?"

"Shut up, Derrick," Lynne said and punched him in the bicep.

I held my breath, my eyes stayed on Niya's. Dark brown, mocha. The blonde frosting at the tips aside, she was born elsewhere. Olive-complected, maybe Italian or Middle Eastern, a hooked nose that might have embarrassed at puberty the way my stammer did me. Shyness finally overcome when the butterfly revealed itself from the cocoon. In my case, no cocoon but a fanatical weight lifting combined with my growth spurt at fifteen that left me just under six foot. An outsider like me.

"OK," Niya said.

Lynne squealed, scooped up the bills.

* * *

The five of us piled into a teal Subaru Forester. The duffel bag warranted an uneasy look from Lynne while I stowed it in the back. I could tell she wanted to ask me about it.

"Don't worry," I said. "No weapons or bombs. Just clothes, shoes, a book."

"*A* book . . . only one?" Niya asked me.

"Bible."

"Oh."

Lynne almost choked on her laugh.

"D-Don't w-worry, I won't try to c-convert you."

"You a born-again Christian? One of those bible-thumpers come around the college every spring?" Glyph Boy asked me.

"No," I said. "A keepsake from my mother when I left home. She thought I might need it up here with you people."

"Us *people*?"

"She believed demons walked the earth and took human forms."

I meant it as a joke. No one laughed. Niya kept her eyes on the road and didn't join in the conversation. Lynne did most of the talking—silly, adolescent prattle, social media gossip. I wondered what college was doing for her. No one in my family got an education past high school. My older relatives quit after grammar school to work.

They talked all the way to Ninevah Road. Music, films or Netflix series, students, and professors liked, "loved," didn't like. Another world, not mine. Glyph Boy tried to include me in the conversation swirling around "serial killers," but my stutter kicked in. I stared out the window. I had other things on my mind—mainly, how badly was Angelo Bucci hurt? Was he in surgery in the hospital? How close were the cops?

Niya turned to ask me where I wanted to be dropped. My only thought to that point was getting out of Northtown and lying low in Jefferson-on-the-Lake, a resort town where transients weren't unusual. Most of the businesses closed until Memorial Day but a few bars and motels stayed open year-round. I'd figure out a next move from there. I named some bar that served beer and fried foods on the Strip. I'd been there with Donnie Perdue.

If you grew up in West Virginia, your vision constricts. It's all up and down, hills and hollers—not many flat spaces. If you're in a car and you get a straight road, you gun it for all your engine's worth. Taking an icy curve with a 300-foot drop a few feet from the shoulder would be a thrill ride to these kids. Lake Erie's shoreline lay a hundred feet away in a drop down sheer sandstone bluffs. White gulls flashed in spirals in a column of light breaking through the clouds drifting past. The sky opened up in ragged patches of washed-out blue the same color as the water. I imagined the skyscraper-sized glaciers that lumbered down from the pole to carve out that shallowest of the Great Lakes ten-thousand years ago. The surface of Lake Erie looked like an old mirror shined to a dull polish. A lakeboat going uplakes created an optical illusion; it floated past my window in mid-air. Only a tiny curl of bow wave broke the illusion.

Lynne was an annoying, nonstop chatterbox—an empty-headed girl with no serious thoughts in her head and a voice had that adopted that irritating lilt Midwestern girls adopted to sound like California girls; every statement like a question. She fiddled with the radio, couldn't settle on one station, sang bits of tunes, and spoke whatever was flitting through her brain at the moment. She ignored me, once it was safely established I wasn't a card-carrying member of the serial killers club.

I envied them, even Lynne, for their safe lives. Having time stand still in prison was one long, excruciating agony of dullness. I trained myself to sleep fifteen hours a day to make it pass. I vowed I'd make my life matter, do only right things when I got out—you know, not the live-life-to-the-fullest crap the TV commercials talk about while shilling some medication. These kids, my almost-peers, had lives full of promise for the future. Mine was limited to the next few hours and the money in my pocket. I felt lightyears from their world and all because of one stupid deed that put a noose around my neck; it tightened as we drove despite the miles between me and that junkyard.

Lynne's voice accompanied a song on the radio, cracking on the high notes. The words seemed aimed like an arrow right at me: *I need a miracle . . . I need a miracle . . . I need a miracle . . .*

"Hey, creepo guy, whatever-your-name-is, why are you wrinkling up your face like that? Got a problem with my singing?"

Yes, your dang screechy voice among other things . . . I thought.

"I remember a different song," I said. "Got a line in it like that."

"Oh yeah, why don't you sing it then?"

I sang a few lyrics from the end of the song I listened to in Denmar: ". . . I haven't prayed since I was young, but Lord above, I need a miracle."

Niya said, "My, you have a nice voice, what's-your-name."

"Thank you."

When I discovered in grade school that I had no stutter when I sang, I sang alone out walking in the woods or squirrel hunting as much as possible without anyone near.

The boy beside Glyph Boy started an argument with Lynne over the song by saying Toca's "Miracle" was actually Coco's. Lynne said it was on Apple, not Spotify. The boy in back with me said he liked La'Tonya Smiley's version over Tara McDonald's. Then Glyph Boy jumped in with an obscure tidbit about Fragma, the German group Coco sang for but wasn't on the remake with Guru Project because she was suing her old bandmates and asked if anyone knew Grateful Dead's song of that title, which was ignored by the rest in a zigzagging conversation among the others about mixes, remixes, extended mixes, dubstep, trap, house, garage, techno, mashups, and a dozen words I'd never heard before. Prison was a time warp. I went in with two kinds of music: rock-'n-roll and country. Nobody paid any attention to the whiggers in reversed ballcaps driving around after school peeling rubber for attention.

I let the conversation swirl overhead. I didn't understand any of it. Like people speaking English suddenly bursting into Tagalog without skipping a beat. This was the same group that couldn't be interested in Maslow twenty minutes ago but knew every minute detail of a popular song's history.

Niya looked at me differently while everyone jabbered about their music. Maybe she sensed something in my singing that spoke to her without words. Or my silence. It was the closest conversation I didn't have with another person in years.

* * *

Niya dropped me off in front of Freddie's Grill, the busiest intersection. Jefferson-on-the-Lake officially opened on Memorial Day, but being a year-round village, too, some places remained open all year. Donnie drove us out here to drink a couple times. He put in a word with Tony when I first arrived in Northtown. Pure chance we met. He was in the BP station down from the Imperial Arms apartments buying cigarettes. I was there looking for a job, any job. The first and last month's deposit had just about cleaned me out of cash. I needed a paycheck and my car blew a transmission on Interstate 90. My goal was to go west to Cleveland to look for work. I hitched a ride with a trucker hauling steel coil who was going east. He dropped me off and I wound up in Northtown. It wasn't too long before I realized Donnie was a sponge, looking for a drinking buddy who'd pick up the tab.

"I can take you right to the Chalet," Niya said. "It's just a couple blocks up. You said you were going to be late for your interview."

"I know, but I'm m-meeting a friend here first. He s-said he'd give me a few p-pointers."

"For a creepo guy with a lot of mysterious friends, you don't seem happy about it."

She saw through the lies. But I'd paid for the 6-mile ride and wasn't too concerned about her feelings or whatever her gal-pal thought of me. I needed to get myself situated, get ready for whatever came next. Every dime of the money I'd planned to send back was going to be needed. I left little behind in the apartment. I'd been traveling light since I left home at seventeen to knock around the world—only my world at the time was so small you could draw its circumference with a fat crayon.

"Good luck—with your interview," she said.

Lynne flipped me a middle digit out the window as they drove off.

I do need a miracle—

Walking around with a backpack and a duffel bag out here wasn't noticeable but it didn't make me invisible, either. I found a back booth in the open-air dining room, set my bags on the opposite seat, and settled in, checked the menu, and went up to the counter to ask for a hot dog and a Coke.

"Whatever you have is fine."

The waitress in a ponytail scowled, handed me a ticket.

"What kind of pop you say you want?"

"Give me a root beer."

Back home, 'Coke' meant any kind of soda. I was already making mistakes. She might remember me.

The donut shop was open but the next three places I passed were boarded up or had soapy windows. I headed toward a biker bar on the other side of the street. Most of the family-fun stuff ended— the go-carts, trampolines, waterslides, and miniature golf games; they'd return in warmer weather like animals coming out of hibernation. Biker bars were like skunks coming out in February, you'll see them open first.

Dwight's Bar was like most bars back home: concrete-block construction, pure shitkicker. The front double doors let in little light and the vertical slit windows cut into the walls made it resemble a World War Two bunker. Damage control evident in the handmade sign over the bar: BEER IN CANS ONLY. No glass or bottles for the inevitable fights that break out. No foreign or craft beers. Bottom-shelf whiskey, Bud, Coors, and Old Milwaukee. All country on the jukebox except for pre-1970 Rolling Stones.

On any night, Dwight's clientele consisted of a mix of bikers, mainly locals but the occasional outlaw biker or fugitive fleeing a bench warrant. Tourists or locals who ingratiated themselves with the bartenders were tolerated. Runaway teens from nearby states hiding from parents or pimps, or women tired of being thumped around by boyfriends or girlfriends might be spotted inside. Always one or two ex-cons holding down a stool or a booth looking mad at the world. The town's summertime population was so full of transients that people wandered in all the time asking "for Dwight," which meant someone wanting to be hooked up for drugs.

More than a few crimes were hatched here, according to Donnie, who liked the place. Dwight himself was off in Chillicothe doing five years for running a gang of teens who boosted high-end cars. Whenever he went off to serve time, a representative from the Chamber of Commerce came by with an escort of deputies from the Sheriff's to remove the small Confederate flag Dwight had tacked to the wall by the jukebox. It was always replaced.

The last time I was here, the place was jammed, tattoos outnumbered the people by fifty-to-one. A dozen serious drinkers manned the bar stools. My eyes adjusted to the dark in case any vice cops were slumming. Word of my rebar-tossing back in Northtown would be all over the police scanners by now.

Ordering a Coors, I chose a stool at the end. Two bikers with vest patches a few stools away were hunched in close conversation. One eye-fucked me as I sat down.

"This is a private conversation here, dude. Whyn't you find another place to drink your beer?"

In most redneck bars, that's an invitation to fight. In Dwight's, it was a polite request.

Picking up my can, I grabbed my bags and relocated to a booth. On a crowded night in summer, taking up a booth like that would have been an invitation for trouble.

I finished my beer, went up to the bar. Only one bartender on duty, a woman in her thirties, plenty of eyebrow, cleavage, nose, and lip studs. Black nail polish and rings on all her fingers except where a wedding ring would go.

"Shot 'n beer," I said. "Any kind."

She brought the drinks. I paid. Gave me a sly look when she brought my change. A transaction taking twenty seconds, yet she'd given me the once-over as thoroughly as nay bartender in any bar I'd been in. She nodded at the bags.

"New here?"

"I used to come here with Bobby La Salle—you know him? Rode with the Pagans."

A safe name.

"Nope."

"Just got served divorce papers," I said, wincing, shrugging my shoulders—a rascal down on his luck. "Looking for a place to stay for a few days without a lot of paperwork. Bobby or Tig, one of them two guys, he told me I could find a place while I'm sorting things out.

Sorting things out meant *running from the law* or *facing the law.*

"Cabins over to Erieview Road," she said. "Follow that gravel road across the street between Dunkin' Donuts and the Chalet. Ask for the manager, guy named Teddy Basset."

Someone heard the name and called out from the back, "Bassett Hound, what's that slimy fuck up to?"

"Mind your own fuckin' business, Jimmy!"

She turned back to me.

"Bassett Hound's an asshole but he'll give you a good deal."

She twitched her fingers, which I took to mean "off the books." I thanked her, finished my whiskey, left half the beer.

Bestview Cabins Day or Week, the sign said.

A dozen cabins either side of the small gravel road separating them. Mock-Swiss with a cross-gable roof and a tiny porch you'd fall off if you were drunk. The third cabin from the cliff edge had *T.M. Basset, Manager* burnt into a wooden board beside the door. Bassett's was the only two-story cabin and that couldn't have been more than a loft upstairs.

The man who answered my knock was in his fifties, bald, and had an expanse of belly that caused him to walk like a man holding a fishbowl between his knees. The nickname fit: wagging jowls, a turkey-wattle below the neck big enough to keep fish in. He put me in mind of my father's old hunting dog. His missing teeth between the lower incisors reinforced the dog image. The reek wafting from inside his cabin was putrid, a mix of dirty feet, oven grease, and reefer smoke.

I gave him a similar version of the story I'd told the bartender.

"Caught you lookin', huh?"

"Oh yeah, it was fast, all right," I said. "One day I'm on the road hauling wire to Nevada. Next day I'm comin' home, my own dog tries to bite me in the ass, and the guy's legs are going out the window."

"Ain't that the way it is with women," he said, grinning. "You can't live with them and you can't kill them."

"I'd like to keep her lawyer from serving me for a couple days," I said, "just until I can get some of my property relocated."

"I know *exac-terly* what you mean. Been married and divorced three times and I'm already lookin' for the next ex-wife."

"Look here, Mister Bassett, the gal back there at Dwight's, she said you could accommodate me. I was hoping we could dispense with the driver's license and all that bullshit. I'd be willing to pay a little more."

I brought my hand out of my pocket holding four fifty-dollar bills from my stash, folded longwise, sticking out from between my knuckles.

"Ain't no problem for me, Jack," he said, and covered my hand with his. "You give me any trouble, say, the law comes round, you got to get out—and I mean hi-de-ho fuckin' pronto."

"Fine by me, sir."

I reached into my front pocket, pulled out another fifty and held it between us.

"I'd sure appreciate a tip, though, if anybody does come looking for me."

Another pass with his hand that left mine empty holding nothing but Ohio air.

"Gimme your cell number. I'll give you a head's-up."

"Wish I could, but, doggone, she kept that too when I stormed out. She's probably checking every email I have."

"My-oh-my, that is cruel," Bassett said. "I will let you know if anybody comes round. You can count on me."

I wish I had a dime for every time my cousin Kenny said that to me. Yet I was the one who went to the slammer.

"I do appreciate that."

I gave it a mushy-voweled, downhome spin—'*Uh-pree-shi-et.*

"Got some Meigs County budder inside you interested."

"No thanks," I said. "Booze is my only vice."

"Ha-ha, I'm doubtin' that, partner."

My new digs weren't spacious but after prison, anything is a castle. I took out some clean clothes, put my razor and bathroom articles in the medicine cabinet in the tiny bathroom. I shoved my bags under the bed. One way in, one way out—not good. A fast exit with a go-bag up and out through the bedroom window was the best I'd manage if I did get a tipoff from the manager, which I absolutely was not counting on despite what he said.

As for Mister Bassett Hound, I didn't trust him as far as I could throw him. I took out some bills from my remaining stash for walking-around money and put the rest inside a Ziploc bag and slipped it into my pillowcase.

Sitting on the bed wrapped in the flimsy duvet around my shoulders, I couldn't think of a way out. I could ad-lib for so long before it all came crashing down like a house of cards under strobe lighting. Being on the run, jumping from one spot to another wasn't my idea of a good life. At the same time, my paranoia ramped up. Once you start realizing the US Marshals can come crashing through your door at five in the morning, it changes your attitude about a lot of things.

I did what generations of Cardels had done before me. I walked to the nearest liquor store for a bottle of cheap rye to get drunk on. The clerk gave me a sour look when I asked her for a roll of quarters.

"I got a ton of laundry to do."

On the street, I passed clusters of people walking about, a few tourists, mostly locals and lots of young people Niya's age. I saw shamrocks on clothing, in windows, and advertisements for green beer. Tourists wore green sweaters or sweatshirts with slogans like *Kiss Me I'm Irish* and *Shut Up You Stupid Mick!* Happy couples held hands, out for a stroll despite the brisk wind off the lake, plenty more people occupying benches up and down the Strip watching passersby, oldsters in matching outfits and rowdy teenagers with tattoos and green-dyed hair, who looked at one another with suspicion or interest. Everywhere, the phone zombies. I thought of Dwight's as an oasis. If you tried to take out a cell phone in there, you might pull back a bloody stump. They'd figure you for a narc at the worst, a harmless lookieloo at the least.

Payphones weren't obsolete out here yet.

My Aunt Ida answered.

"How is she?"

"She's dying, Wade. You don't need to ask about that."

"She doing her regular chemo?"

"She said she ain't gonna be doin' that no more. It won't let her keep nothin' down. She's all sticks and bones as it is."

"Where's Dad?"

"Off drinking. Where else?"

"Tell him . . . will you please tell him I'll send money when I can?"

"You should be tellin' that yourself, Wade Cardell."

The sob bubbling up from my esophagus wouldn't stay down. I coughed.

"What you say?"

"Nothing. Got a little cold is all."

"You heard what I said, Wade?"

"Can't right now," I said. "I got a little deal up here to straighten out first."

"Like that last one?"

She meant my dealing with Kenny.

"You Cardells and your big deals," Ida huffed.

"Be sure to tell him, Aunt Ida."

"You got gumption, boy, telling me what to do."

"I'll call again when I can."

"I won't be holding my breath . . . That no-good Kenny called. He was askin' about you."

"What did he want?"

"Didn't say."

The clipped staccato, the snapped-off replies—so familiar. Memories of home that tripped off a pang of anguish.

"You tell him?"

"I didn't tell that no-count jailbird nothin'! He's a lowlife—"

I heard a voice in the background, a deep growl—my father *"Who you talkin' to, Ida? Gimme the phone . . ."*

"Who is this?"

I'd had years of watching my father drink himself half to death. Once a union miner who made a good wage, he was a drunk, a laughingstock. I blamed him for my mother's cancer. I knew some of the money I sent back went to pay for his boozing in Clarksburg. He bought drinks for his friends, strangers, anybody who helped him squander his money.

"Hey, Dad."

"Wade."

"Did Aunt Ida say what Kenny called for?"

"Nope. I didn't know your cousin called . . ."

The long pauses in our conversation were always awkward, as uncomfortable for him as for me. I hated talking to him on the phone. It made me feel awkward like a kid again, a time when I used to look up to him.

He broke the silence first. "All that trouble was Kenny's doing, not your fault."

Trouble . . . He meant going to prison, having a record that kept me back.

One word could hold a powerful amount of meaning sometimes.

"It don't matter now, Dad."

"You comin' home anytime soon?"

I squeezed my eyes shut: the old man's roundabout way of saying my mother's condition was worse than last time I called.

"Thinking on it," I said; "might could. Have to get something done here first."

Talking through plexiglass shields in prison made my speech degenerate fast into dialect, those old expressions we say among ourselves while doing the "No, sir" or "Yes, ma'am" to strangers. Family and kin, a vise grip on your soul.

Aunt Ida's voice in the background telling him to hang up on me.

"Shut up, you!"

"I've gotta go, Dad."

"OK, OK, see you."

"See you."

I walked back to the cabin sick to my stomach. I shouldn't drink, but I knew I was goddam sure I was going to. I tried to pace it. By ten o'clock, when the nightlife had picked up with the crowds streaming into the bars for St. Paddy's and the traffic was full of cars, mobs of people going to restaurants and bars up and down the Strip, I was tempted to join them to get away from myself, but

I was too drunk. No matter how much I put down my gullet, I couldn't erase the image of Angelo crawling through the mud with his face drenched in blood.

The last image in my head before I passed out on the bed was my cousin. Two years older, bigger, more reckless than I could be on my craziest day. Many people—not just family or cops—thought Kenny Cardell was crazy dangerous, not just wild-acting. Every stupid thing you can do as teenagers to raise hell on a weekend, we did. Some of it was criminal, none of it was for anyone's good except Kenny's and mine. He taught me to steal, fight dirty, smoke dope, and too many things I tried to put out of my mind in the years since we used to run around tiny Salem, West Virginia, and later, when we got into drug dealing in a big way, in Clarksburg, a dozen miles east on Highway 50.

Kenny arranged my first sexual experience with an older girl he sold drugs to—and never let me forget it. I can still see the smile on his face as he turned around in the driver's seat to watch Korie-Jean Lomax's head bobbing up and down in my lap. *Bitch can suck the chrome off a trailer hitch*, he laughed, ripping off Willie Nelson's line about an old girlfriend. Didn't faze him he had a girl up front giving him head at the same time.

My parents warned me, even some teachers who thought I had promise and could make something of my life. You'd think he was the devil trailing sulfur and brimstone in his wake—all except for the girls. Of Kenny, no one said good things or made any predictions that weren't grim: *That boy's headed for Mount Olive*, meaning the state's maximum-security prison. . . . *No, the cemetery's where he's headed . . . ain't nobody gonna hire that boy, he's too goshdarn wild for his own good . . .*

Too wild . . . too crazy, they all said. But Kenny thrived and he had no shortage of followers, including me. And he did it all with a smile, the one that made you think he was your best friend and would always have your back. That is, until you felt the blade going in.

I never thought I'd hear those things said about me, too, until I was in too deep with the dealing. I was half-stoned every day. I never noticed how Kenny held back, kept his wits about him. I let him lead, and like a Judas goat, he led me right to the kill chute with my eyes wide open.

When he came back to Salem from his first stint in a real prison, he seemed different. He'd done time before in Weirton for possession of drug paraphernalia and intent to sell; he was ordered to remain in the Boone-Hancock juvie facility until his twenty-first birthday because his parents were missing in action. His dad off in Brushy Mountain, his mother living with whoever she'd shacked up with. He was heavier from the starchy food, but it was his inside his head that was different—meaner, quieter, still the big smile he could turn on and off like a lamp. But something dark inside him had been turned loose, and he was pretty content to go along with it.

When Kenny came home from his level-2 prison for an armed robbery of a pizza parlor in Clarksburg, we were celebrating his release at the place where we often took girls and drank. He said that he'd heard a rumor Ray Hennig was dating his girl on the sly. I admitted I'd heard the same rumor. I recall how he'd stopped guzzling his beer, turned slowly to gaze at me, and said in a voice I'd never heard him use before: "But you never told me that in your letters, did you, Wade?" I told him I didn't to upset him, which was true. I was hoping Ray—a guy I knew and liked— would come to his senses and end it before Kenny heard about it.

The long and short of it was that one day while we were cruising around Clarksburg, Kenny asked me to go with him to settle a score with Ray. I tried to talk him out of it. It wasn't because Ray had been an all-city linebacker for Liberty High. Kenny was family. I figured we'd jump Ray, Kenny could get in a few good licks, then we'd run off laughing, and that would satisfy him.

I was wrong. We waited for Ray to leave work at the welding shop and get him in the parking lot at his vehicle. Kenny had me hit him low from behind, he'd hit him high—"convict-style takedown," he said.

It was ugly. I remember Kenny coming up to him with a smile on his face: "Hey, Ray Hennig, how you doin', boy?" Ray said, "Ken Cardell, what's up?" And that was the last thing he said because I tackled him, both arms wrapped around his thighs. Kenny slammed a forearm into Ray from the front and he doubled over backwards. I was afraid to let go. Ray had a reputation. I heard several sounds, none of which sounded like punches: *thwap . . . thwap . . . thwap—*

My cousin had some kind of homemade sap with a beavertail. He was slamming it down on Ray with all his might. When I felt Ray's legs stop struggling in my grip, I saw the damage. Kenny's face was a mask of pure rage, just a bug-eyed, spit-flecked demon sucking air after his workout with the weapon. I thought we'd murdered Hennig. I let go of Ray's legs, rolled over, and jumped to my feet. I caught Kenny's arm before he could bring the sap down one more time.

"You'll kill him!"

He tried to use it on me then. No reasoning with a rabid dog. Somehow I dragged him away, pushed and shoved him toward his car and we drove away.

Kenny never spoke a word on the way home; his eyes glittered the whole way and he had an expression on his face that said he was watching whatever was filming behind his eyes—and liking it. Something, not joy exactly, but as close to joy's evil twin brother as you can get.

"What the hell's wrong with you?" I shouted. *"You tryin' to kill him?"*

He turned to look at me—or through me—and gave me that old Kenny smile.

Ray never told the police who attacked him. He spent a month in the hospital for a fractured skull and had to have a couple hundred stitches to close the wounds in his scalp and face. I heard he left town when he was released from the hospital.

Kenny wasn't satisfied. Missy Debevec, the girl who cheated on him, was tricked into going to a sleazy motel on Highway 50. He used one of her girlfriends hooked on drugs to lure her there. Missy was drugged and taken to a room where three men were waiting, all ex-cons or friends of cons serving at Kenny's former prison.

"That bitch, she's a three-hole wonder," he laughed, telling me later. *"Got it all on video."*

"I don't want to see it."

"Too bad," he said to me as we drove. *"You'll be about the only one in town who hasn't. I made fuckin' sure her boss at work and her parents got a copy."*

That was my cousin. Three weeks later I was ordered to come out of my house through a bullhorn, hands behind my head and face the wall. It wasn't for Ray Henning, as I first thought. It was a stupid break-in of a bike shop in Clarksburg.

The place had no alarms—Kenny was right about that—but it did have a CCTV system; my mug was on the loop and cops had no trouble convicting me. Kenny backed off from going with me at the last minute. He said he "had the shits" from a weekend of binge-drinking.

"You can do this one, Wade. I can't be holdin' your fuckin' hand every time."

My car was about to be repossessed. I needed money. I told him I was up for the challenge—or some foolish brag like that.

The thing that galled me worst for the two long years I sat in my cell in Denmar Correctional in Hillsboro was that Kenny had set me up from the git-go. We never spoke again, but I knew why and had plenty of time to think about it in my bunk: *That's for not telling me about Ray Hennig and my girl.*

Bad dreams in my sleep that night. Screech owls in the stand of fir trees. The rhythmic sound of waves rolling up on shore below the bluffs. Every sound from footsteps on gravel through drunken laughter or the couple in the next cabin fighting knocked me closer to wakefulness, but I could never get all the way up, like jumping into deep water with your clothes on. Morbid thoughts of my mother wasting away in a back room, cops crashing through the door. I woke hearing the sound of waves beating up against the shoreline below the cliffs and realized it wasn't that; it was the blood pressure thumping away in my ears.

Birds at dawn. Not the ones I remembered as a boy in Salem—mainly pigeons, starlings, and grackles. Gulls make a racket with their godawful banshee screeches. I dressed and left the cabin to walk toward the cliff's edge at the end of Erieview. Gulls with their elbow-bent wings wheeled in the cold air. The morning sun painted their wings and bellies silver-white as they circled and dove. I watched them form a circling spiral over the blue-gray water before plummeting for a school of shad or perch.

Past the manager's cabin, I headed down to the Strip for the first place that served coffee. I had to go all the way to Freddie's that early. I wasn't dressed for the morning chill. The gutters were full of St. Patricks' decorations, paper hats, and even vomit from the night before, a dismal symbol of all that forced jollity. A few people were up and about like me, mostly workers at shops and diners.

I drank two cups of black coffee. My mood and stomach didn't improve. After last night's binge, the best thing was hair of the dog. On my way back to the cabin, I decided to call home again to check on my mother's condition. Aunt Ida would be up this early. The woman never slept.

Someone picked up on the first ring—not Aunt Ida or my father. A deeper male voice blasted through the receiver: "Rise and shine, motherfucker, time to do crime!"

The same greeting I'd heard for years. Cousin Kenny . . . son of a bitch.

Chapter 3

"Fuck me, Wade, I ain't talkin' about this on the goddam phone, especially on your Daddy's phone," Kenny said.

"You expect me to forget those two years I spent looking at ceiling stains and smelling farts from the guy in the bunk below?"

"Christ, you one scared little bitch. 'Wah-wah, my pussy hurts.' Time to be a man, Cuz, grow the fuck up. Auntie says you got inked at that pussy prison Denmar. Question now is, do you have the balls to go with it?"

You watch your smart mouth, Kenneth Lee Cardell!

"See what I mean, Wade?"

"I'll call you back later," I said. "I got something I need to do first."

"OK, but the offer don't last much longer. I got places to go, people to see, you know what I'm sayin', dude? You want somethin' from Kenny, you call me back before four today. The offer's gonna expire one minute after."

"Give me your cell number."

"Fuck that," he said. "Call this number I'm givin' you . . ."

* * *

Except for leaving my cabin to go to the grocery store for energy bars and potato chips, I hit the liquor store for a six-pack and stayed inside my cabin, thinking long and hard about the call home. The decent weather lasted exactly one day; the cold spring rains of March returned in a fury, pounding the streets and sidewalks, driving everyone off the streets.

Around 2:15 hunger made the decision for me. I held my flimsy windbreaker over my head to keep from getting soaked on the run down to Freddie's. My hair and shoulders were soaked anyway by the time I got there. The girl who took my order was a different one from yesterday. I ordered the same thing and took a two-person table near the back door. The place was packed with people at tables and booths waiting out the rain. A few sipped from liquor bottles in paper sacks; some looked to be taking the hair- of-the-dog remedy for a bad hangover I thought about myself. Despite the rain, the atmosphere seemed tense as though people were enduring daylight until the night's drinking commenced.

I gave fate a hand in my decision: turn myself in to the law or find out what Kenny had in mind.

I wanted to turn myself in, do the time more than I wanted to re-connect with my cousin. Every instinct in my head said *You can't trust him, he's a pack of lies, a con man, and a psychopath to boot.* Knowing him since we were boys, and being kin, I thought we had a bond. It wasn't until I got I went to prison that I realized Kenneth Cardell was all about Kenneth Cardell, nobody else. He had no more concern for another person's welfare than the tissue he blew his nose into.

On impulse, coming back from the liquor store, I saw a Lake cop and began approaching him to turn myself in for the short ride back to Northtown. I even made eye contact—but changed my mind at the last second and kept walking past him. It struck me as wrong or goofy to surrender to a part-time cop holding on to a bicycle.

I wondered how much time I'd get for an agg assault charge. I figured, if I was lucky, a halfway decent lawyer could get me down to a year or two at most. With good time, every week an extra day deducted, I'd be out in less than a year. Denmar shaved three more for every month—sooner if I made the right impression at a parole hearing.

My heart was lighter with the choice. Angelo was a prick, and I didn't regret putting him through the pain. He'd have a story to brag about and a few battle scars.

Three-fifteen by the black street clock across the street. I took it as an omen, possibly a good sign: 'That everyone who believes may have eternal life in him.' John 3:15.

The skies were clearing again and people were leaving their booths and getting up from their chairs to venture back out onto the Strip. The air was tinged with that ink-smell after a rainstorm.

I walked toward the pint-sized precinct where the half-dozen Lake cops were housed in tourist season. Sucking into my nostrils street aromas: French fries dashed with vinegar, steaks smoking on grills, fried taco meat, cotton candy, shish kebab cooked on sidewalk grills, pizza, beer—nothing healthy, but scents I'd miss in lockup. If the Buccis had the clout everyone said, I might draw more than a light sentence. It might be years before my nose and palate were treated to these scents again.

I walked on, a grim set to my mouth, not aware of the people passing me. I'd grab my bags, cross the street, and make the last hundred yards so that I'd arrive at exactly four.

Approaching the newspaper kiosk, the headline of the top paper in the stack jumped out at me, as if the boldface words in huge type could grab my eyes: *Employee Sought in Salvage Yard Killing.*
Shit, piss, and holy fuck—
Angelo Bucci dead. I killed him . . .

If World War Three had broken out, the size of the print would be only a tad smaller. I stared hard as I passed the kiosk, then picked up my pace. My driver's license photo, grainy and dated, inserted into the middle of that three-column article below the fold. My name everywhere now. My photo.

It was like some shitty cop movie where the fugitive reads of his own crime and then makes a run for it chased by citizens and cops who all recognized him at once.

Those college kids in the car . . . all that mindless chatter about songs and serial killers . . .

Just like that, the relief at the tough decision to turn myself in gone. I was a rabbit on the run, a gutless, stomach-churning mess of a rabbit. I kept walking, averting my eyes, terrified someone across the street would shout and point at me any second. This was no one-year sentence in a county jail or a minimum-security joint I was looking at. This was murder, second degree, voluntary manslaughter—only if I was lucky. So far I was lucky to be outside without shackles. In Ohio, with my prior conviction, that would possibly mean LWOP, life without parole, until I was so old the state would kick me out to save money.

Fuck that—

If I could make the call home before four, I'd demand Kenny come get me. I'd be beholding to him, no doubt about that and all the auld-lang-syne shit he'd throw in my face to cover his betrayal. He wouldn't have to sell me on his 'sure-fire money-maker' of a gig, whatever it was he hinted at when we spoke.

I really need a miracle . . .

* * *

"Four-oh-seven, jackoff. What did I say?"

Ten rings before he answered, each ring a punch to the heart: *Pick up, pick up, Kenny, you bastard.*

"I was fixin' to leave, Wade. One foot out the door you caught me at the last possible second."

More likely, he was standing next to the phone letting it ring.

"I'm in."

"That's good, that's good. You won't believe what a sweet deal—"

"There's one problem."

"What one motherfuckin' problem?"

"You to come get me."

"Where you at?"

I told him.

"Jesus fucking Christ. Lake fucking Erie! Fuck you, I don't need a partner that bad, I got to drive all the way there."

"That's the deal," I said. "Come up, get me, I'm in all the way. You owe me, motherfucker."

More automatic cussing, which was his way of wrapping his mind around it, assessing the guilt, my demand, what was in it for him if he did or didn't do what I asked.

44

"Stop dicking around, Ken. You'd have told me to fuck off by now. You're coming. We both know it, so write down what I tell you."

"Pushy little prick, ain't you? Grew some balls in the joint, I 'spect. OK, fuck it. I don't need to write down directions. Baby's got GPS."

"Baby?"

"You'll meet her."

"I'm ready to go right now."

"Fuck you, I ain't. Be where you said, tomorrow, one o'clock latest. Pack your shit and don't make me wait on you or else."

"Or else what?"

"You recollect old Ray Hennig, right?"

* * *

Moving from one group to another, staying in a crowd and keeping pace with it, I walked past Erieview a good hundred yards before turning back the other way.

I saw all the way down to the manager's cabin but not as far as mine, which was catty-corner to the others at the end of the opposite row. The cars that were there when I left were still there— same models, same number, in the same position. When Kenny was mentoring me in the fine art of thievery and other related vices, he taught me to upgrade my surveillance skills: *Know your baseline normal. See anything different? Then it's time to cut and run . . .*

The developer left a stand of fir trees behind Bestview Cabins extending to the edge of the steep slope. I made my way through, ducking low beneath the branches whenever I saw a lit window from an adjacent cabin. Behind Bassett's, a window in back seven feet off the ground, was uncovered. I'd have to do a chin-up with my fingertips on the ledge to see into the interior.

His broad backside, wearing a Hawaiian shirt with palm trees. I didn't figure him for a Proud Boy. Taking punches from all sides while naming five kinds of breakfast cereal was hardly a ritual initiation that stopped a real prospect. But some fat guys could handle themselves. Maybe Bassett was one. He stood near the front window, leaning. He pushed the curtain aside to peek out. I held the grip on the ledge long enough to see him repeat the action three more times—jumpy, nervous as a cat.

Before I dropped back to the ground, I glimpsed something in his right hand: a cell phone. On a rumpsprung couch were my bags. Only one reason he'd have my stuff and be watching the road—to see me stepping up to my cabin.

Kenny's words rang in my head like ugly ringtones: *Wade, you dumbass, you can thieve all right but you can't read people for shit . . .*

I didn't know to a certainty, but I could guess the reason; the article about me I was too scared to stop for must have included a phrase like "reward for information" or mentioned a tip line. Given my brief experience with my landlord, I figured he wasn't a ratting me out because he was a standup citizen. He planned to keep my money as a bonus.

Think, Wade. The trap would be sprung when I got there, not before. He didn't want cops lurking among the trees or hiding in my room. He wasn't worried about being exposed as a grifter or a doper. The female bartender back in Dwight's clinched his reputation. His only concern had to be keeping me off the books. The cops could report him to his boss and he'd be canned no matter what reward was offered. Being known as a snitch to the bikers might not worry him much, but he wouldn't want it shouted from the rooftops. Bikers have long memories to go with their short tempers. Cops running around with weapons drawn and sirens caterwauling down the Strip worked in my favor.

I was counting on that hunch. But I had to get inside to get my money and that was the immediate problem. I wouldn't get far without it.

Retracing my path through the trees, I headed back to the gravel road. I had an advantage for a short time; it wouldn't last. Gorgeous afternoon sunlight blurred the edges of everything in a soft golden light. I brought everything into sharp focus or I'd be leaving this crappy resort town in the back of a cruiser. *You want me to come barging over to your cabin, hollering about my missing bags, knowing I wouldn't call the cops. OK, fat man, we'll play it that way—with one difference.*

As I passed Bassett's cabin, my peripheral vision caught the glint of something reflected through the glass at head height—just where a cell phone would be if someone were to talk into it. Keeping my pace slow and easy, I resisted looking back. I strolled up and down on the tiny porch, lingering for a moment, as if I couldn't resist basking in the golden light.

The countdown in my head started. *Now—*

Inside the cabin, I went straight to the toilet in the closet-sized bathroom, lifted the tank lid to retrieve the cellophane bag of bills I stashed before leaving.

Shit McGee. No cellophane bag, no money.

You dirty dog, Bassett Hound. I didn't give you enough credit for being a clever snoop as well as a scumbag.

I stepped outside, my face blank, stretched, yawned, looked off down the gravel road toward the cliff's edge. His curtain flapped when he saw me turn in the direction of his cabin. Let him think I didn't see the missing bags under my bed or the stolen cash yet.

Standing by his window, probably cursing the cops. *Got him a front-row seat, the thieving prick.*

The road ended in the cul-de-sac overlooking the lake where I'd strolled early that morning. I moseyed toward it, just gawking at the pretty day breaking through after all that rain. Someone taking his time, in no big hurry. As soon as I reached the guardrail secured at each end by a heavy metal bollard, I hightailed it out of range of his vision.

Then I bolted for the last cabin on Bassett's side like a running back on a Jet Sweep. I swerved for his cabin and came up on the blind side. Still packing momentum, I threw my shoulder against the pinewood door and smashed it off its hinges—splinters flying every which way, some blasting into Bassett's face. His cell phone flew out of his hand.

My blitz attack propelled him backwards off his feet onto the floor. It sounded like a piano falling from a balcony. Proud of myself, sitting on his chest, big belly jiggling clamped underneath my thighs. I brought the hard edge of my curled fist down on his nose. No point in risking those delicate metacarpal bones to inflict a little well deserved pain.

"My money! Where's my money?"

Blood spurting in the air. Grunting, wheezing, snorting. A hog under the butcher's knife.

"I'm waitin' on your answer!"

His eyes watered, blood flowed from both nostrils.

"I don't—I don't—"

Blood dribbled over his chin onto his tee-shirt. He tried to heave me off. I dug my knees into the flab around his ribs even harder.

"Don't try bucking me off, Bassett. Where's my money?"

"I'm choking on blood!"

"My money. I'll smash your nose right into your brain you don't tell me, fucker!"

My second punch traveled a foot, if that—a right hand that clipped his jaw and snapped his head around.

More groaning, louder. His eyes rolled back.

I thought he was playing possum. I was thinking Id hurt him worse than I thought, which was my second big mistake after trusting him. For a fat man, he had power. He swung one chubby arm the size of a tree branch into my ribs to move me off him enough to thrust a hand into my crotch and squeeze. I howled. That was all he needed to shift my weight and buck me off.

Somewhere in my lizard brain, I heard sirens wailing. Coming this way. No more time, I had to go.

Bassett wasn't even in my head when the bullet sizzled past my right ear. I heard the gunshot a split-second afterward. I was already out the door and running at top speed.

That was no cell phone, you dumbass Wade, I told myself.

I was halfway down the gravel road by the time my brain kicked in. Nothing like being shot to find your full-tilt boogie gear. I thought I'd left it behind when my days with Kenny were done. Bassett took another shot, even with cop cruisers barreling toward us.

Zigzagging close to the tree line away from the gravel road, I sprinted for better cover. My arms found that piston rhythm on their own, my head steady on my neck. *See a cheetah run?* Coach *Krażcik* used to say, *thass how you do it* . . .

My legs pumped hard despite the years of smoking, boozing, and drugs. My breathing steadied—no slug plowing through my body, no vital organs converted to stew meat by a lead projectile at Mach-1 speed. My eyes were pinned to a point ahead on the Strip. I had to blend into the crowd before that first cruiser turned up Erieview, or I'd be trapped on a dead-end road.

I just turned the corner, slowed to a canter, then a lope. I put the brakes on and speed-walked up to the small crowd, my only camouflage until I figured out the next move.

They passed us, running dark—no lights flashing or sirens. Two Northtown County Sheriff's units. Two more minutes tussling with him on that shitty brown rug would have trapped me.

Broke, hunted. Spilt milk, as Aunt Ida would say. No point crying over it.

Sundown coming fast despite the warm day. The night air would have a late-springtime chill to it. I couldn't risk going far even with wheels under me. Dwight's wasn't safe. Foot patrols would be looking for me from one end of the Strip to the other.

I stayed a few steps behind the crowd, like a tagalong kid brother. Need be, I'd slip into the pack or duck into an arcade if I saw a Lake cop or real heat coming my way. Freddie's Grill a few dozen yards ahead. One thought left: intercept Kenny tomorrow before he turned down Erieview and found himself surrounded by police pointing guns.

The question now: How to do that without being seen myself in a street crawling with cops?

Not Kenny this time but my old man's words in my head. *Nothing's ever easy.*

Jesus, Pop, if you only knew.

* * *

Insomnia didn't keep my eyes open that night. As soon as I could peel off from the nighttime crowd—mostly college-aged drinkers with fake IDs—I slipped down the sloping road, half cracked asphalt and sand blown up from the beach behind Freddie's. By that point, I'd walked up and down the Strip a dozen times, crossing and recrossing the street, blending in with pedestrian traffic, trying to stay calm every time I spotted a cop ahead or a pair of them talking on their shoulder mics.

The road had a few houses and a diner with a sign out front that looked like a B & B. Then it petered out into a winding sandy path leading down to the beach. The village didn't believe it was necessary to update the lights this far from the main drag, so I had no worries about being seen this far from the Strip as long as I avoided the yellow cones of light they cast onto the ground.

What sounded like love-making going in the dark behind a vacant lot where overgrown grass and stunted trees took over the land. The last structures I passed were barely lit up by the last streetlight—the ruins of cabins, their white paint almost disintegrated into flakes that reminded me of an albino alligator's hide.

Donnie told me coal miners from West Virginia and steelworkers from Pittsburgh and Youngstown used to bring their families out here on vacation from that era to hear Tommy Dorsey's swing band play on the Strip. The men took in the Burly-Q next door to Freddie's, another abandoned hulk, and catch Gypsy Rose Lee or Jennie Lee spinning her nipple tassels while Mom watched the kids wade in the water or play on the swing sets down by the beach. Kenny's father had a faded poster of Tempest Storm tacked to the wall of his garage.

The last cabin on Erieview overlooked a steep decline down to a rocky shoreline without a beach. Down here, a half-mile from Erieview, a spit of beach was formed by wave action from ancient times. Red buoys bobbed a hundred yards out to mark the swimming area, although the only people who swam were members of some Polar Bear club doing it for charity. Donnie liked to come down here to ogle the girls in bikinis during summer. He complained about mothers with saggy tits and varicose veins, screaming children running up and down the beach. "Bread snappers," he called them

I hoped what I remembered from one trip in summer was still here. I made my way down the path in the dark and immediately felt the change in temperature. The wind picked up and the air had a bite to it. Canada was out there in the blue-black where the water ended.

Distances over water are deceptive when you're stumbling around a sandy beach in pitch-black. It's not easy to find a building, much less what I was searching for. Waves crashed to the shoreline on one side of me, sounding like marbles skittering across a tile floor. On the other side of me, high above the path I came down, I could barely make out the muffled sound of voices from the night life on the Strip. An orange haze hung where the sodium arc lights mixed with the dozens of LED advertising signs and old-fashioned light bulbs of marquees, all combined to create a luminous disk of gauzy light from one end of the street to the other. Down here, alone and cold in my thin windbreaker, I was invisible.

My boots were filling with sand from tramping. I hugged my chest to keep the chill off but every minute out here exposed was increasing the chances of hypothermia.

Then I stumbled right into it—an abandoned lifeboat left there to rot on the sand. Donnie told me some drunk was found dead under it once. The main thing was that I had a place to hide in until I could meet Kenny tomorrow afternoon.

I've gone to sleep in strange places, woke after a hard night drinking in strange cars, other people's campers, truck beds, rooms, and girls' beds. Once in a tent with a girl from Sherman, Texas. Drinking and drugs turned me into a rudderless boat.

This life boat was by far the worst. Chiggers and sand fleas devoured every inch of my exposed flesh. Holes in the lifeboat let in chilled air all night long. I considered giving myself up just to get to a warm jail cell by the time the first light of dawn penetrated the gaps in the wooden slats.

Worried about some early morning jogger or an occupant of an early vacation cabin looking out the window and seeing me crawl from under an abandoned lifeboat on the beach, I rolled over in the hard sand to pull out my dick to urinate. My bladder was on fire. The relief was instant. I wound up with sand in my shorts to add to the long night's misery.

Time is a strange thing. You know that saying about when you're having fun, it flies, right. There's the other side of that coin, also true. I had too much time to think, lying there shivering, thinking about my fucked-up life, my family, the choices I made, especially the bad ones—and God knows, a whole bunch more yet to make.

My friends from high school all settled down and raised families. Big, tough Kenny and me, for all our bullshit, where were we in life? Those guys didn't take stupid chances for easy money. They went to work every day, they raised kids, had real lives, not this nomadic shit I chose. Shaving, cutting my hair, hoping my jailbird past didn't come to light, all to convince some yabbo in a bow tie to hire me for minimum wage. Before I gave up and headed north, I saw plenty of that type smiling across their big desks and saying, ever so politely, "I'll give you call if there's an opening." *Sure, they would.* What they meant was they'd call someone like me when hell froze over. I felt humble underneath that lousy windbreak of a shelter. I was a fucking zero, and the people I thought I was so much smarter than were worth ten of me.

Self-pity isn't a trait you'll find in people from my neck of the woods. The people on TV, the reality shows, they don't play well with mountain folk. They call us hillbillies but we see the fuss outsiders make over a cracked cuticle, the moaning and pissing over the least things, the over-analyzing of everything, and the rat race to get more sparkly stuff from Walmart. Why, I wondered, do people with money seem so intent on finding reasons to make themselves miserable?

My thoughts turned to my cousin. Where was he right now? What kind of "sweet deal" did he have in mind for me? *God, not some gun-pointing heist in a bank*, I hoped. Would he get to this resort town without doing something stupid like get drunk or get in a fight on the way? Kenny had left me in the lurch many times in the past because of some cooze he'd picked up. I never knew with him. The biggest question of all: would I get to him before the cops got to me?

Seconds dragged inside the lifeboat. I had no sense of clock time. I was aware of the light increasing only when I blanked out and refocused my eyes. At first real light, I saw every inch of that dirty lifeboat a hundred times over. The fact some guy died where I was didn't faze me at all.

My stomach gurgled constantly, no food for half a day. The energy I'd expended to get under this boat, running, hours of walking—all of it combined to send my body into revolt. I horked up a ropy string of yellow phlegm. Then nothing came but a choking sensation in my esophagus like a sick cat trying to vomit up a hairball.

Prison taught me to be still. Contrary to what Kenny said, Denmar was no country-club; it could make you stir crazy. Despite my mother's best effort, religion didn't take with me. That night, though, I felt God was punishing me. My eyes burned from the salt of my tears, thinking I had betrayed the only people who loved me.

A sound stopped me before I turned myself into one of those Hollywood assholes on the talk shows: someone else on the beach. Not someone—several people. Noises, voices carried by on the wind into holes of the lifeboat. I hoped it was only tourists searching for beach glass, maybe joggers who liked to run when the sun came up. Windsurfers, people training for the triathlon event in August, but no swimmers, not for a couple months. I knew it had to be cops.

One voice became louder, drifted closer on the wind; it was followed by a tinny radio crackle.

My breathing stopped, my body turned rigid. *Don't move, don't breathe,* an order from my neocortex.

An hour passed; it could have been ten minutes. Nothing happened. No more voices.

Everything inside the lifeboat was clearly visible now. Like a miniature version of those big rays from the clouds at sundown, tiny beams probed the holes of my coffin and exposed everything like the Daddy Long Legs in one corner, the big yellow spider feasting on a midge in another, a fly mummified in a cocoon for future dining. The sand teemed with insect life. If I died here and no one found me, I'd provide sustenance for thousands of black flies and beetles to the nth generation.

I leaned on my elbows to put my eye to a hole to see what was out there. An empty beach at dawn with normal sounds: waves coming ashore in a steady march, gritty, wind-blown sand ticking against the sides of the boat. Humpbacked sand fleas, little crabs, crawled over the tiny sand dunes beside me like lost travelers on some desert. No people sounds now.

My body ached. I was racked by spasms and muscle tremors. Hypothermia was setting in. I didn't have much time before I'd be too weak to do anything. The thought of being unable to crawl out from under this rotting hulk the same way I got under it sent a shockwave straight to my heart.

This really could be the end of me, I thought.

Donnie Perdue would be telling the story in bars as long as he could cadge a drink from it.

The odds were against me if I left now with no one about; leaving, however, was necessary if I didn't want to die. I couldn't hoist one side of the boat off me to crawl under it when I first tried. My arms shook from the strain. I tried again with the same result. I lay on my back panting like a dog. Another hour and I wouldn't have the strength to lift it as far as I did. My muscles balked without food, and I had more willpower than physical strength.

When I had my breath back, I positioned my hands and twisted my body for a final heave—now or never. I thought my eyes would pop out of my head from the strain. I eased it slowly, an inch at a time, across my chest, ignoring the splinters tearing into my flesh. My whole body a wounded snake trying to slither from under a rock.

By the time I was able to get a really good grip and use both legs, I'd scraped the bulk of its weight free of my chest and shoulder, ripping buttons off my shirt front, tearing my pants—and raking more of my flesh. But I was finally out. I had to get up off the sand as soon as possible, but I couldn't stand up for a long time like some groggy prizefighter who'd been decked to the canvas.

Up at last, I staggered back the way I'd come last night—a week ago, it seemed. If anyone had a good look at me, I'd be taken for a drunk coming off a bender.

Inside Freddie's, I walked unsteadily to the counter to order. My reptile brain was taking over. I needed food, something warm inside me.

I looked at the waitress, she looked at me. The same one who served me the first time: Swinging Ponytail. I blinked under the harsh fluorescent lighting, my eyes tearing up.

"What'll you have?"

"H-hot dog, coffee—b-black."

My voice was rusty.

"Can you pay, sir?"

I looked up at her, understood, nodded.

"Yesss, misss—hissing like a basket of snakes from both he cold and my stutter.

"What?"

"I c-can p-pay."

I dug out my wallet, fumbling at it because my numb fingers made such a chore of it. Giving up, I opened it to show her the bills.

Without a word, she reached into a plastic holder and dropped the plastic card with the number in red on it. Number 1. There was no one else in the place. She turned her back to me and went to the grill.

Taking a far booth, I slid to the end close to the wall. Passersby, a few at a time. They couldn't see me without entering the dining area. I didn't get much time to enjoy my refuge because the dry heaves hit with a vengeance. I muffled the sound with my hand over my mouth but that was ineffective—shoveling shit against the tide, as my father used to say for anything hopeless.

My body seemed to bend itself, and I banged my forehead on the metal edge of the table. I couldn't control my gag reflex. My stomach kept spasming. Pain from the exertion rip-sawed across my forehead like someone drawing a filleting knife across it. A ragged red curtain clouded my vision.

My brain screamed: *Stop making a scene, you fool!*

The one and only thing above all to be avoided—yet there I was, making vomiting noises like some drunken teenager hugging the toilet. Kenny mocked me whenever I couldn't hold my liquor: *Got you a greasy cheeseburger, Wade.* Then he'd mime me upchucking. *That's you, Wade, calling the Irishman . . .*

Might as well be a big black arrow hanging from the ceiling pointing at me, thought between spasms.

Voices, people milling around. Before I could lift my head, hands clutched me, holding me roughly under the armpits—*cops. It was all over.*

"Get him out of here . . . damned drunk . . . every St. Patrick's, the same thing . . ."

I could have wept with relief. They didn't realize who or what they were grabbing, Wade Cardell, wanted man. College boys, a short order cook in a white apron. Staff, not cops. They frog-marched me to the sidewalk and turned me loose.

"Don't come back, loser!"

Walking helped straighten my body. I cast a backward glance and saw Pony Tail smirking. A look of someone who saw through to the core of your being and weighed it up, your worth, and didn't see much value like a cop's stare, an auger that probed through to the lies you hid there.

Stepping up my pace, terrified others on the street were watching, I walked in the direction of the cabins on Erieview. My brain wouldn't help, nothing helped. It was all I could do to walk without falling down. After a hundred yards or so, I managed a decent stride. I caught my reflection in several windows. My eyes looked like pissholes in the snow. Little wonder the staff back there took me for a boozer or a doper. My hands and face grimed, clothing ripped, bloodshot eyes, ribbons of my windbreaker fabric hung in strips as though a jungle cat raked a claw across my chest, blood-smeared and full of wood splinters.

But the strangest thing happened, that miracle I prayed for: no one *saw* me. I mean *me*, the guy the cops were chasing. I was less than human, unworthy of a second glance, some draggletailed homeless person to be avoided on the street. The few people at that hour of the morning crossed the street seeing me approach, fearing a panhandler or a mental case.

I might make it yet, I thought, if I could keep it together until my cousin arrived. With Kenny, you could never tell. I gave him showing up 50-50 odds. He didn't do for you, you did for him. It was never any different.

Fifty yards from Erieview, I was still a jerky puppet on wires; my body sensed the danger before I saw it—a Lake cop o n a streetcorner. I resisted the urge to bolt, even if I had the legs. Donnie Perdue used to sneer at the Lake police, called them rent-a-cops, mall security: *These guys'll bust you for jaywalking just to have something to do . . .*

The painted yellow lines of a crosswalk just yards from the gravel road. I felt eyes on my back the entire time.

Now what?

Only one thing to do and one place to go where I wouldn't be thrown out at once.

I reached for the door latch of Dwight's Bar. Locked. Too early even for the veteran boozehounds. The cop across the street was looking at me, his eyes bored holes in my back right then. I could almost hear him saying it to himself: *It's him, that guy the Northtown cops are after—*

The door flung itself open like magic.

I stood there, rocking on my heels, unable to move let alone run.

"What, you? Push the fucking door, you want in."

The bartender in her black leather vest stood in front of me. She fixed me with a look that took in all the damage.

"You're the guy asked about the cabins. What the fuck happened to you? You look like you were rode hard and put away wet."

"I got into a fight. OK if I come in for a minute? I'll pay."

"You better," she said. "Cops are all over the place after you."

Oh fuck a duck. What do I do now?

"Don't stand there like a fuckin' deer in the headlights." She stepped back to let me in.

"You read the paper," I said.

"Didn't need to. When the pigs come into Dwight's, they're serious. We don't tell 'em shit from Shinola."

Two deputies had been in shortly after "the fuckup" at Bassett's cabin.

She told me to sit in a booth up front.

"What happened?"

"He stole my money," I said. "Then he shot at me. I ran off."

"I don't mean that," she said. "Bassett will cornhole a dead dog for a few bucks. Everyone knows that. That guy in Northtown you killed with a pipe."

"I d-didn't mean to k-kill him."

"You're cold," she said. "You look half-dead."

"No, I stutter."

"So?"

"He tried to drop a m-magnet . . . I got fired . . ."

Babbling like an idiot.

"You're not making sense—and you look like shit on a stick."

"Can I sit down, r-rest a couple minutes?"

I was talking to the only person in the whole town, maybe the county, who was willing to risk harboring a fugitive. Why? Just to hear his sad story? I didn't question her motives. I was glad to be somewhere warm, safe—if only until she decided to turn me in. Even if she said she was going to do it, at that low point, I would have stayed where I was and waited for them.

I told her what happened at the junkyard, a short version, leaving out the escape, the break-in of Bassett's cabin, the lifeboat.

"That doesn't explain why you're sitting here talking to me."

"I got thrown out of Freddie's . . . They thought I was still drunk or stoned."

"So you weren't in a fight?"

"No. Are you going to turn me in?"

"I'm thinking about it," she said. "Really thinking about it."

"If you do, would you tell me your name?"

58

"So you can come back here and kill me after you get out?"

"No. . . . You're only the second person I met on the run who's been kind to me."

"Who was the first?"

"Some college girl, she gave me a ride out here."

"From the looks of you, she didn't do you any big favors."

Dwight's was shabbier in the light like most bars when the lights come on. This one made me wonder why I ever thought any bar was a good place to do my drinking.

"Name's P.J.," she said. "Short for Patricia Jean. Don't even think about calling me that."

She was older than I first thought, crow's-feet. Hair dyed Spanish black. The white cami beneath the vest cut low to reveal the tops of her breasts, natural to her body size but squeezed for extra cleavage. I'd known women who duct-taped their breasts like that. Tiny blue veins running across the backs of her hands. A handsome woman growing old in a dim bar.

I don't know why she didn't whip out her cell phone and call 9-1-1 right there. What was the point of running, I thought, only to be caught so soon? She stared at me, thinking her own thoughts. Then she decided something about me. That little electric charge of tension between strangers evaporated.

"You lied about the divorce thing, too, didn't you?"

"Yes."

"What do you want from me?"

"My cousin is coming by today to pick me up."

"OK."

"He's going to turn down Erieview. I need to catch him before then."

"Your cousin, he in trouble with the law, too?"

"He usually is, but not right now. No, I don't think so."

"So you want me to head him off for you, tell him you're here?"

"That's it."

"Call him, what the fuck."

"I don't have his cell number. I don't have a cell phone even if I had his number."

"Christ, you're a hopeless mess. What's your name anyway?"

That was as good a description of me as anyone could give. I told her my name.

"All right," P.J. said. "All right."

"I don't know how to thank—"

"Shut up," she said. "I don't like liars or bullshitters."

I shut up.

"What's he driving?"

"Last time I s-seen him, he drove a Silverado with a hundred dents from baseball bats being slammed into it and a cracked w-windshield. I don't know what he's driving now."

"That doesn't help me much, Wade."

Hearing my name on her lips—not spitting it out like bird shit—made me feel good for the first time in days. I described Kenny but left out the last time I saw him in his underwear and a wifebeater, standing in the doorway of the rented house we shared. He had a bottle of beer in one hand and his shit-eating grin watching the cops cuff me up.

"I have to get the place ready. Dwight was here, he'd kill the two of us just for talking. You stay out of sight."

"Where?"

"Out in the back where the coolers are. Customers will start showing up in an hour or so. I'll keep watch. That's the best I can do. No promises."

"If the cops come back, tell them I'm here."

"In a heartbeat," she said. "I'm not going back to Marysville."

The women's penitentiary near Columbus. "You did time?"

"Axe-murder. God, don't look at me like that. I'm joking. Shoplifting. I was using at the time."

"I know how it is," I said. "I've been in the system myself."

"Every customer I serve but some of the tourists have that same shitbird look."

I went behind the bar and sat on a stack of beer cases. I had hours to kill before I had to worry about Kenny or which direction he'd come from. If he took Interstate 90, he'd be coming from Northtown driving east. If he drove up through Columbus to

Cleveland, he'd be coming into town from the west. Either way, she wouldn't know until he was right there across from the bar ready to make the turn. If she were behind the bar serving, she'd never make it to the door unless he was held up by traffic. I sat on a couple cases of beer and leaned against the concrete blocks.

When I heard customers in the place, I realized I must have dozed off. The lunchtime drinking crowd filled half the booths and all the tables. Every seat at the bar was occupied. P.J. stopped in to check on me. I hadn't moved.

"I didn't want to wake you. Hey, you want a beer—a shot, take the edge off?"

I thought a shot of whiskey might kill me. "Water would be nice."

She brought me a bottled water and a couple bags of potato chips.

"You look like you could use something to eat."

"I'd like to pay."

"Fuck you."

She went back to work; another bartender showed up. I heard P.J talking to him about kegs and the delivery truck.

I guzzled the water, ate the chips, licked my fingers, greedy for every greasy drop. I started to doze off again when she came rushing into the back room, wiping her hands on a towel.

"Hey, I think I seen him, your cousin, whatever."

I jumped to my feet and walked behind her to the front of the bar. A dozen eyes tracked us. She opened the doors and stepped back to let me look.

A Dodge SRT Hellcat, black-over-red, racing stripes was waiting on a line of cars to pass before turning. I couldn't see the driver because of window glare. He'd come from the west and had to wait for traffic to pass before he could turn onto Erieview.

I hesitated. Every swinging dick in Northeastern Ohio cruised the Strip if he had a car worth showing off. Running out there was a one-shot deal, no turning back. I'd be exposed to every car, cop, pedestrian, and straight-arrow citizen if that wasn't Kenny behind the wheel.

The chassis was pocked with dents and scrapes. Only my cousin would drive a beautiful set of wheels into the ground—

I ran out the door like a hunchback, my head lower than the roofline of the Challenger. The last car was about to pass. The driver throttled in neutral impatiently indifferent to the sign posted in front of Erieview declaring 15 m.p.h.

I slapped my palm on the passenger side window twice. The driver swiveled his neck, seeing me. I looked right at him. His face was expressionless.

Jesus, he doesn't recognize me—

"Kenny, you lunkhead, it's me, Wade."

He grinned, reached over, and let me in.

"Cuz, long time no—"

"Don't turn! Don't turn! Go straight!"

I curled into a fetal position on the seat, half my ass squeezed down to the floorboard.

"What the fuck, Wade?"

"Kenny, drive. Cops."

I didn't need to explain. That word did it all for me.

He jerked the steering wheel back to straighten out the car with a squeal of rubber.

I wanted to raise my head up, look back at Dwight's to see if P.J. was there watching.

"Fuck's wrong with you?"

"Got a little problem. Tell you about it on the road. Keep going this way."

"Why you keep lookin' back like that, bro?"

"Like . . . what?"

Kenny to a tee. Tell him you have a problem with cops and he'd be keen to see what he could get from it like a hyena spotting a limp on the savanna.

"You look like you was a fuckin' baby had the nipple snatched away."

"Just sorry to be leaving this place," I said. Many wonderful memories."

"Fuckin' liar."

That was Kenny to a tee as well.

* * *

Chapter 4
Salem, West Virginia

"Why the fuck you keep itchin' your crotch like that for? You got the clap?"

"Got sand in my clothes from the beach."

"The beach? Fuckin' March, dumbass. Who goes swimming up here in March? This ain't Florida."

"Since when did you start caring when I go for a swim?"

We were halfway there, and I'd avoided telling him anything. He'd find out soon enough on his own. The landscape of Southern Ohio looked more like home with the hillocks, yellow buckeyes and sycamores growing on the slopes, small farms, horses roaming behind fences. I didn't feel safe until we were entering the Columbus innerbelt. I saw junction signs for Westerville, The Ohio State University exit, and Marysville. . . *I'm not going back to Marysville . . .* We all had places we couldn't bear to go back to.

Kenny pulled into a truck stop. I ate a full breakfast—pancakes, three eggs over easy, rye toast, a pot of coffee. Dessert was caramel cream pie. Kenny ordered a cheeseburger and fiddled with a cigarette, twirling it like a tiny baton between his fingers.

"Watching you scarf up that food," he said, "I'm wonderin' when you last had a meal. I seen guys pack on the pounds in chow lines, but you beat 'em all, Wade."

"I didn't get a chance to eat yesterday."

"Yeah, you said. It's what you ain't said that's got me wondering."

"Don't wonder. I told you I'm in."

"Glad to hear it, bro. But I meant that business about the cops. What kind of shit you step in?"

I told him about the savage yard, the rebar, left out the important parts about being wanted for murder. I left off at the part about banging on the Challenger's window to avoid a bar tab.

"That saves me having to talk your ass into my project. Like the old days. Me leadin', you followin'."

That rankled but I didn't say anything.

"Whatever, Ken. We do this together, we take the same risks, same everything. Same shares. You ain't got to worry about me putting in the work."

"Talking like a true gangbanger."

"Just sayin' is all."

"Don't be such a touchy bitch."

"Talking like a true ex-con," I said. "But I do 'preciate you driving up to get me."

"That's better, fucker. Not much, but it's better."

He ratted me out and I wind up apologizing, I thought.

"As long as you're in the appreciatin' mood, how about you take a shower in this place while we're here. I mean, not to put too fine a point on it, you stink like you been rolling in shit."

"If I do, will you stop playing twenty questions. I'm too tired to talk right now. You can tell me how much dope you had to sell to buy that car."

The restaurant had a 24-hour country store attached to it. I bought a new set of clothes from money Kenny loaned me. After a shower and shave, I felt human again. Yet that deep, plunging kind of sorrow also hit me again like seeing that headline and knowing I killed a man in fit of temper. I'd have to think of that and live with it all my life.

Kenny took me up on my suggestion to talk about "Baby" once we got back on the interstate.

" . . . Redeye's better than a Scat Pack, in my opinion," he said. "Got a wider body, better aerodynamics. I mean, fuck, a three-ninety-two Hemi, four-eighty-five h. p. Baby's starts at three-oh-five, goes up to seven-ninety, for shit sake."

"How much?"

"Thirty-thou, can you believe it?"

"You street-racing the shit out of it, I suppose."

"Pope shit in the woods, dummy? 'course I'm racin' it! You probably heard about the legend of Kenny Cardell up here in the frozen North, huh? This motherfuckin' dreamboat left a Shelby so far behind last week driver needed a GPS to find me. Made a thou off that pussy."

"I noted the dings all over rocker panels."

"Badges of honor, dude. Like a fightin' pit bull with his scars."

I thought of a nature show in the rec room at Denmar about a venomous spider called a Brazilian Wandering Spider, six inches long, muddy brown color, races along the jungle floor. Overly aggressive, the voiceover said; *it will even attack small pets . . .*

My cousin and his shiny car reminded me of that, a monstrous-sized predator without fear or a conscience. I listened to him go on about Baby, his deals, his bigger-than-life bullshit. All ego and then some. *He hasn't changed at all,* I thought.

The talk shifted to people we knew, relatives, friends we'd grown up with and gone to school with. He told me about classmates who'd died in car crashes, some from drug overdoses.

"We're the fucking opioid capital of America," Kenny bragged.

Death, violence, sex, scams, and his appetites, all favorite subjects. He mentioned one guy we both knew, a kid named Johnny Beavers we called "Bo" for some reason. He had a sweet temper, got bullied a lot. Kenny told me he was murdered by his wife two years ago.

"Carol just fuckin' lured him out of a bar with a story their little girl was taken ill. He follows her home, walks inside—and she gut-shoots him right there with his own thirty-ought-six."

Some had moved away—Texas, Florida, Nevada; most stayed.

"Aunt Ida," Kenny said, "that mean old bitch will never die."

"She's taking care of Mom all these months."

"Yeah, I reckon. No disrespect, Wade, but your pa, he ain't worth two shits when it comes to taking care of things. I mean, how hard you got to drink before they kick you out of the fuckin' V.F.W. in Clarksburg?"

"I heard."

"Bobby says you been supplying him with the cash to drink hisself into a blind-ass stupor every night."

"Bobby Cranson said that?"

"Bobby's an Afghan vet. He drinks there. Don't get mad at Bobby. Your old man says that, too. He tells everybody where his drinkin' money comes from like he's proud of his only begotten son."

I said nothing, stared out the window.

"Don't get all hissy now, Wade, or I'll stop this ultimate driving machine and pull over and beat your ass into the dirt."

The pressure of knowing my father was wasting that hard-earned money got to me. I exploded: "That money's supposed to go to my mother's medical bills, not down his gullet! Me and him, we're gonna have a little talk when I get back."

"Hey, calm down there, boy."

"I don't owe him shit."

"You owe him your beating heart, dude. He made you."

Scrimping and saving my shitty wages so he could drink it up. Now I was facing a murder charge, my mother was worse off. What was the point of anything?

I looked at my cousin.

"What's that grin on your ugly face all about? You think I'm being funny?"

"No, I don't think you're funny at all. I think you're the Devil himself."

"Shut the fuck up."

We were back on the road, coming down Interstate 77 into Parkersburg.

"Look at me, dickhead," Kenny said. "I'm serious as a heart attack."

He could turn it on and off like a switch.

"Your money problems are soon over. You and me, we're a team again. I got this juicy motherfucker of a score lined up you just ain't gonna believe. Candy from a fuckin' baby. You'll have enough money to pay off all your mother's bills—including the fifty bucks I loaned you back there for the new duds."

"I've been listening to you brag for the last two hundred miles about all the gash you've had, this hot-shit car, what 'Baby' can do— blah-blah, your connections, blah-blah. Who is this dude you say lined you up for this sweet job? He has a name, I reckon?"

"Yeah, dude has a name. But he don't want every motherfucker using it. He's Brand and you don't fuck with the A.B. . . ."

Great, I thought, *Kenny's mixed up with the Aryan Brotherhood.*

Denmar was medium-security, spanned by razor-wire and high-tech surveillance; however, budget cuts meant first-time offenders with felony convictions like mine were also shipped there. Kenny did time in "the big-boy places," he bragged, whereas Denmar was "a candy-ass joint."

"This one fuckin' guy came in, see? First thing, he begs the deputy warden, 'Don't put me in a pod with Brotherhood. They know me, I can't do time with them.' They didn't listen because they don't give a shit, number one. Number two, you're a con, so fuck you and the white horse you rode in on."

"Let me guess," I said. "They get him in the chow line. Now he's got a neck that looks like a zipper."

"Better than that. Two weeks in, he thinks he's OK, word gets to him, *all's forgiven*. They caught him in the shop, razored off every motherfuckin' A.B. tattoo on his body. And the guy had *mucho*. He come out of the hospital lookin' like he was baked in a toaster oven. You don't fuck with the Aryan Brotherhood."

"This deal we're doing. It's for the Brand? So we're 'associates,' which means we do the job, take the risk, get a lesser cut, am I right?"

"Not a hundred percent," Kenny replied, still smirking, driving with a single finger the way he used to back in high school.

"Jesus, Kenny, tell me you're not a member."

"Wisht to hell I was. Those boys do crime on a big scale. Being in prison don't mean shit."

"That money you loaned me, that Brand money, because I'll pay you back as soon—"

"Keep your panties on, Wade. Don't sell me short. I ain't just a gofer for them boys. I have my own projects—lots of irons in the fire."

"You're a venture capitalist, like my bunkie at Denmar would say."

"Don't mock me, boy. I'm your salvation."

It sickened me to admit it, but he was right. Only getting as far away as possible from him, my family, and this part of the country would save me from him—and myself. I was thinking Wyoming or Montana, somewhere I could disappear. Maybe snow crab fishing in Alaska.

"I'm still waiting to hear what the big project is—you know, the one where I'm going to be wallowing in pig shit right after."

"We're coming up on Salem. Old home week for you. We won't have time to talk once we get there. What say we pull off for a drink? We can talk over a cold one."

* * *

My strength was coming back. I wasn't there yet mentally speaking, but I felt better than I had since the day Tony fired me.

Kenny's big plan went past B & E into burglary, a night-time entry into a person's home, even if the occupants were gone. Nobody around to get hurt, he said. *Easy as taking candies from a Pez dispenser*, he said. He talked big money—a hundred thousand, maybe more, he said. Discounting my cousin's lifelong tendency to exaggerate, it still sounded like a big risk, anything but easy money.

Nothing's ever easy. My old man was dead right about that.

"OK, I'm good for it. My word. I need your word this isn't going to be a clusterfuck like that last 'project' you involved me in. You know, the one where I did two years practicing my letter-writing skills and reading old paperbacks from the library."

"That was your choice, Wade. All your choice. A man can learn a lot in prison if he wants to. I learned tig welding."

"You've never welded anything in your life."

"I have better things to do. Come on, motherfucker, let's hear all your objections, get it out of your system."

"This couple we're going to—liberate their cash from. They live simple lives in some shitburg town on the Ohio River. You say they go to casinos in Wheeling and Pittsburgh every three weeks like clockwork."

"Fuck, I done said it five times now."

"They keep their winnings in shoeboxes stashed in their house."

"That's what my inside guy told me," Kenny said. "Shoeboxes, not banks. They don't like to declare."

"Even I know the casinos send tax forms to the IRS if you win big."

"I don't give a shit about whether they pay taxes or don't pay taxes. What the fuck are we talkin' about here?"

"I'm having trouble understanding this couple we're gonna hit. Two successful people—one's a retired dentist, the other's a paralegal—"

"Lawyer," Kenny corrected.

"You said 'paralegal' at dinner. I remember that."

"Para-motherfuckin'-lawyer-paralegal, who cares? I misremembered it, so fuckin' sue me."

"These two quiet, God-fearing people, living quietly in this small town—which you haven't yet named—they spend all their time on junkets to gambling casinos."

"You're putting words in my mouth now. I'm gonna knock you flat, rip your head off, fuck you in your empty eye socket, then take a shit on the stump of your neck."

"Yeah, yeah. Put the convict talk aside and just listen to me. We're risking serious prison time if this goes sideways. It'll be a big jolt in maximum for both of us. You, with your felony record, you're gonna get a Buck Rogers sentence. Your folks won't see you until the next century."

"My folks don't see me now. I can do jail. No big thing to me."

"I can't do twenty years," I said. "I'm a career criminal like you."

"You did one shitty bid for two years. What are you talkin' about? Continue with your annoying questions."

Telling him I was wanted on an Ohio murder charge would only put me deeper in his pocket. I didn't understand why my cousin wasn't answering simple questions about the job. He wouldn't name his source, give me details about the robbery. Last time I talked to my dad about Ken, he said my cousin was sent away for armed robbery but won a new trial on appeal and then pled to a lesser charge for a lighter sentence. I couldn't get my mind around this wacko couple stuffing huge amounts of cash into shoeboxes or handbags or whatever and leaving the money lying around on closet shelves. No professional couple does that.

"My guy said this, not me, so don't blow a gasket—he said we might have to follow them from the casinos to make sure they had their winnings on them."

"So they can add another shoebox of cash to what's in the house? Why don't you pull my other leg, the one with bells on it?"

"Wade, you was always a rockhead when it comes to doin' what's simple and what's right there in front of you. These people—"

"—don't exist. I smell a ton of bullshit coming at me."

"He knows, motherfucker! My guy knows the score!"

"Your score makes as much sense as a rat fucking a grapefruit."

There was no talking to Ken after he lost his temper. We drove the rest of the way into Salem in stony silence. The closer we got to home, the more my stress level increased. The US Marshals could be there already waiting for me to show up. Kenny said nobody cared about a stupid assault beef, and called me a dozen names, but finally agreed to making a couple passes of the house and drop me off around the curve ahead where I could check it out from the slope above the house.

Kenny's relationships with people all go one way: he had something on you, something he held over head, some drugs you needed, whatever it was, he turned into your pimp, not your friend or your family any more. You became his whore. One way or the other, there'd be a big price to pay when the dust cleared.

* * *

These hills, these people. You see their shit-sucking lives and you wonder why they stay. The old ones, what choice do they have? The young want out. Some of them do get away with sparks flying from their shoes. Many come back with their tails between their legs. Or like kids who stick their toes in the deep end of the pool want to go right back to the shallow end. Coming home like this was like sitting on a hot-iron brand. Family, blood—how do you escape?

When we got to Main Street, Kenny pulled into a store to buy more cigarettes. I thought about my first girlfriend in Salem. We held hands at the Applebutter Festival but we never kissed.

Kenny came out fifteen minutes later.

"Took you that long to buy a goddamn pack of smokes?"

"*Whee-yew*, I can see homecoming has loosened your tongue. How about a tour of the big house while we're here?"

He meant the Jennings Randolph house owned by Salem University. They gave tours and sponsored conferences for the historical preservation society.

"Kiss my ass."

"I remember you telling me one time you was goin' away, and you said you was comin' back to buy the place."

"I said a lot of dumb things when I was a kid. So did you."

"Yeah, but the difference is I did most of mine."

"I won't argue with that."

That line in youth, somewhere around fourteen, fifteen, I'd say, that golden time when you think you can do anything or be anything. Kenny was going to play for Bobby Bowden's Salem Tigers, turn pro, and make a fortune. I was going to go to the college, get a degree in engineering, make a name for myself. Kenny played linebacker one semester before he got kicked out for rape. I managed the last part two days ago.

"Fuck me sideways, I'm tired from all this driving. You want to go right home? I was thinkin' we might hit Bill's for a quick one."

I was sinking into depression, but he'd gone all that way to fetch me, pluck me out of the lion's mouth, as Aunt Ida would have said.

Bill's Tavern near the tracks was a twenty-minute walk to my house right before Main Street curved off into the hills and up a dozen switchback trails into the hollers where the real Mountaineers occupied houses their great-granddaddies had built and they were born in.

"You ain't got any money," Ken said. "I'll be buying, I suppose."

"Got it in one. That diamond-sharp mind of Kenny Cardell is amazing, folks."

"OK, buttercup, let's see if Laydean in there can put some of Bill's whiskey down your gullet and make you the sweetheart you really are deep down."

"Hurry up before I change my mind."

* * *

Kenny was halfway to shit-faced when I told him I was going to walk home to surprise my mother.

He barely acknowledged me. "Fine, Wade, you do that. Call you tomorrow."

He went right back to another one of his convict adventures, usually something violent or with plenty of smut involved in the telling. He liked being the show wherever he was whether to classmates, other cons in his pod, or to a bunch of old farts and barflies, regaling everybody with his jailbird tales full of comic disasters and mayhem.

I stayed long enough to catch part of the one he was yabbering on about—some booty bandit from Weirton or Morgantown who had a fondness for "clean old white men," one old con in particular. The men at the bar listened with rapt faces as Kenny told them how the old guy would grease himself up to make his body too slippery for the ass-bandit to hold onto. The old men and even some wives laughed. One old man at the end of the bar shouted down: "Hey, Kenny, did ya'll have any trouble escapin' that old boy?" Kenny roared.

I recognized some of them, men from my father's generation. Farmers, ranchers, miners now in their sixties and seventies. One old dairy farmer still had on his coveralls and Wellingtons smeared from stepping on cow patties all day.

The same kind of clannishness I found in the working-class bars in Northtown and in the salvage yard. I thought it might be one of those déjà vu things, but I could have sworn two old-timers I knew from my past were planted on the very same stools as when I left town years ago to do time.

I walked down Main Street just as the big red disc of sun was dipping behind the hills. Light and shadow all around me. I would never get this sight out of my blood. Instead of passing the house in a car, I made for the hills in front of it in case any strange cars were parked in the driveway. Thing was, I didn't know how long it would take law enforcement to track me here. They could still be scouring the Strip for me for all I really knew. I thought about P.J. up in her bar and wondered if the cops had hassled her if somebody reported seeing me leap into a car right out front of Dwight's. A hundred thousand things had to fall into place at their exact moments in time for me to have grabbed that rebar and swung it at the cab and put me in a car with a cousin I swore I'd never see or talk to again.

My family house was a small ranch built on a slope like every house not right off the busy part of Main Street. The woods behind were mostly ash, Norway maples, and locust trees with a few scattered garbage trees, like Trees of Heaven here, already showing color while the rest lingered awhile longer in post-winter budding.

I left the trees to approach from behind. The back door was never locked, no matter what season it was.

I trotted up to the back window and looked inside the house: nothing, no black-clad SWAT or US Marshals. I didn't want to give my Aunt Ida a scare so I slipped around to the front and knocked.

"Lookee what the cat drug in!"

"Hello, Aunt."

We hugged. We made small talk in the kitchen before the subject came up.

"She's sleeping upstairs. She ain't got long to go before the Lord calls her, Wade. It's a good thing you're here."

"I might not be able to stay long, Aunt."

"Figures."

"What does?"

"You being a Cardell and all."

"I'll just go upstairs and look in on her."

"Don't make noise. She has a hard time sleeping."

Upstairs, the banister rail was smooth from four generations of hands rubbing it. Her bedroom door was cracked open and the last sliver of light from the setting sun fell on the hallway carpet beside her bed. It was an image burned into my brain from the seventeen years I lived there.

The morphine drip and the tube connected to her arm were the first thing I saw. I had a catch in my throat when I looked at her all shriveled and wrinkled up from cancer and a hard life that would stay hard until she breathed her last.

Life, fucking life . . .

* * *

In the morning I drank coffee with Aunt Ida in the kitchen

"She recognize you?"

"I think so," I said. "She tried to speak to me."

A car horn out front disturbed the calm.

"That's Kenny," I said. "I have to go."

"He'll wake the dead, never mind your poor mother. . . What for you got to go? You just got here."

"He's got a job lined up for me."

Her sour face said she knew what kind of work that was likely to be.

I picked up the paper sack on the floor where I'd stuffed some clothing, extra socks and underwear, and one other item I'd hid behind the iron vent in my old bedroom before I went away to Denmar, a Ruger .22. Only a stupid burglar takes a weapon on a job. That makes it a class-2 felony just about everywhere. But Kenny Cardell sat out there in the driveway and, truth be told, he scared me more. No matter what he said about packing on a burglary, he'd be armed to the teeth. I'd be crazy to trust him after whet he did to me once.

74

Aunt Ida was standing at the foot of the stairs when I came down. I didn't look at her.

Kenny's horn blasted another salvo.

"A Cardell to the end," my aunt said.

I went out the door wondering if she meant me or Kenny. Probably us both.

* * *

Chapter 5
New Zenith, Ohio

New Zenith is 15 miles from the town of Fly on the Ohio River. Both towns are a speck, more like recreational rest stops where hunting, fishing, and camping in summer are the chief commerce. Like Jefferson-on-the-Lake up north, the place locks down in winter, crawls out of sleepy hibernation with the warmth of the sun.

"Ain't nothin' but a barbed-wire fence and a lobo wolf between them two towns."

We had just crossed the bridge from West Virginia into Ohio between Gallipolis and Point Pleasant.

"Mothman flies around here somewhere," Kenny said. "You believe that shit."

I told him I believed in a lot worse.

"Don't give me the fisheye, cousin. Hey, a guy I did time with one time, he's from Illinois. He said he seen these big flying creatures called 'The Mythic Child-Stealing Thunderbirds of Kickapoo Creek.'"

"He's a lying sack of shit."

"He said 'Ohio' was Japanese for "Hello."

"Chatterbox this morning, ain't you? Why don't you tell me something useful about this fucking job where we're going?"

"Shit McGee, I get close to money, my dick starts a-jumpin' in my pants and mouth gets watery—*whoo-hoo-didley-dee*!"

"This inside man, your Brand brother, how much of a cut is he expecting?"

"You ain't got to worry about that none, Wade. I done all the work except stuff the money into your pockets. You just along for the ride."

"Taking care of kin like before."

"You had a large bug up your ass ever since I fetched your ungrateful self in that resort town you was in. I pick you up, I feed you, I give you money for new clothes, and now I'm bringing you in on the score of a lifetime. This is the thanks I get."

"I forgot I was riding with the Dalai Lama."

"Who the hell's that?"

"Forget it."

My cellie was a CPA, but he read all kinds of books in lockup to keep his mind active. All I wanted to do was sleep. Sleep those two years away and wake up when it was over. He had all these different paperbacks in the Walmart totes we kept under the bunks. He told me one afternoon about the Dalai Lama as the spiritual leader of Tibet, how he was born in the Wood-Pig year on the fifth day of the fifth year. He told before lights out that he'd explain what it meant to be the "fourteenth incarnation" the next day, but he got stabbed up in the chow line out of the blue. The convict grapevine said he'd had a conversation with a jailhouse lawyer over his appeal, and that he refused to pay the man who turned it over to the Aryan Brotherhood for collection.

"Tell me we ain't driving into a town with a population of a thousand in broad daylight, a place we intend to commit felony B and E, in a car you see coming for miles off."

"Relax, fuckface, your cousin got this covered. . . . You ever notice, you get back home, you lose that *duh-duh-duh* stutter of yourn. That must mean something."

Trying to pin Kenny down wasn't easy; he slipped my questions, distracted with convict jibber-jabber or juked and head-faked the way he did with his body when he was all-conference. When all else failed, he'd push the button marked *Family* to shut me.

"I hear my aunt ain't got long to go."

"You been talkin' to Aunt Ida?"

"Why would I talk to that hatchet-faced bitch? She's like steppin' on a fucking water moccasin every time you ask a simple question."

"Your aunt—my mother—is dying."

"Sorry about that, Wade. I liked your mother."

"She ain't dead yet, Ken."

* * *

Kenny left Highway 7 to follow a river road. I think even the GPS was lost. He wheeled the Hellcat over roads that weren't on any map I could find in the Atlas where my finger traced his pencil marks, arrows, and notations in his scribbled shorthand.

"You know where you're going?"

"Yep."

He followed what looked like a farmer's back road for three miles and then turned down a road that looked like quad bikes and two-wheelers made. Stones rattled under the chassis; for fun, he dogged out the last half-mile between a canopy of trees, the big engine sashaying in the muddy tracks. He drove expertly, showing off his skills.

"Where the fuck are we?"

"Shut up, bitch. . . . We're here."

We broke through into a clearing.

"Smell that?"

Rotting fish, diesel oil. The Ohio River up ahead somewhere beyond the last stand of trees we were emerging from, slewing and swerving the way Kenny used to do when he turfed lawns. A campground entrance off to the left. Closer, scow barges piled with refuse and sand plowed against the current. One bulldog tug pushed a barge loaded with iron-ore pellets, taconite from the Minnesota mining region.

"We park here," Kenny said.

"Where are we?"

"Matamoras," Kenny said. "Our base of operations."

Off to the left inside the campground were several dozen cars and SUVs lined in rows. RV's were parked opposite them in a semicircle of their own. Men in waders carrying fishing tackle and rods milled about, some talking, others unpacking fishing gear.

"They got separate parking for trailers with bass boats parked down by the landing," he said.

Not bad for Kenny, who was usually as subtle as a rain-wrapped tornado. We were going to blend in with a fishing tournament.

"What kind of fish?"

"Who gives a flying shit?"

"Somebody talks to me, I ought to know whether I'm after catfish or bass."

"As I recall," Kenny said, "you couldn't catch a fish if it jumped out of a fuckin' pond and landed in your lap. Grab your gear and them two Shakespeares, don't talk to nobody, and follow me."

He opened the trunk and took out a canvas backpack and started walking toward the RV section of the parking lot.

Signs announced the tournament was starting tomorrow at 5:00 a.m. Three thousand dollars apiece for biggest catches in the largemouth and smallmouth categories. Second and third prizes were a drop down: a six-drawer tackle box with Rapalas, Thundersticks, a Mepps Black Fury, and a Hummingbird fishfinder, the least expensive one on the market. Every participant, the sign said, qualified for a ballcap and tee-shirt imprinted with the tournament logo.

"Whoop-de-fuckin'-do," Kenny said passing the sign. "Senko worms and shad dancers, you want to catch largemouth."

"Where we going?"

"You'll see."

A small trailer, slightly humpbacked in the middle, like a decaying barn, occupied a corner of the lot. He went straight up the steps and took out a small ring of keys, inserted one in the door and shoved it open. He turned around to look down at me:

"Don't know why anybody bothers to lock this. Who'd steal this piece of shit?"

There was a microwave and a coffee pot on in the kitchenette in back, a small spring frame was hooked to one side and dropped down from a pair of latches bolted the wall. A rolled up mattress leaned in a corner.

"No electric, so don't bother askin'. You're sleeping on the floor, buddy-boy."

"I never doubted it," I replied. "This doesn't explain how we're going in."

He held up the key ring. "Transportation provided."

That man I'd bunked with at Denmar popped into mind at the strangest times and now, in the strangest company. Like me, Kenny was the opposite of an intellectual: uncouth, ignorant as pig shit, a fixed belief in his way of thinking. If he got anything right, it was owing to the same odds of a broken clock being right twice a day. That man explained the differences between different kinds of beliefs in Asian religions like Buddhism and Hinduism. He used big words like *satori* and *bodhi*, words I'd never heard my teachers use. "You talk about 'bliss' and 'enlightenment' and all that hifalutin shit," I said to him one day when my anxiety and loneliness were pressing in on me like boulders stacked on my chest. "You're in here for check kiting. What makes you think you're better than me because I broke in with a crowbar to steal money while you used a pen?" We stopped speaking much after that. Then came the day he mentioned the Dalai Lama. After he went to the hospital, I had the cell to myself for ten days.

Right then, however, I had a gut feeling my old cellie would call a *premonition* in his fancy way. Kenny had everything he needed.

So what did he need me for?

* * *

One pass, that's all, then we come right back. No mopery with intention to gawk. Got it?" He handed me the joint and parked his Challenger behind the trailer. A dinged-up tan Toyota was left with the key in the tail pipe.

"Ken, I don't like this. You're treating me like a mushroom. In total dark and covered in bullshit."

He ordered me to stop talking once we approached the couple's street. He didn't want to risk more than one quick pass, let me glance and go back.

"Someone could be looking out a window, remember this car."

"So what? You said your inside man had no trail back to him. This car's a dime a dozen. You haven't been here in two weeks. What if there's something going on next door the night we go in? This is stupid, Ken. Plain stupid."

"Like what? A fuckin' block party?"

"Tough titty. I want to see this place for myself. Give me that backasswards map you drew up."

"I ain't slowing down so take a good look, God damn it. We're going for food right after. Fuck what you say."

I wanted to pull my hair out, but what were my options at that point? Go back, turn myself in and hope I got out when my dick still worked when they released me? That fucked-up pizza parlor robbery of his that got me jugged for two years was so involved with details and surveillance you'd think we were taking down Fort Knox.

At least Ken's guy provided the right kind of ride for the job, a beat-up Toyota. Nothing like a beige Camry if you want to be inconspicuous on the road. Thing was, as I tried to explain to my thick-headed cousin, you're going to be on closed-circuit camera somewhere, sometime no matter how hard you try to avoid it. I'd talked to enough guys in the slammer who got jammed up like me because the camera nailed them at or near the scene. Knuckleheads learned to leave their cell phones at home when they were out doing crime, but there's nothing you can do about Ring cameras on every third house on every street nowadays.

Guys in prison studied crime shows and took notes. They laughed at the bozos who went to Walmart with a list of their purchases that a rookie prosecutor out of law school could demolish a defense with. The average person doesn't buy bleach or plastic 5-gallon gas containers, much less tarp, ropes, and nylon ties unless he's got some unbelievably bad ideas rolling around in his head. Those ceiling-mounted, hi-def cameras can read the list in your hand while taking out your wallet to pay.

We passed a modest, middle-class street with decent houses, nothing special, a little smug in the frou-frou landscaping but every one of them in the $150,000 to $200,000 range. Their house, "Mr. and Mrs. Lucky," as I was calling them in my mind, had the biggest house on the street—a spacious, two-story brick-and-wood Tudor with a turret, a landscaped yard with trimmed rose bushes beneath the windows and a twenty-foot flagpole out front. In the long driveway was a late-model, cobalt blue Navigator.

"That's for show," Kenny said as we passed it. "To keep thieves away while they're out gambling. They take their second car, a big-ass Escalade."

"Lucky people."

"Not so lucky," Kenny quipped. "My inside guy saw them cashing in at the teller's window after a big payout at the Mountaineer Casino."

"Horses, too? These people ever work?"

"Anybody ever tell you, hoss, if you like what you do, you never work a day in your life?"

"You oughta knit that on a sampler next time you do time. How much exactly are we going to find in there—according to your inside man? And if he knows so much, how come we're going in blind?"

"Questions, questions. Bags of cash he said. Listen to old Kenny you want to get rich and stop your bitching. I swear to God, Wade, I want to be nagged like this, I'll get married. Think of the poon you'll get with that money. No more hot dates with the Palm sisters because of that s-s-stutter."

He added a punch on my upper arm just like high school.

"Time to put the feedbag on, boy," he said, "and don't give me no more of your *Forensics Files* horseshit."

"I'll pick the place. That last place you chose gave me indigestion. You see the letters AUCE, you think it means good food. It's rattling the stick in the swill bucket is what it means."

"Fucking, ungrateful moron, you . . ."

It wasn't the bad food roiling up my stomach, it was my cousin jabbering away non-stop, not giving me time to think. He didn't let me out of his sight long enough to get my Ruger out of my bag and stick it in my pants.

Maybe Kenny was right. Ever since I learned I was a killer, I was short-tempered and paranoid. Maybe he was right about my ingratitude, too. I thought of my condition before he picked me up. I never heard from my cellmate when he came out of the hospital because they put him in SHU for his own protection. A guard told me he was released when I asked. I still had six months left of my sentence. He liked to quote Shakespeare. One of his quotes stuck: 'How sharper than a serpent's tooth it is to have an ungrateful child."

But who was the child, who the adult?

* * *

I couldn't finish the submarine sandwich and dropped it into one of the barrels placed around the campground on our way back to the trailer.

"Hey, you better fetch that back, Wade. Got your DNA all over it. Cops'll be jumping on that garbage can like chickens on a June bug."

Trying to josh me back into a good mood, the stupid ape . . .

I turned around and got in his face. I was still steaming.

"I can't believe you were going to make a cell phone call," I said. "You know they can track those tower pings and put your ass right the fuck here on this spot."

"I know all about that shit, Wade. Cons in every joint I been in love that show. You ain't tellin' me nothin'."

"Apparently I got to, bonehead."

He told me he was calling some chick back in Clarksburg he was seeing on the sly from his regular girlfriend. I didn't know what to believe and I wondered how many times he'd made a call since he picked me up at the house. I turned around and took a few steps ahead. I never heard him behind me. He used a leg sweep to the back of my knee to send me sprawling in the dirt.

"Don't make me fuck you up, Wade."

I got up slowly, brushed the filth from my shirt and pants, and looked at him calmly and did a half-turn, gesturing at the fishermen out and about, chatting, comparing notes, and jawboning with one another. The atmosphere before the competition was festive.

"No one saw that—let's hope. You want to get into a dustup when we're this close?"

"You're right about that, cuz. We gonna settle this business later. I'm up to my eyebrows with your bullshit."

Kenny's face was mottled with blood, almost russet in coloring. He was unlike his blond-haired, fair-skinned family in complexion and build, all except for the blue eyes. Family rumor for years was that his mother, my Aunt Della McDuff, was known to have a wandering eye. His black hair and blue eyes made him stand out like a young Elvis Presley, a comparison that did nothing to tamp down his arrogance. No doubt it added luster to his attractiveness to girls and women. When I described Kenny to my cellmate back in Denmar, right down to that extra knob at the top of his spine, he said my cousin might be a Melungeon. I asked him, "What the fuck's that when it's at home?" He told me it was somebody mixed up European, African, and Native American genes. When he started talking about Neanderthals mating with Homo sapiens, I laughed. "That's my fucking cousin, all right."

My stomach burned worse. It wasn't the anger with Kenny's half-assed planning, so much as watching him stow away the food without a care in the world; he packed away enough for both of us: Swedish meatballs over egg noodles, wedding soup, a roast beef sandwich and a slice of custard pie. He bought a plastic bag of chocolate chip cookies for later. Watching him eat in the car made me nauseated and envious of his robust appetite this close to a job. Cardell males were prone to bleeding ulcers and cirrhotic livers, although the latter was self-inflicted.

"Relax, homey, as the brothers say. Just havin' some sport with you."

Inside we made up our beds. Kenny sat down and swung his legs over. His bulk collapsed the thin mattress and made the springs squeal. He reached for his backpack at the foot of his bed and stuck his hand inside. He tossed a couple glossy magazines at me on the floor.

"Check these out. These'll help you relax."

Score, Juggs.

"Why am I not surprised at your choice of reading material?"

I tossed them back up to him.

"No, thanks."

The confinement and shared quarters brought back ugly prison memories. The absence of women made prison tough. Skin magazines made doing time tougher.

On that subject, Kenny agreed: "Guys in the joint go batshit over lingerie pics that get past the prison censors. They get their girls to send beaver shots and they all wind up in the Gang Intelligence Unit. Those horny bastards at my last place enough to fill a swimming pool with jackjuice. Even the cruelest, most vicious guy I done time with never once wondered who might be snappin' them shots."

Back to shooting the shit again like bros. His talkativeness was his way of apologizing, or so I thought.

"If you're planning to whack off that cashew between your legs, try to keep the moanin' down," I said.

"Wade, don't make me release the python. That's all I got to say about Jumbo. I'll have to fire off a couple shots. Might get some on your face while you're dreaming. In the morning, you get hungry, you can peel 'em off, eat 'em like potato chips."

Convict talk, soldier smut—the same everywhere. "You got anything else in that backpack besides fur books? I could use a nightcap. We got a few hours to kill before we leave."

"Just so happens I do have a bottle of JB in there."

Stupid move—putting alcohol on top of a sore spot in the stomach lining, but I was feeling more depressed than ever. I was knee-deep in crime, something I promised my mother I would never do when I got out.

"Take a swig a this, settle your nerves."

He swung the bag over to me. It hit the planking floorboard with a metal sound.

"What's that?"

"Binoculars, some shit we might need tonight."

I stuck my hand inside and came out with a pint bottle of Jim Beam wrapped in bubble wrap. A couple packets of Trojans secured by a rubber band. I fished around some more at the bottom and came out with a cellophane bag of weed and a small bag of powder. If Kenny started using meth, too, this was worse than I thought. Another reach inside the bag brought out a couple box of .22 ammo for semiautomatics.

"You really think we'll need these—long-round hollow points, Glaser safety rounds?"

I'd gone hunting with Kenny many times and saw him explode squirrels with hollow points just for fun. Bits of fur, bone, not much meat left, no carcass.

"The weed, yeah. I never do a job without a little toking after to celebrate."

"What about the meth?"

"I'm holding that for a friend."

"Where do you keep it?"

"Got me a secret hiding place in Baby so the staties can't find it if I get pulled over, which has been known to happen."

"They call in a dope dog and bust you, what then?"

"One time, this hound, he goes around Baby sniffing and sniffing. Damn dog knows it's there, trooper eyefuckin' me in his ten-gallon hat and shades knows it's there—"

"Save that for your memoirs, Ken. The gun, where do you keep it?"

"Same place, fucktail."

"I see you on that cell phone again, Kenny, I swear to God I'll shove it up your ass."

"My legs get all tingly when you talk like that. Blow me."

I drank more, big swallows—*fuck that big dummy.* The fire scorched its way down my throat and set off a wicked hurting deep in my belly; then, like molten electricity, it flowed through my whole body. In my hardest drinking days, I'd get night sweats something fierce; the booze would leak from every pore and I'd wake in the cold dawn hungover as hellfire hearing them starlings settin' up a godawful racket. All my regrets would come thudding home, stepping on my heart, as Aunt Ida said. I couldn't change then, I couldn't change now.

No, that ain't true. I can slip out of here while he's sawing logs and run like a motherfucker.

But I didn't.

I closed my eyes and thought about that couple's house and the money in it. Money wasn't going to get the US Marshals off me or any cop with a computer. But it might get me off this hamster wheel of going nowhere except into more trouble and bigger trouble. I wasn't book smart or any smart, for that matter, yet I knew one thing for certain: people talk about happiness way too easily. It's got too many meanings for any dictionary to handle. Like them dumbass cons hankerin' for photos of the vertical smile, we never stop askin' for it. And when we get it, we don't even know we're worse off than before.

* * *

"Rise and shine, motherfucker, it's time to do crime."

Despite everything going on, I'd slept. My body or my mind, whichever, just got tired enough to knock me out.

"How long we been out?"

"Me, a couple, three minutes. You, three hours, snoring like my old man. Now get your ass off the floor so I can get up. We ain't comin' back to this dump 'cept to pick up Baby."

"Jesus H. Christ, I slept that long. What time is it?"

"Wade, what the fuck you doin'? Get up, soldier. Time to get rich."

Kenny said the couple wouldn't be returning home for another day. He was sure of it, but like everything else I asked about, he wouldn't say how he knew except to say "my guy" knows.

He burned me once. In Kenny's mind, that was payback for not telling him about his girl cheating on him. That was *my* betrayal, not his. It got me for two years. This time was different all around. It smelled from the start. We'd dealt drugs with more planning. His mysterious Aryan Brotherhood source in lockup somehow knew the couple's habits, but not where they kept the money in the house and how much money they had from gambling. Which was another problem. Gamble enough, the law of averages catches up. The house wins. This was no break-in job with crowbars or bolt cutters. We were parking in the couple's own driveway and going in the front door, thanks to Kenny's guy whose name he never revealed, joking about it: "I tell you his name, Wade, I'd have to kill you." This AB convict even provided Kenny with a duplicate key of the front door, the Toyota and the camper we were using. It was *supernatural.*

Kenny never shared unless he had to, and when he did, he got the lion's share. Anybody who did all that his magical contact could do from prison would demand a full share of the swag. Yet my cousin insisted he was OK with that. I knew enough from Denmar to know the Brand used "associates" on the outside, but they didn't consider them equal. Kenny was hired help, like me. So what kept sticking in my craw?

Which brought up the $50,000 question for the fiftieth time: Why bring me in at all? Kenny made it sound like all we had to do was walk in, find the cash, stuff it in our Levi's and walk back out the door. *Easy-peasy,* he said. "You don't need me if it's that goddamned easy," I told him. He blew me off with some ass-headed saying he bollixed up about "looking at a horse's mouth," the dumb shit.

If I hadn't been so desperate back in that Ohio resort town, half-frozen and starved, with a warrant out and cops looking for me, I could have given this whole thing more thought. I should have. My mother dying back home in her bed was eating at me constantly. Now it was too late. I had to play out the string. The river card was dealt just like in Texas hold 'em.

"Read it and weep, motherfucker"—just like Kenny would say.

* * *

Chapter 6

"You've been here before," I said.

He looked at me as if I'd fallen out of a tree and landed in the seat beside him.

"Of course, I've been here before, asshole."

"I mean, you've been here before—this town, the way you drive. You know these streets. Even in a one-horse town, you drive like a regular citizen. Yesterday, when we did the recon, you turned down that side street like you knew there might be a patrol car sitting at the intersection."

"You're full of shit," Kenny growled. "You think I'm not going to drive extra-careful, huh? I'm not as stupid as you think, Wade."

Kenny wasn't like my cellmate with his Rubik's Cube. I'd known him too long. He was all animal intelligence. Put a book in his hands and he'd fall asleep. For all his size, though, he was light on his feet and you best not try to sneak up on him. Cagey, sly like a fox, he stepped in the shit himself because of his arrogance. He'd fight anybody in any bar on a dare, but he liked to come out from a direction you weren't thinking about. He'd get there fast all the same. I'd seen him in bar fights. He got real quiet, not mad or angry like most guys who get their dicks in a twist and start ripping off their shirts, like that's got something to do with it. Bump into him, spill his beer or say something contrary, he might fight or he might make a joke. But if he wanted you busted up, he'd make sure you didn't see it coming until it was too late.

"These houses, look at them," Kenny remarked suddenly, as if we were sightseers on a jaunt. "Mortgages, lawns to cut, kids to feed, bills to pay. Got them little dwarf things with the pointy hats from China, whatchamacallits, them ceramic things peekin' out from fences and lilac bushes."

"Yard gnomes, for Chrissake."

He gave me that smile, one that made the girls respond.

"Can you smell that money? I sure can."

* * *

My heart picked up a faster tempo the later it got. My hearing became acute as if I could hear every sound inside and outside the car, the clang of that sewer grate we drove over—everything too loud or too quiet.

The car hadn't been washed much by the owner, but it had a good engine from the steady purr of its measly 6-cylinders. Someone had taken care of it.

Birds roosted invisibly overhead in the maples and oaks lining the pleasant street. Streetlights revealed pigeons roosting, hunched together on the wires like football players on the sidelines. I caught the gleam of cats prowling in yards, their luminescent flash of gold-green caught in the car's beams as we turned into Old Beaver Road, the residential part of New Zenith. Too early for fireflies; the air close to the river had that fuggy smell. It seemed like a place where cats could roam freely, a nice place to live.

We were going to make it a not-so-nice place soon. It would change the atmosphere after we left. Nothing's the same after a house robbery. *You hear the Barretts got robbed last night . . ."*

Breaking into a house at night increases the punishment if you get caught. When Kenny told me we were doing this at night, I tried to talk him out of it.

"Let's go in the daytime," I said. "get some uniforms, slap a decal on the side of the car like we're furnace men or landscapers. Nobody'll pay attention to us and we won't be stumbling around in the dark without flashlights."

All that got me was a sneer. "We go at night just like he said. I'll find the fuckin' money without lights no matter where they hid it. We ain't changing nothin'."

I figured Kenny was acting on Brand orders, maybe the only ones who could make him obey, tamp down his bullrush instincts: *Do it the way we told you.*

Every third house had lights on, TVs glowing behind curtains, many dark from the front. A couple houses on both sides of the street kept their porch lights on as well. No traffic this late but no feeling that people had gone to bed after the late-night talk shows or Netflix, whatever people did at night to avoid sleep or relax after the kids were put to bed. Kenny dropped the speed to 20 m.p.h. as we drove down the couple's street.

"Not too fast, not too slow—just right, like Goldilocks," my cousin said. Probably the last book he read.

I kept my gaze on the lighted windows, watching for any hands pushing the curtains aside to see if their teenaged sons or daughters were coming home this late after curfew. Every neighborhood has a Nosy Nora, some woman or man, a bored retiree or lonely widow, who knows everybody's business and whereabouts, the person who's always the first one the cops want to speak to after a break-in.

"There she is," Kenny said, pointing through the windshield up ahead where I could just make out the shape of the Navigator in front of the garage doors. "Wide open, dripping like a wet pussy just waitin' for my cock to fill it up with hot jizz."

You can take the boy out of the prison, I thought, *but you can't take the prison out of the boy . . .*

* * *

We got out, walked up to the front door. Kenny put the key in the lock, and we walked right in. *Nothing's ever easy . . .* I blocked out my father's words and tried to breathe deeply. My heart was pounding like a bongo.

"Wisht I had them night-vision Army goggles," Kenny whispered, once we were in the foyer.

The couple had timer lights that enabled us to see but also be seen from the street if we moved in front of a window. "Told you we could do this easier in the dark."

"You told me a lot except who your man is and where the money's stashed."

"Keep your panties on, boy. We got all night to find it. You look around in the closets downstairs. I'll go upstairs."

I made a quick search and felt stupid opening cabinets, sideboard drawers, behind the cushions as if somebody would hide stacks of money anywhere like that. A tall mahogany secretary was in view of the picture window out front. I'd check it last if we didn't come up with the money before then. The house was neat, comfortable, middle class. Everything in its place. They didn't leave any dirty dishes in the sink when they left. Nothing unusual, nothing out of place. I suspected the garage would be as neat. A door off the kitchen led to it. I took a peek. Hammers, drills, saw lined up by size. Not the kind of people who feared banks or the IRS, not the kind compelled to stuff money under the mattress.

Keeping an eye on the windows every time I moved, I headed for the stairs after Kenny.

He was sitting on the edge of a bed in the master bedroom.

"I found it," he said and pointed at the walk-in closet.

I stepped over to see, dreading what I'd see. He wouldn't be sitting there calmly; he'd by stuffing it into the bags we had on us.

A floor safe. *Fuck a duck*—

A stainless-steel box you can buy at Lowe's for a few hundred bucks. Maybe two, two-fifty in weight.

"What now, genius? Your man, is he a powder monkey, too? Because you and me don't know jack shit about blowing a safe open."

"Dunno, Wade."

"*You don't know, you lummox, you're sitting on the bed like King Farouk*—"

"The old lady across the street might not have heard you. Why don't you say it louder?"

"Let's grab the fuckin' thing and go. We can carry it out of here, the two of us can haul it easy. Bust it open later."

"Go ahead, try to lift it," Kenny said.

I squatted in front of it and gripped the bottom. Bolted to the floor.

"You fucking son of a bitch and your fuck-ass convict source."

Taking a deep breath, I said, "OK, it's bolted down. We can rip up the floorboards. Get off your big ass. Let's find some tools in the garage. It's a fucking Home Depot in there."

I flew down the stairs, two at a time. Maybe we had all night, maybe not. But cutting the safe loose wasn't going to happen on its own, and even I knew it would take a couple hours; even then, we needed the right tools.

Shoeboxes—that motherfucker—and stupid me, I believed him . . .

Putting a light on in the garage was risky, but hell's-holy bells, I figured we'd parked out front behind the couple's Navigator. Any neighbors or police passing by would see people were at home.

The owner had a rack of tools on all three walls. *Thank God, a do-it-yourselfer.*

I scoped what I needed. If I could take out a transmission from beneath a truck while lying on my back on a stack of junk cars, this wouldn't be that difficult.

Grabbing the power drill on a small bench first, I located a sledge leaning against a wall, then a jig saw, a claw hammer, awl, and a foot-long shank punch on another bench. I scooped everything into my arms like some sweepstakes-loving yahoo who just won the hardware contest and had a minute to grab as many tools as he could carry. I hit the light switch with my elbow and hauled ass for upstairs.

My thighs burned from racing up and down like a hunchback. I stumbled into the bedroom, dropped everything on the bed.

Kenny just looked at the tools.

"Hope you found all that without lights."

"Everything we needed, right there."

"Lucky dog, you."

His nonchalance was pissing me off. We were trespassing the second we exited the car. Then it became housebreaking when we walked in, key or no key—a serious felony. Going into a house without the owner's permission with intent to steal and then you add in the safecracking we were about to undertake and that leapfrogged the crime by enough to triple the time behind bars if we got caught. My cousin didn't just risk violating parole for felony possession of a weapon, thanks to his black throwing knife tucked in his boot. That added "deadly weapon" to aggravate charges. We didn't have to steal a dime to both go away for ten years.

"You mind giving me a hand here, Mister Cool?"

I drilled holes at an angle in front of the bolts and used the hammer and awl to punch out enough wood to cut the jig saw blade in.

"What if he's got it concrete behind them bolts?" Kenny asked me.

"Holy shit, you actually care about the job? Not likely, unless he's fixing to have a three-hundred-pound safe come crashing down on his head while he's having spaghetti dinner with the missus."

Fuck me, I was sweating hard. The cramped space in the closet made it hard to work. I thought of my time under the lifeboat, wiggling in the sand all night, straining every muscle in my body. I took off my sweatshirt and tossed it to the foot of the bed.

"You mind helping me, Ken, or do you have something else to do tonight?"

"You pussy, stand back, and give me that fuckin' sledge."

The floorboards were tongue-and-groove, not the shitty laminate over planking. Hardwood, cherry or walnut—very tough to penetrate because the sledge had to be swung at an awkward angle. Kenny wasn't worried about his carpentry skills.

"We ain't making a fuckin' piano here. Get the fuck out of my way."

He blasted chunks out of the door jamb and sent chips flying, punched holes in the drywall with shots that ricocheted or missed altogether. I spelled him whenever he whacked the metal undercarriage too hard—like a bad hit in baseball that made your hands sting from the impact's vibrations.

He handed me the sledge again, looked at his watch.

"Fuck Almighty, Ken, we been at this an hour and more—what gives?"

"Goddamn iffen I know. I can't budge that motherfucker."

"I'm OK with calling this off."

"Nossir. No fucking way. We come for money. We're leaving with money."

"Even if we get it loose," I replied, "we still have to haul it down them narrow stairs. How the fuck are we gonna get that heavy bitch into the trunk of a Toyota with the whole neighborhood up sipping their morning coffee and watching us from their windows—not to mention the rest of the town when we drive by with the ass end of a stolen safe hanging out the back?"

"Wade, let me explain something to you. We leave empty-handed, it won't be cancer killing your ma and your daddy, or us neither. Nobody's gonna die in a four-poster bed handin' out stocks and bonds to the grandkids."

"What the fuck are you tellin' me?"

"Them guys I'm working for—we're working for—don't tolerate failure."

"I can believe you'd drop me in the shit because you did it before. But my folks got nothin' to do with this business."

"That's the way it is, so you better come up with another plan."

I stood there looking at him after that jaw-dropping statement he'd uttered as calmly as though I'd asked him for the time. He sat on the bed and took out a rolled marijuana cigarette from his shirt pocket.

"Judas Iscariot has got nothing on you, cousin."

"Go downstairs and fetch us a beer while I ease my mind and think on this a minute." He lit up.

Shit, piss, fuck.

I left him there calmly smoking as if he was sitting in a rental cottage and had all the time in the world.

I went down the steps like a man walking to his doom. I eyed the door, thought of making a break for it. Let him try to find me. Instead, I headed to the kitchen. With my shirt front in my hand to avoid fingerprints, I opened the fridge and grabbed two green bottles of beer by the neck.

The digital microwave clock said 3:15 in the morning. By then, I felt as if I'd been born and raised in that house.

Upstairs again, I handed a brew to Kenny.

"Remember to take it with you—"

"Yeah, yeah, you CSI motherfucker. Shut up with that shit."

I waited while he sat on the mattress and guzzled the beer.

"Breaktime's over, Ken. Union rules. Back to work. Your turn with the sledge."

"Nope. We wait."

"Wait? Wait for what? The cops? You want I should start breakfast so we can all sit down and eat while they write up the charges because there's gonna be a truckload of them."

He looked at me in a way I hadn't seen yet. "We wait for them."

Jesus, the owners . . .

"Kenny, look, no shit now, we got to go—"

"We wait for those motherfuckers to come home. I'll make them open this thing up or I'll open up their fucking skulls one at a time."

His grin froze my blood.

He reached around and from the back of his belt he pulled out a semiautomatic and rested in on his knee, a finger not on the trigger but close enough.

"Don't make any foolish moves, Wade."

Too late for foolish moves. I'd made a shitload of them by then. Forget second-degree burglary, hello aggravated burglary. Right there, that moment, I knew I was well and truly fucked.

* * *

Chapter 7

Now I understood why the car in the driveway didn't bother Kenny. Why he was so cool about being in the house. The car we drove was usually parked there. And it was usually parked there because whoever drove it most of the time lived there. In the house. It was part of the baseline normal of this particular neighborhood.

The gun rested on his knee, his fingers big enough to make it disappear like he'd just mashed a tarantula on his leg.

"I don't suppose you'll take it kindly if I turn around to leave, me being family and all."

"You ain't going nowhere, shithead."

"That's what I thought."

"Sit down over there on the floor next to that end table and keep your mouth shut."

Live and don't learn, I thought.

Thinking back, I knew my instincts were right. *Trust your instincts*, Kenny told me often enough when we were in the dope business. Mine told me in so many ways this was bound to happen. I knew what those people felt like when they fell for one of those Nigerian prince scams on the internet. I should have seen it coming, but I wasn't paying attention. I was looking too long at other things, not thinking about what I should have seen all around me. It should have been me finding out about those things in myself I was missing all along.

Squeezed between the table and the bed posts, I was getting cramped at the knees. Kenny didn't pay much attention to me. He just sat there smoking weed, casting a glance at me every so often but content to sit and look at his wristwatch as if he had an important meeting to attend.

"I told you we'd have to settle our business, Wade."

"What business?"

"Lordy, I ain't got time to explain it all. But, hey, no hard feelings."

If he expected me to scream or beg or curse him back to Adam, he was disappointed. That wouldn't amount to much anyway. The light leaking into the room from the beneath the closed drapes enabled me to see the gun, a matte black Taurus. Long as I'd known him, Kenny was a fiend for S & W's, Glocks. His favorite was the SF with .45 ACP ammo. But the gun didn't put as much fear in me as the ammo. With hollow points, it had all the stopping power necessary and wouldn't go through the walls and kill the neighbor's toddler. It was strictly meant for close-up killing.

"I don't have any hard feeling toward you," I said. "I'm curious why is all."

"Kinda obvious, ain't it, dummy?"

"Maybe you could explain a little bit."

"I owe you that much, I s'pose. Cousin to cousin, one jailbird to another."

"The problem I got is money, a shortage of it at the moment. You sorta fell into my lap when you made that phone call home."

"That don't explain much."

"A little birdie told me you stepped into some deep shit in Ohio. I was afraid you'd get picked up before I had a chance to—"

"—to put me to good use. I get it now."

"Good. Glad we're on the same page." He checked his watch again.

"Who you waiting on?"

"I think that's enough chit chat for now. I got to secure your hands. Don't make me shoot you. All that forensic horseshit you were so worried about—well, let's say there's a time and place for everything."

He reached around and took some nylon cuffs from the same place where he'd kept his gun.

"I want you to stand up, real slow, and put your hands out together like this, see? Stretch 'em out toward me. That's it. Don't take a single step, Wade. I don't got to tell you what a hollow point can do to your face if I so much as nick you."

I tried to rock to my feet, my back hitting the wall. I slid back to the floor.

"Sorry. My knees locked up from cramp. I been sitting down here too long."

He pointed the gun at my head.

"You need to get on your feet right now. I can kill you here. It's all one to me."

I stood up, still rocking on my feet. I stretched out my arms for him to apply the ties to my wrists.

"That's it. I really appreciate you bein' a good boy about it."

I kicked him in the crotch.

He let out a *whoof* of air from his lungs and then swung the semiauto at me.

Fight the man, not the weapon . . .

Nothing like pure animal fear to give your body the adrenalin boost you need. I hit him low, in the knees, and he stumbled backward but didn't fall. I was clinging to his legs with every ounce of strength I could muster. If I took him to the floor, I could go for his eyes, claw my fingers down his face—

He brought his gun arm down hard aiming for my head but it skimmed off, missing the back of my head. Rolling over him, I was back upright, on my feet, running low for the doorway, not seeing anything else in my tunnel vision. I aimed my body like a missile down the hallway for the stairs where he wouldn't have a clean shot.

My brain might have recorded the shot, I don't know, but a basketball-sized chunk of drywall exploded over my head and powder dust blew up behind me.

I was halfway down the stairs when I saw them, the three of them—the family—although that's an exaggeration to say I *saw* them. The image was recorded in my neocortex like a blip.

A man and woman standing stock-still in the foyer of the house—a family portrait of people just arrived home—a middle-aged woman, a man in a checked sport coat, the young woman, a daughter, between them. Three stunned faces seeing me flying down the stairs being pursued by a madman with a gun—in their own home.

She remained the clearest in my mind's eye: full head of light brown hair parted in the middle, a blue nylon jacket with a striped scarf that reaches her waist; she stands in front of them—not to shield them from him, a strange man racing down their stairs at breakneck speed. All three of them have their mouths wide open, as if they were singing the same song from a choir hymnal. This weird tableau, these three people I never met and never meant to harm, fixed in place as if they were mannequins nailed to the floor.

The stairs have a landing cut at a right-angle to the foyer. I couldn't slow my momentum and grabbed for the landing dowel to swing me around to clear the last half-dozen steps and point me toward the door leading to the garage. Instead, the dowel came off in my hand. I slammed into the wall, collapsing in a heap to the floor as another explosion of powder rained down on me. This time, I felt bits of plaster hitting me in the face, but they didn't sting at all. I was too flushed with adrenalin to feel any pain. One thought coming from my reptile brain: *Go, get out, out, out, go—*

I scrambled to my feet and dove to the bottom of the steps in a belly flop. I didn't bother looking up to see if Kenny was coming down or aiming for another shot.

Those three people were going to save my life. I intended to ram into them like a bowling ball and hoped I'd get out the front door in time before Kenny had a clear shot at me fleeing. My human shields. I didn't think about their lives at all. But, yet, I did it. At the last possible second, I veered, swerving for the kitchen and the door to the garage.

I still see it in my mind's eye like a jumpy film: *I see the door. I'm running for it like the finish line with the baton in my hand*—and my right foot slips on the tile flooring.

My cellmate in the joint told me physicists can parse seconds into nanoseconds, and split that some kind of time-unit even shorter in something called a particle collider. My brain saw it coming—the edge of the table before I slammed into it, then blindness, red colors like floaters in my vision in slow-motion . . . I'm going down hard, my chest and ribs taking the brunt of the impact.

Here's the part I had to put together long after those split-seconds of time: someone's voice, shouting words my brain can't take in because there's a black vortex sucking me down. A girl's voice, not yet a woman's very clearly as though the words were cast in bronze. But they are locked in my head: "Kill them . . . Shoot them all now!"

Summoning all my remaining strength—am I reaching for the doorknob to flee? Am I trying to get the lifeboat off me again? It's fuzzy, mixed up. Then everything goes haywire, like a 4th-of-July sparkler, before it turns black. *I'm stretching out my hand to take the baton for the last quarter mile of the 4 x 440 meter. Coach Kraźcik knows I'm better in second position. I run to the back stretch and move into the inside lane . . .*

The memories are mixed, like chips of colored plastic in a kaleidoscope. Just when they start to make sense, something twists the tube and the image blurs, disappears in bright flashes of color. I can't pull them together to make sense. I see my hand, I see blackness like a curtain dropped on stage after a farce comedy where pratfalls and shouts are the whole point.

I remember coming to on the floor, blood dripping from my nose and mouth from the face plant. The side of my head feels like I got hit with the sledge. Three of my ribs are scorched, like a branding from a red-hot poker. I wonder if I'm dying on this floor, if dying is supposed to feel like this. But the pain makes me realize I'm still alive, still breathing. Then, oddly, I think of my mother in her upstairs bed waiting for death in a bar of sunshine. I lay my head back down on the floor. I wait for it to happen to me.

This is better than going back to prison. . . . as fucked up as a Chinese wedding in the T'ang dynasty.

Not me, Kenny. He said that. More whackjob prison gibberish . . . I think I must have tripped carrying the safe to the car. I don't remember the people—except for that girl's voice and her strange demand for someone to shoot. I can't think anymore. I decide to sleep.

* * *

Chapter 8

Head wounds bleed. Mine bled enough to keep Kenny from putting a fragmentation round into the back of my head and finishing me off on that floor in a godawful mess of blood spatter, brains, and bone shards—at least, that's what I think happened before I woke up and stayed awake. Half my face was stuck to the floor from the dried blood around my head and the blood that leaked from my nose and mouth.

How crazy the brain is with its own thoughts. It made me think of Elmer's glue and doing pictures from magazines when I was in kindergarten.

I came awake fast that time, like waking from a nightmare—only to see you're still in the nightmare and all your senses are working, colliding at once.

Swallowing blood when I smacked my jaw on the floor and it poured down my throat, I leaned over to vomit it up. I was lucky I didn't choke to death if you can call anything like that luck. I felt around my head with my fingers sticky from blood. My head ached like the worst migraine I ever had times ten. My hand came away stickier.

I stuck my finger in a hole back there. I didn't know whether to laugh or sob. That shot from the landing must have hit a wall stud, a fragment ricocheted into the back of my head with terrific force. I thought I was shot, but I remembered getting up and running as though I had a rocket strapped to my ass.

Standing wasn't easy. My legs weren't working and breathing through cracked ribs was a new torture to go with the rest. The digital clock on the stove blurred, settled into a meaningless row of bright digits that didn't mean anything yet. I wanted to rest before trying to walk again.

With the elaborate effort of a decrepit 90-year-old man with a dozen hitches in his step, I tottered, my vision reeling then clearing, a bit more with each passing second, I held on to the edge of that heavy kitchen table.

The collision had moved it four feet, gauging from the indents the legs made in the tiles. I leaned over to heave again; nothing came up except blood-flecked spittle. The blood on the floor was drying, but I couldn't tell for how long I lay unconscious. The edges were starting to turn a rusty brown. It would turn black in time. *Why was I alive? Where were those people who walked in when my cousin was trying to kill me?*

The biggest question was the obvious one: *Where the hell were the cops and why wasn't I in custody?*

I'd been on the floor too long for the police not to be here. My first real thought was that Kenny took them hostage after he forced them to open the safe and give him the money. Then I remembered hearing that girl shout those words before the lights went out.

The answers came, not at once. I was still too groggy and in an agony of pain from every direction to think clearly.

Stumbling from one piece of furniture to the other for support, I moved to the front window and pushed the curtain aside. No cops. No cars. No neighbors pointing at the house—after all that ruckus? It seemed impossible. A woman walked a Schnauzer past the house.

Staggering to the downstairs bathroom, I splashed water on my face and washed blood out of my hair. The mirror showed me a face I didn't recognize from the bruises, swollen flesh, puffiness on one whole side where I'd slammed into the floor. I put a finger in my mouth and felt a couple loose teeth. Cleaning up as best I could, I walked back out into the living room. My shirtfront was sopped, and splattered in blood.

I had no plan. It didn't seem any use to think beyond the next five minutes. My extra clothes were back in the trailer with my useless gun. I winced at the memory. I could have used one of those Japanese *satoris* the moment I felt that box of ammo in Ken's bag. I didn't even bring a knife to a gunfight.

I wanted to get into clean clothes; nothing else mattered. Deep down, I knew the cops were on their way. They had to be. I wanted to be in clean clothes when they arrived with sirens screaming at me to come out with my hands up. *At least I won't be a bloody mess when they make me do the perp walk for the cameras . . .*

I was working my way toward the banister, walking like a cripple, when a voice in the living room almost knocked me off my feet: *Sylvia? Sylvia? Did you forget we had a meeting with Pastor John today? Give me a call.*

My heart caught up with my brain—the answering machine.

Yeah, Sylvia, I thought, *where the fuck are you—and your husband and daughter?*

The girl, the daughter. Kenny's "inside man." The knowledge finally wiggled through the haze. I could have puked at the treachery. *Who else? You big dummy.* She must have driven off in one car, Kenny in the other. The car we used was hers.

Maybe not a full-blown *satori* or a—*what did my cellie call it—an epiphany.*

Kill them!

Her words to Kenny. A set-up. Not just a set-up to kill, her parents but a set-up with a patsy. Me, of course.

That made me what my instincts were trying to get through to my brain ever since Kenny left me in the car at the rest stop to go back inside. *Use the shitter,* he said. *No, you lying fuck, it was to call her, the daughter.* And how many other calls did he make between then and the minute we rolled up in her family's house—*to kill her parents.*

Jesus, shit, fuck . . . I was so stupid, stupid.

I walked up those stairs like a man walking up to judgment on the Last Day.

Framed photos on the wall placed at geometrical angles. Father, mother, daughter: Sylvia beaming for the camera in her wedding dress. Her new hubby with a full head of hair. Higher up, the daughter appears. First, a baby in her mother's or father's arms, then a toddler in a Minnie Mouse tee-shirt. Close to the top of the stairs, she's transformed: a gawky teen with her face breaking out, budding cones of breast, braces. No more Sears or Walmart family photos of the three in similar attire, however. She's alone, caught at moments unaware of the photographer, except for one photo of her and another girl, Corinne awkward, shy, squinting, whereas the tomboy her age beside her looked boldly at the camera, both standing in front of horse stables. No big toothless smiles post-adolescence.

Finally, a last photo of her. She's an unhappy young woman in her twenties with a sheepdog haircut, heavy lids, full lips in a tight smile more like a sneer. Dressed for church services, standing in a pew with sunlight illuminating a stained-glass window behind her. I knew the scene: The Garden of Gethsemane. Jesus praying near a boulder, weeping blood-red tears.

I could have written captions for the last two beneath her hard stare: *Fuck off* and *I Hate My Life.* Trouble in the family home. It led to this, to me standing near the top of the stairs in a house I had no business in. If my face didn't hurt so much, I might have wept then.

All those thousands of subterranean forces working away in the dark. Me in the salvage yard—that was a part of it, too. Me back in Denmar. Me creeping into my own house in Salem. Every goddamned thing I did and everything she did came together to make this happen. Harold would have called it "karma" or "kismet." I thought I had free will like every other asshole on the planet who thinks he's in control of his own destiny.

Right there, I had a better words for it than destiny; my bastard cousin, the snake let in twice.

Flashback to my cellmate reading another Shakespeare play. Me, trying to sleep, aware he's talking—no, he's reciting like some dingbat college professor to a student: '*Look like the flower, but be the serpent beneath*' . . .

Annoyed because my insomnia is making me jumpy as a cat, I lean over the bunk and bark: *What the fuck you laughing about?*

Lady Macbeth, he says, laughing. *She's one hellcat of a woman. Listen to this: 'Come to my woman's breast, and take my milk for gall, you murd'ring ministers'* . . .

I'm tryin' to sleep here, Harold. Keep it the fuck down . . .

A last slap in the face: The final family photo, maybe the last time they all smiled together, showed them standing near the camper when it was new and the paint fresh; the girl stands between her parents as she did, as she always will in my mind. The same rust-bucket I spent last night in.

I found clothes in his drawer that fit me well enough although the pants were too short and sagged in the belly so I had to cinch the belt up.

Shirts too tight in the chest, short in the arms but clean. 'Better than the white robe of righteousness,' as Aunt Ida would say.

I hobbled downstairs, one step at a time like a toddler, on the same wobbly legs I came up. I was famished but leery of eating with anything with a concussion. Hunger won out. I ate an apple from a basket on the counter and drank orange juice from the fridge. White bread with a little butter seemed a safe bet so I took my time eating, assessing the rumble below in case I had to upchuck. I didn't want to experience again that searing pain across the forehead from the heaves.

Sylvia, Sylvia . . . dear, where are you? Give me a call . . .

How long before they all come trooping over here to find out what's up with this family?

I played the rest of the messages in case someone was heading over to check on the Barrett family. I found out their name when I was upstairs rooting around. The father had underlined the monthly figure on the cable bill and scribbled a note for his wife: *Sylvia read this.*

Not anymore, Mr. Barrett. Sylvia's done all her reading in this life, like you, sir.

But not your daughter. I'm thinking she'll be underlining a whole other kind of figure—the one on your life insurance policy.

What had he done with them? Or, more accurately, their bodies?

Kenny was a lot of things in my imagination—kin, braggart, athlete, womanizer, hunting buddy, mentor, bully, dope dealer, crime partner, traitor, backstabber. Now I had to add one more: hit man for hire. Hired by the daughter of a family she wanted to kill but couldn't do it herself. She could be dead, too, for all I know, but the closed safe upstairs told a different story; whatever money was in there, it wasn't the reason for Corinne to summon a badass like Kenny Cardell to break it open for her. No, she wanted more: their insurance payout, the house, car, and every dime the family had. Whatever she promised my cousin, it had to be big enough to account for the consequences of a double homicide. Those people had to die and their bodies had to be discovered. She wasn't going to wait years for the courts to declare them dead. That had to be the scenario that made the most sense. For one thing, it was the only one that allowed her to stand in close proximity to my cousin and keep breathing air. Kenny wouldn't risk touching her. If she didn't pay up, he'd do something then, no doubt about it. But until she had the money in her hands, it was a stalemate. Like a remora fish under a shark's belly. Neither one could rat out the other, especially Kenny with his record; he'd take the steel ride if convicted. Being young, and having a first-class lawyer, she might could do a deal with the state and get parole in her late middle age.

I played the rest of the messages. They added up to what I suspected. This was an ordinary family. They paid church dues, joined civic committees, paid their bills on time, carried a reasonable credit-card debt. Had good relationships with friends and family out-of-state. The only gambling either one probably ever did was to choose between brands of toothpaste. I found old papers in a file folder that showed Mr. Barrett once owned the campground and a bait shop before the state bought it from him.

Your average family. That is, except for Corinne.

Or, as I began to call her, Macbeth's little bitch.

* * *

Chapter 9

I felt like a shitheels for doing it. Money was the only way I had to bolster my slim-to-none chance of escaping this dumpster fire without a belly shackle. I went back to poking into drawers, rummaging through clothing, searching for loose cash, valuables, anything to hock. Upstairs in the bedroom, I started pulling out the bottom ones out of habit. Kenny's voice in my head: . . . *you don't waste no time, see, shuttin' them if you go from top down* . . .

"Little late for that now, cuz," I said to the empty room.

I looked at the ripped-up floor, the safe nicked but undamaged and still unopened. A ruse, a trick to keep me busy until they came home. My corpse had to be fresh when the cops arrived. . . . *You, cocksucker, Kenny, I'll find you if I survive the day.*

In a sock drawer, I found a roll of quarters, a tiny billfold with ten $2 bills with Thomas Jefferson's portrait. The jackpot was in Sylvia's underwear drawer. Beneath a dozen white cotton panties, I found a wad of bills secured by a couple rubber bands. Almost $400 dollars. I took the quarters, put them in a heavier sock, and the roll of cash.

The front door opened downstairs. *Someone coming inside—*

Jesus shit fuck. Kenny back to finish me off. I held my breath.

Steps in the kitchen. *Heavy tread—a man's not a woman's. A male voice. Not Kenny's—*

Calling out from the bottom of the stairs, a deep bass: "Daniel . . . Sylvia . . . Corinne . . . Anybody here?"

Bad. This is bad.

"Oh my Lord, what's happened here?"

110

He saw the blood in the kitchen.

"Hello, are you up there? Did someone have an accident?"

Don't come up here . . .

Stair steps creaked, one halfway up. Still holding my breath, I looked around. Tools lying on the floor in the same place before Kenny got tired of playing his waiting game until she arrived with her parents. Ken's sly phone calls at the campground, tracking the family's movements.

The sledge on the floor . . . *No, too weak to lift it.* The claw hammer. *No, I don't want another murder on my conscience.* The pry bar.

He moved down the hallway, tentative, cautious, calling a timid "hello, hello" as he came, maybe thinking "prowler," maybe the couple having sex, but the sight of that blood downstairs propelling him forward.

First door on the left, her bedroom. "Hello? . . . hello?"

Slowly, I reached for the hammer, straightened up, took a lungful of air, and moved away from the doorway where he couldn't see me unless he opened it most of the way.

Not shouting like before, whispering, approaching the bedroom.

"Syl, Dan, again. . . anybody up yet? It's Pastor John. Evvie Peterson called—"

The door opened halfway.

"—she was worried . . . she didn't hear from you."

I waited, my mind blank.

"—she asked me to look in on you. . . . I saw blood on the kitchen floor—"

The door opened, and I stepped around it.

Pastor John and I stared at each other for half a second. He bellowed something, an animal cry. I brought the pry bar down on his head, flat end to make the contact. I didn't want to kill the man, just stun him into submission.

But not hard enough. His hand flew to the top of his head where I'd struck him, and he staggered backward into the hallway. An obese man in his sixties, dressed in dark clerical garb.

"O-O-O-O."

That's all he said before he collapsed to the floor.

He scooched backwards to the opposite wall on his rump, his shoe heels digging into the carpeting as though that would propel his great bulk. Whimpering, he slumped against the wall, one arm bent upward toward me to ward off another attack.

Torn between helping him and giving him another whack, I stood in front of him, slapping the bar in my palm.

"I don't want to hurt you, Mister. "I have to tie you up. Do you understand?"

He mumbled gibberish at me like a man speaking in tongues and curled his bulk on the floor to make himself smaller with his arms covering his head like man being attacked by a bear.

I tried again. "I have to tie you up. I don't want to hit you again unless you make me."

No better than my thug cousin.

I pulled the sheet off the bed and used the awl to rip sections of it. More whimpering noises, gargling—words tumbled out, prayers. He'd wet himself as I leaned over to tie his hands and feet. I thought about hogtying him but I didn't have enough strength in my arms to roll him over. Besides, I was afraid he might suffocate with his weight pressing on his lungs in that position. He looked like a heart attack wasn't far off as it was. *God damn, no calling back the dice.*

"People will be coming for you," I said. "Give me your car keys."

He heard me but he was far away. I rooted in his front pockets, found his keys, and left him lying there saying prayers faster than I'd ever heard a man of the cloth do before.

I wagged the pry bar at him. "Don't you move, hear me?"

Walking down the stairs, still light-headed, I thought of Kenny's remark about preachers: *All them fuckers is phony. All they want is money. Ten pounds of shit in five-pound sacks, the whole bunch of 'em . . .*

I thought of grabbing some food from the fridge on my way out the door but changed my mind. Banging that bar down on an old man's head, tying him up and terrorizing him was the most brutal, mind-numbing thing I'd ever done to a human being. I was sick to my stomach as it was.

Stepping out of that door into the bright sunshine of a spring day was like walking through the gates of hell back to life itself. His car, a gray Honda Civic, seemed a long way off. I had to concentrate on getting there, feeling my way along the driver's side fender like some beat-up TV cowboy feeling his horse's flank.

I had all the pastor's keys on a ring with the PAX symbol. I stood there trying to find the right one, half-bent over, fumbling, until it dawned on me to click the key fob. I never learned to boost cars like Kenny. He practiced holding car keys in his hand so he could tell the ridges from the valleys by pure touch. My self-disgust didn't do anything for my mood.

Salem was a long way away, too far for me to drive in my condition. My vertigo worsened behind the wheel. I let hate concentrate my focus on the road back to the campground. I fantasized getting to my gun just before Kenny drove up with his murdering partner in the passenger seat. I didn't mean to kill Ange Bucci. I definitely intended to kill my cousin even if it meant three hots and a cot for life. I'd take the needle and burial in potter's field to get that sweet revenge.

* * *

Chapter 10
Matamoras, Ohio

I was more dead than alive by the time I pulled into the campground and passed out. I nearly crashed twice on the way. Smacking a guardrail woke me up in time. Another two miles down the highway, and a state trooper would have spotted me swerving like a sleeping driver. My reflexes were too slow taking sharp curves. Several times I found myself drifting toward the shoulder. But I made it and parked. No Challenger, no shitty Toyota in sight. From my vantage, I couldn't see any movement. The tournament was still in full swing. All the trailers were lined up, bass boats in the river.

Walking toward it from an angle away from the windows, I came around from the side and stepped up to the door. If Kenny were hiding inside, I had as much chance of fighting him off as finding the lost head of John the Baptist.

Unlocked.

I looked in, still wary of ambush. The sock with the roll of quarters dangled from my hand at the ready in case I needed to swing at anybody coming at me. Hitting a older man with a dog collar showed me I'd crossed another line.

No paper bag of clothes and no gun. Nothing. The bed springs were attached to the wall again, the mattress rolled as it was when we walked in. Nothing of our time short there remained, even the food wrappers gone. Not cleaned, just empty. I had a fear I'd find Corinne's parents inside with my prints all over the place. I still didn't know how the two of them planned to use me—rather, how to get the cops to investigate me as the killer if my corpse on the floor of their kitchen was all they had to work with.

The ride back to Salem seemed more like a dream than something I did in reality. Turning off Highway 50 once more, down into the valley was no second homecoming. I drove past Bill's Tavern and couldn't help myself from checking out the parked cars for a beige Toyota or a dented Challenger. I wouldn't put it past the scumbag to stop off for a cool one to celebrate what he thought was the perfect crime. I still didn't now how the daughter was going to play her final part: was the plan to have her discover her dead parents and the killer, also dead, on the kitchen floor? Was she supposed to come home, rip her clothing and give herself a nosebleed and a couple bruises to show she'd fought off her parents' killer before killing him? Even a dim-bulb like my cousin knew that theory had too many holes for even small-town cops to buy. They'd turn it over to BCI as soon as they found the bodies.

It was easy to imaging Kenny driving around with their corpses in the trunk of his car, stopping off at a DIY to buy a shovel and a couple bags of lime. As Aunt Ida said about him often enough, you can't do anything about stupid.

I kept going past my house unwilling to stop. An old pickup and a cherry-red Nissan with the back window slathered with NRA stickers. No cops, no SWAT vans. That didn't mean anything. I took the next curve and stopped in front of a swing gate leading to a pasture. If anybody got curious or a cruiser decided to check it out, I'd see from the stand of trees coming back from the house.

I made the same entrance as last time after peeking through the windows; this time, however, the door was locked.

I knocked.

Aunt Ida opened the door. Her grimace told me everything. "She'd dead."

I nodded, shook my head to stifle tears, and asked if I could come inside.

"Your house now. . . .What happened to you?"

"Car accident," I said. "Who's in here?"

"Our cousins from Clarksburg. . . . Wade, cops been comin' around lookin' for you every hour. They wouldn't say. The phone's been ringing off the hook. Everyone suddenly wants to know where you're at."

"Where's Dad?"

"Off drinking. Where else?"

"My cousin stop by or call?"

"He wouldn't dare with me here. What kind of trouble are you in?"

"Big—but I can't talk about it now. C-Can I see her?"

"The hearse from Nallen's Funeral Home just picked up the body. Maybe they might could let you see her if you—"

"I can't. I can't. I've got to go."

"Aunty Ida, come here!"

One of the cousins shouted from the living room.

The TV was on. The news from Clarksburg was on. A young woman anchor said the words "A Salem man has been named a person of interest regarding a recent murder in Northtown but authorities have not yet identified—"

I didn't hang around to hear the rest.

I left my aunt standing in the kitchen looking at me in the strangest way I'd ever seen as if she'd just been caught talking to one of the Four Horsemen she used to yammer about from her bible school teaching days.

I was qualified to be one. I was carrying all the plagues with me.

* * *

I stopped by the shed out back for a Phillip's.

Zigzagging my way to the tree line, I saw no one parked near the preacher's car. I'd do my grieving later. Running was the priority of the moment. I walked, slipped, and made it to the bottom of the slope. My clothes were uncomfortable to move in much less climb up and down slippery gulleys in.

It was too soon for any news about New Zenith to make it to the channels or the papers, so I had time. Not much, maybe enough.

The first thing was to ditch the Ohio plates. I drove Highway 50 into Clarksburg. It seemed I had those two cartoon figures on my shoulder. The white angel said, "Go back, give it up. It only gets worse the longer you run." But the other one, the devil, had Kenny's face. He said: "Loser, you'll never find me."

Downtown Clarksburg looked normal and I wondered for a moment how that could be. How can these people come and go down the sidewalks, enter restaurants, do shopping, head for the tall office buildings and not know what was happening. It was like the world was ending and nobody cared. All of it in my head. My life, my woes and troubles and sorrows, meant nothing. I drove past the brass plaque commemorating Stonewall Jackson's birthplace. Still there, despite the protests of Charleston liberals, all funded by Hollywood commies, according to the patrons in Bill's Tavern. If a great general's memorial was a single marker on an office thousands of people passed every day without looking at it, why should anybody give a shit about me? I had to start thinking like Kenny, let the rat instincts come to the fore.

I checked the big parking lot behind the municipal building. The mounted CCTV cameras on the corners behind the building looked too new, too good. I headed for the Walmart on Emily Drive. Their exterior cameras were good but not wide-ranging enough to focus on the farthest parking spaces. With my plates tucked under my arm, I found a small Hyundai sandwiched between a couple SUVs. It would hide me well enough from passersby and the cameras but the Ohio plates would stand out too much. I chose an SUV with a baby seat. A busy mother might not notice too soon. It took about three minutes to remove the plates and replace them.

Having a stolen car in another state didn't mean you were safe from BOLOs. Nearby states had a sister relationship when it came to crime. WV plates might last a little longer. I wasn't kidding myself.

Where next?

Food. My appetite was coming back. In the rearview mirror, my eyes looked sunken in my head, my right eye a slit now from the impact with the floor. Blood congealing beneath my eye. My forehead was hot, a low-grade fever. The vertigo was subsiding but that didn't mean I didn't have a low-grade concussion. The hole in the back of my head I'd felt with my finger was pulpy. I left the Supercenter and headed back on to Interstate 79. Being on my own for years and living off fast food, I could find places to sell me bottled water, pizza, and bags of snack food where no cameras were if I were blind-folded. My heart raged for revenge. My body said, "Eat when you can."

When I'd scored enough supplies to eat and clothing and blankets from the Salvation Army to rough it in the car, I drove down to the park near the West Fork River. Something in my belly, a cat nap and I'd be good to go—if *good* was the right word for someone in my shape. The place in the back of my head still felt mushy. My I took a few bites of a Slim Jim and fell asleep with the opened water bottle in my hand.

I dreamed I was back in prison. I bumped into Angelo in the chow line. "*Che cazzo*, he exclaimed spotting me: "You got some balls coming here, Cardell."

I wanted to tell him I was sorry, I didn't mean to kill him with that rebar. I had no answer for why I threw it. I took my food and sat down at a table far from his. He was sitting at the Brand table. He said something to them and they stopped eating at once to glower at me. I went back to my cell to look for my shiv, a toothbrush with a straight razor soldered into it from a Bic. I couldn't find it. I knew the AB would send an enforcer to my cell. I was rummaging in my tote, checking the vent grates, running my fingers along the metal bunk frame—nowhere.

I was down to seconds, before my "demonstration" came, "the hard candy" that Brand enforcers deliver to cons they want punished, their so-called three-knee-deep message to all not to break their rules, which usually meant repeated stabbing short of killing. I asked my cellmate to help me find it, but he was hunched over a metal tray rolling joy sticks, weed treated with PCP, which I'd sold after high school to support myself. He seemed pleased with himself despite my lurching terror. "I can get Xanax and

Valium from the dispensary," he said. "The new shift guard is selling it to me. Ever kitty-bend, Wade? Ketamine and Xanax, it's a trip, I'm telling you . . ."

I wanted to reach for his throat and choke the life out of him. My terror couldn't have been greater when the Brotherhood's enforcer showed up holding the bottom of a sock packed with something heavy like cans of mackerel, a common bartering item in joints. My mother stepped out from behind him.

"This is what you deserve."

When I woke up, hitting the steering wheel hard and sending a lightning bolt of rippling pain into my damaged ribs. The water bottle fell from my hand. I watched the water pour out onto the seat cover. I was too hurt to reach over for it.

And I was the one going after big, tough Kenny Cardell. The ghost of my mother sounded in my ears as she had so often when I ignored her pleas to straighten up before it was too late: *Pride goeth before destruction and a haughty spirit before a fall.*

I know, Ma, I know. But everything's too late now . . .

$$* \quad * \quad *$$

Payphones are deader than Julius Caesar in Clarksburg unless you deal drugs. Before cell phones became commonplace, you'd be lucky to find one that worked downtown without having to compete with a steady crowd of "unfortunates," as my Aunt Ida would say. Kenny's version of America's decline in the post-pandemic era was more colorful, rabidly racist: "Country goin' to shit—just lookit that white skank pushing her abomination in the stroller on her way to the welfare office. Motherfuckin' scum, welfare hoes, illegal *Messicans*, white-boys wearing a doo-rag and talking that rap trash to their homies."

He was happy to sell drugs to every one of those people he despised, however. That was the time we started to deal weed to the high-schoolers or stronger stuff to the ones who liked to bump up their drugs with combinations like bazookas with crack and marijuana, or candy blunts—marijuana and cough syrup.

Smartphones and emojis were assisting every step of the way as they showed in every kid's backpack: Kenny's symbol was the laughing emoji with dollar signs on his eyeballs and tongue. Reading the sequence of emojis was like learning a foreign language, but when you got to know your customers, you could read the screen at a glance and deliver the goods inside an hour.

It changed when opioids hit town—hit the whole damn state like a tsunami and business suffered. Pill doctors became the new drug dealers. Kenny wanted to get in on it, expand to more serious dope like "white girl," fentanyl—the newest and most dangerous high yet. He said he had a contact in the Dirty White Boys. "Them boys is always lookin' for guns," he told me.

I was on the verge of deciding to get out when the pizza job came up. The money from drugs was nothing like I thought it would be from TV. It was non-stop bullshit morning, noon, and night. Up early, going until way past nightfall. People wanted dope but couldn't pay. I got tired of seeing them squirm and fidget. Watching meth freaks twitch made Kenny laugh; he'd take sex for cash from the most desperate girls. Cutting into our stock and profits didn't faze him. It was around that time, tool, that I saw the dark side of him emerge. He gave freebies to pretty girls all over town, groomed them to go to harder drugs, and when they were at their most desperate, he'd use them in rough sex. He filmed gang bangs. If a girl rebuffed him at first, he'd bide his time until he had her at his mercy. One night he came home and whipped out his cock, showed me the blood on it. "I wasn't good enough for that bitch in high school. I made her do anal for her fix." I told myself that was it. I'm done with him. By the end of that week, I was posing for y first mug shot.

I was used to living off the grid but a phone was essential, so I found one downtown on the side of a CVS pharmacy that was usually free of lowlifes.

A skinny male stood a few feet from it, leaning against the wall and smoking as if he'd just found the last cigarette in the world.

I parked and walked over to the phone; still working but tagged with more graffiti than I recalled.

"Hey, man," the smoker said, giving me his tough-guy eyefuck, "I'm waiting on an important call."

"Just give me a little privacy here."

He mumbled something but shifted his position and assumed the identical pose a dozen feet from the phone. I hit the buttons and heard him mutter "Go fuck your mama."

I remembered Steve Dufresne told me his brother had moved back here from Buckhannon. He saw combat in Afghanistan and drank at Post 573 in Clarksburg like most of the vets in town who weren't too fucked up in the head or had all enough limbs to get up the steep concrete steps out front. Tommy was a part-time bartender at the V.F.W.

"Tommy, what's up. This is W-Wade. You remember me? Steve and I ran track together."

"Wade Cardell?"

"That's right."

"You're all over the news, Wade."

"Yeah, I didn't mean to k-kill the guy—"

"Guy?"

"Yeah, what they're saying about—about what happened to that guy in Northtown."

"I don't know about a guy in Northtown, man. They're talking about a double homicide in New Zenith just over the river. It's all over Channel Twelve, man. A couple bodies found in a garage . . ."

I hung up.

Son of a lowlife motherfucking bitch—

I never looked in the garage.

Kenny's Voice ringing in my ears: "That's why you're a loser and I'm a winner."

* * *

The Clarksburg-Harrison County Public Library has a modern, two-story building that looks like a gigantic crashed-landed spaceship from behind. It offers computers for public use, but you have to sign in. Clarksburg is a big enough city to have its own population of wandering vagrants, druggies, and transients who take advantage of the public space to gather there out of the cold, sit in a chair near a window and pretend to read a newspaper or arrange a minor drinking binge with anyone who has pocket money and is willing to share a bottle. I'd found my father there, chatting with people he met there. When he was short of drinking money, my mother said he was "at the library," which usually meant he hitched a ride with someone driving to Clarksburg that day so he could hang out with his "new friends," meaning the derelicts, single welfare mothers, their boyfriends, and anyone able to work past a caseworker to get lodging in the high-rises off Main Street by the railroad tracks.

I had no trouble passing for one of these people. The regular patrons and staff cut their eyes from me as soon as I walked in. *One of them, these garbage people* . . . I could almost read the words like a cartoon bubble over their heads.

Pretending to be looking over the New Arrivals shelf, I spotted a row of teenagers and adults busy online. The desk clerks had a clear view in case anyone attempted to look up porn. A spotty teenaged boy intent on his game, wore headphones and monopolized too much space. The adults on nearby computers gave him a wide berth, cast irritated glances at him whenever he twitched. His monitor burst with color and action. Bizarre figures, part-human, part-animal, scooped up objects never used on this planet, then died or morphed into new shapes with gravity-defying antics. A schizophrenic's world.

I took a ten out of my wallet and crimped it between my fingers as I tapped him on the shoulder.

"Hey, man, I'm using this one."

"Can you help me? I'm trying to find the newspapers online."

"There's a whole rack of them over there."

He pointed to a spindle rod where a half-dozen papers were doubled over it. The trouble was that a dozen people were sitting in the chairs facing it. I'd be in plain sight. It might take a minute to put my current face onto a mug shot. I didn't want to chance it.

"Here's a ten for a couple minutes of your time."

"OK but that's all, dude, five minutes."

I waited for him to step away before doing my search. *The Exponent-Telegram* piece had just enough details to nauseate me. The article said "brutally murdered"; the bodies of Mr. and Mrs. Daniel Barrett were found in the garage. Both were shot to death, executed. One person of interest had been named, "a former resident of Salem, West Virginia."

The paper lagged behind the TV station, but it wouldn't be long before all the media were describing me down to my toenails.

The news report confirmed my suspicion. The use of "brutally murdered" was a cliché for any and every double murder. If Kenny used the hollow points, I'd expect something grimmer in the details. That round was meant for me only, and only because he'd lost his cool and was trying to put me down before I escaped. Now he had two weapons at a crime scene for the police to puzzle over. Maybe that's why he couldn't use that weapon to finish me off while I lay unconscious on the floor.

No remorseful "suicide" blasts a couple fragmentation rounds in a house for fun after a failed robbery and then blows his own head off after knocking himself out sliding into a kitchen table. My cousin and the girl were playing a forensics game on a timetable, and it backfired because I got lucky and kicked Kenny in the balls. That meant the Barretts were murdered with my .22. I had to be left alive after that carnage or it wouldn't work.

Alive or dead, I was as valuable as a used condom as far as my cousin was concerned. But if he wanted to collect from Corinne after the insurance payout, he had to leave me alive. I had a teacher, old Mrs. Decker in Civics, who would call that a Hobson's Choice. I asked her what it meant. She said it meant no choice at all.

Kenny, boy, I'll be coming for you until the last dog dies.

* * *

Chapter 11
Ckarksburg, West Virginia

My parking spot by the West Fork seemed safe enough as long as I didn't park in the same place every time and made sure to leave by sundown. Just another citizen looking at the ducks on the river and contemplating his navel. Cops always did a sweep of the park at night and closed it off at ten p.m. That's why we never used it to sell dope.

Sitting still, doing nothing, thinking about the mess I was in, I started to feel better—if better was the word for it. At night, I drove to the Clarksburg General and parked as close to staff parking as possible. Cops and private security patrolled the parking lot twice during the night and the emergency room always had a uniformed officer around. From where I was, I could see him sneak out to grab a smoke. Sometimes a nurse would join him. Probably the most criminal thing either one of them had ever done.

My fever had gone up a notch; my hand came away from my forehead damp and sticky. A bluebottle fly was buzzing around me. Little wonder. I needed a shower. My armpits stank. Dashing into a gas station restroom required a key. I had to sit in the car and wait for somebody to use it so I could get right in after, splash water on my face and under my arms, then leave fast before anybody inside got curious enough to write down my license.

The side of my face was sensitive to touch, although I'd cleaned all the powder and grit out the first chance I had to wash thoroughly. The back of my head was sore where that chunk of stud rocked me. I felt with my fingers and touched bristles of wood sticking up from my hair back there.

Jesus, I must be sight—driving around in castoff clothing in a stolen car with a beat-up mug and a chunk of wood stuck in my head.

The rearview mirror showed me something worse every time I looked. With so much else to think about back in New Zenith, I didn't pay attention to it when I noticed it above my left eye at the house. Now it was a tiny zigzag, shiny crimson in color, and itching like mad. Not a cut—a staph infection. *Nice irony there*, I thought. Survive being shot at with hollow points and die of a simple staph infection. Hunting Kenny had to go on hold while I got myself tended to.

I made another call to Steve Dufresne last night. He told me I was on both the 6:00 news and WBOY's 10:00 p.m. broadcast.

"They have more details than yesterday?"

"They said the daughter called police to do a welfare check on her parents because she was out of town somewhere and couldn't reach them. They found a minister all tied up hollering for help. What did you do?"

"Look," I said, "I can't explain it right now. I'm using a public phone. I had no choice. I had to get out of there. He just barged in on me."

"It's bad, Wade. You're like Jesse James now. Everybody's reading this shit in the papers and talkin' about you."

"I'm looking for my cousin Kenny Carcell. You or Tommy seen him around?"

"Nope, and I don't care to. Your cousin scares the living shit out of me. Look, I can't help you no more on this, bro. You got to stop calling my house. I got family, man. I can't get mixed up in this."

"I understand, Stevie. Thanks for talking to me."

"Take care, Wade. Good luck."

Luck, hell, I needed that miracle, and I needed it now . . .

* * *

Thought I'd beg the Devil in hell a favor before I asked my old man for help. But there was no one left. *You have to risk it to get the biscuit* . . . Seems I'd never get Kenny's voice out of my head.

The short drive back to Salem created another problem. I needed gas—more exposure there from CCTV cameras. The money I stole from the Barretts was dwindling like melting gutter ice.

Back home again, like that proverbial dog that returneth to his vomit, as Aunt Ida liked to say, I'd drop in at the house. My mother used to scold her for being so hard on me. It never stopped the sisters from quarreling about me then or until the day she died. Their love for each other never failed in the worst of times. That's what family was supposed to mean, not killing your parents for money or sending your cousin off to prison.

I parked at the gate as I did before. Everything still looked normal baseline: spring wheat planting going on, a dozen white-faced Herefords chewing cud near the gate and looking at me. I waited another five minutes. No cars or pickups rounding the curve. Just a quiet spring day with everything beginning to bloom. If I wanted to get up the slope before a car turned the corner, I had to hurry.

Bolting from the car, I made it faster than the last time: my strength was returning if not my former speed.

I made my way into the tree line and followed the same route to get behind my house. Pileated woodpeckers *tatt-tatted* trees for bugs. Blue jays squawked at my intrusion. Squirrels hopped from tree limbs, chittering, annoyed. Ground insects whirred around with the return of warmer weather. Maples dropped their helicopter seeds and the leaves were darker now, losing that lime green for a deeper color. My father took me bow hunting around the knobs near Cheat Mountain when I was twelve; the snow remained on the lee side of the pines at higher elevations. The world was renewing itself, I was going in the opposite direction: rotting.

When I reached the small gulley I had to cross, I stopped in my tracks, froze like a buck getting an unfamiliar scent. Footprints in the slushy earth—not mine. Two pairs of male boot prints, bigger than size tens and fresh tracks.

I pivoted slowly. *Run*, my brain said.

Instead, I slid down the gulley to the trickle of water at the bottom and hunched low. I headed up the gulley for fifty yards before slowly climbing out after popping my head up like a prairie dog. I couldn't see the house but anybody watching the house might be visible from here. I hoped cops looking for me wouldn't circle around this far up the hillside.

Two men in khakis and black windbreaker. One had binoculars in his hand. The other had a walkie-talkie. I didn't need to see their badges to know they were federal, not local cops. F.B.I. or Marshals. There'd be somebody inside the house, too—probably getting an earful from Aunt Ida.

That was that. If my father was inside, there was no getting to him.

I couldn't go into Bill's on the off-chance he was welcome back there. That left Clarksburg and his "real friends," as he described them to Aunt Ida when she launched one of her attacks on his drinking. Kenny called them rednecks, coalfield white trash.

Dad had an eclectic group among including some disabled Vietnam vets and a few younger guys who fell out of society through bad luck, drugs, or alcohol.

The hair on my neck rose once I left the tree line and stepped into open sunlight. I aimed for the car at a gallop. If they had snipers positioned up there, I'd be duck soup.

I drove the speed limit on Main, left Salem behind me and turned right at the ramp once more for Highway 50 and headed back to Clarksburg. The odds of my father being around the downtown weren't that good. He might do his drinking and carousing there but he always came home to sleep. I thought of risking a call to Aunt Ida at the house and thought better of it. The phone might be tapped; she'd never lie if asked by any agent in the house who was calling.

Swinging past the library, I saw a few men gathered outside in the parking lot enjoying the sunshine. I drove up and hit the window button.

"Any ya'll seen Wayne Cardell today?"

A few grunts. Not much greeting.

I let a five-dollar bill creep over the lip of the window ledge.

"I'm his nephew," I lied. "Lookin' to give him a ride back to Salem."

"I seen him at the high rise an hour ago," one grizzled old soul replied. "Him and Emma Jones."

Snickers, looks exchanged.

The bill fluttered in the warm breeze as I hit the closed button; four pairs of hands reached out to catch the green butterfly.

Emma Jones—what did I care who she was? Aunt Ida used to mumble about Dad choosing satin when he had lace at home. I didn't understand what she meant until he was twelve.

I parked near the high rise. The cameras in the lot and in the lobby were for show. Half the closed-circuit cameras in town were. Trouble was, which ones weren't?

There were three *Joneses* on name tabs, all handwritten in block letters. Emma Jones was the only female.

I pressed the buzzer.

Static squawk. "Who is it?"

"Miss Jones, I'm looking for Wayne."

"Ain't here."

"I have a sympathy card with some money for him."

"What you say?"

"From Mrs. Cardell's church group. I'm supposed to hand-deliver."

"Who is this?"

"Can I come up?"

"Wade, that you, boy?"

His voice sounded rusty, as though he'd come off a binge or a nap. My father's latest liaison was too recent for cops to get wind of her yet—I hoped. But every second in the lobby with people coming and going past was making my stomach churn with acid.

"Comin' down. Wait up."

Shit, Dad, for once in your life, help your boy out . . .

I watched him get off the elevator with three other people. Trying to count who was a resident and who was just "visiting," meaning illegally crashing at a government-funded housing project, was like herding cats. Welfare moms had boyfriends and exes coming and going every day. It was known to be a hunting ground for federal cops looking to serve warrants or catch fugitives. Back in the day, Kenny and I delivered *mucho* product here to residents, legit and "visiting."

He always seemed like a giant to me. He'd been a basketball star from his high school days in Weirton. Not so tall now, gray, going thinner on top, still rangy, the same ropy forearms that used felt like steel bars when I was a boy. Despite the years of mining and hard drinking—and I mean everything from beer in the morning to Mason jars of white lighting hidden in the shed, he hadn't acquired that old-man stoop yet.

"What's goin' on, Wade? I hear you're in trouble."

"You talkin' to Aunt Ida?"

"That witch."

"Dad, I need help."

"What was you sayin' a moment ago about some money from Caroline's church ladies?"

"I said that to get you to come down."

"No money?"

"No money."

"Damn it. I told Emma I'd have some for her."

"I'll give you some."

I reached for my wallet. His arm snaked out and pinned my hand tight to my hip. Same lightning reflexes that made him third-team all-state.

"Not here, gosh. These people see you givin' me money, they'll be all over me like flies on a dead possum."

"Let's take a walk," I said.

"I don't care to."

In my father's lingo, that meant *Yes, fine*. While we walked along facing the parking lot overlooking a deserted part of town. Shops and houses boarded up, a few hanging on by a thread, he slumped a bit, as if the sunshine was irksome rather than welcome.

I told him in a few sentences what I needed him to do for me.

"You know anyone like that? Got my build or my age?"

"I s'pose."

"I'll meet you back here in an hour. There's a hundred apiece if you can get someone."

"I told Emma—"

I pieced him off with a couple twenties.

"An hour, Dad."

He didn't say anything; he looked at the money. He never asked me what happened, why I looked like somebody threw me into a trash compactor. If it had been a gold coin, I think he would have bit it with his teeth.

*   *   *

"This here's Aaron," my father said.

"Pleased to meet you," I said. We shook hands.

Aaron didn't look much like me—shorter by a couple inches and twenty pounds, wrong eye color, too. But he looked like a junkie, which was good. Being addicted is one hard grind. I've seen plenty, helped make more than a few in my time dealing. They work at it all day long to support their habit: boosting small stuff from local stores they can sell for pennies on the dollar, scavenging metal to take to the trash, panhandling—anything and everything short of selling their firstborn to get the blast from the powder in the little baggie. Junkies don't read much news.

"You know what I need?" I asked him.

He handed me his Social Security card, a driver's license (expired by three years), and the Medicaid card: Ronald Aaron Runyan.

"You're going to wait for me, Aaron," I said. "When I come out, I'll give you the cards back and the rest of the money."

"How about the rest of mine?"

I gave my father the $80 I promised. He took the bills without looking at them this time and tucked them into the fifth pocket of his Levi's.

"I got to go," he said. "Be seein' you around, son."

I watched him walk back down the sidewalk toward the lobby and Emma, his new woman. . . . . *Your wife isn't even laid out in her casket yet*, I thought.

Stop it—Kenny's voice with a dash of vinegar—*You actin' like a little bitch.*

"Is it your eye?"

"Huh?"

"Your eye," Aaron repeated. "You got a black eye. Is it your eye you need this for?"

"I need a doctor's prescription for it."

"Little old black eye ain't nothing," he said.

"It's worth a hundred bucks to you."

* * *

The receptionist took my cards—Aaron's that is, checked my ID and glanced at me once and told me to take a seat. The doctor would call for me "in a minute."

Forty-five minutes passed. It was all hurry up and wait.

I got up from the bingo chairs we were sitting in near the vending machines. It was a long wait. Squalling toddlers, overweight mothers in their twenties, most of them with biracial babies; a few had boyfriends, black and white, accompanying them. No jobs to go to in the middle of the day. One woman brought all four of her children and struck up a conversation with a pasty-faced obese woman whose little boy's complexion was a greenish shade cast like old brass. The TV set played cartoons on Nick Jr. but the kids weren't interested. A high school artist from Robert C. Byrd High had done a seascape mural on one wall. Two of the older children were pointing tiny fingers at the drawings and competing with each other in naming them: "dolphin!" "octopus!" "whale!" . . .

"Sorry about the long wait, Aaron," I said. "I'll make it up to you."

"Fuckin' better. Fuck this shit."

He was already twitching. A mother snapped her head around to glared at us.

A nurse stepped through the pneumatic doors of the emergency room and called out "Ronald Runyan." She escorted me inside and pointed to a small wooden stool near a stretcher bed.

"Take a seat."

The ER doctor who came strolling up was my age and had curly black hair peeking out from his scrub cap. He looked at my face. I thought he was going to mock me like Aaron for wasting his time with a lousy black eye.

"I've got this above my eyebrow."

He swung a lamp closer to me and tilted my chin.

"No problem," he said. "I'll write you a prescription for Bactrim and another NSAID. We'll bomb it for a week. That should clear it up."

"I have a swelling back here, too," I said

"I see it. What happened?"

He looked at it, felt around it with latex fingers and then told me to get on the electric bed.

"Come here, Nurse," he said.

I lay flat while the nurse tilted the light directly on the back of my head. His fingers had hurt but the hot light was soothing.

"Check this out, Nurse."

The nurse ceased fiddling with the light and leaned closer to get a better look.

I heard her suck in her breath.

"What is it?" I asked.

"Maggots," the doctor said. "Myiasis. A fly laid maggots inside the wound back there. How long have you been walking around with this?'

"Couple days. Got hit with a two-by-four at a job site."

"I'd say you got clobbered with it. There's a piece of wood sticking in there about half-an-inch deep where maggots burrowed." I remembered waking up in the car with that fly buzzing around my face.

"Can you fix it?"

"That's why they pay me the short money," he said. "Maggots eat dead flesh."

"I know that." Hunting with my father, I'd seen deer poached and field dressed in the trees hanging from limbs. Hunters took the parts they wanted and left the rest. If they left the buck on the ground and it was big enough, possum would bore through the anus and settle in like a family home. Nature's not pretty. Look at us.

My head was shaved, sterilized, and the doctor worked on my for a long time. The nurse assisted with sterile pads to mop up blood as he worked on me. I tuned out everything but one thing: how many ways I was going to make my cousin pay for this, too.

When the doctor finished, he told me I could get off the bed.

"Look at this," he said when I sat on the stool again.

He showed me a small metal bowl filled with something that looked like spoiled cottage cheese.

"That's infection from your wound," he said. "See the maggots in there?"

She regarded me the whole time with lip-curling revulsion as if she'd seen glimpsed hyenas mating.

"Give you fifty bucks to take a sip," I said. "No shit."

I turned to the doctor. "Can I have my prescription now?"

He scribbled on a pad and ripped off four pages and handed them to me.

"Watch those two-by-fours," he said.

I stuffed the prescriptions into my pocket and headed out the doors. Aaron jumped up from his seta as soon as he saw me.

"'bout got-damn, friggin time."

"Thanks for asking, Aaron. I'm feeling great."

Outside we headed toward the car. I gave him his cards back with the other half of his money and asked him if he wanted a ride back to the high-rise.

"Fuck no, buncha deadasses in there. Take me to Puchan's over to East Pike."

I thought it was a Chinese take-out. It turned out to be a bar.

"I used to go here when it was Hummer's Bar and Grill," I said, pulling up to the curb.

"Who gives a shit? How's 'bout forkin' over a little somethin' for the waitin' time?"

I fished out another twenty and handed it to him.

"Appreciate this, Aaron—"

"Good luck with your black eye," he snorted.

He was out the door before I finished saying "Thanks for the help—*and fuck you, too, Aaron.*

A harmless discard from my life, not the way I was to Ken, how he used people like me, threw them away, and moved on. *You ain't movin' on so fast from this one, you fuck.*

The Rite-Aid the next block over on Hickman filled my prescription while I sat in a chair looking at old black-and-white photos of the town from the days of Stonewall Jackson. Horses and buggies. Short, wiry little men with grand facial hair and wives with razor-slit smiles.

My father's expression came back to me once more: . . . *shoveling shit against the tide.*

Always been that way.

* * *

Chapter 12
Matamoras, Ohio

I loaded up on supplies from the pharmacy: a gel pack for the ribs, enough food, water, medicine, toilet paper to lie low for four or five days until I healed up and looked normal again instead of a walk-on extra in a zombie film. With my hair clipped in back, the black eye, and facial swelling I was conspicuous but not resembling as much the mug shot from the Clarksburg PD years ago. Denmar hadn't sent the most recent or else the Marshals and feds figure they'd have me in custody without local law getting in their way

But too many too many people had seen me in town by now either way. It was a matter of time—hours, I figured—before that doctor and nurse started chatting in the breakroom about "the patient with maggots gnawing away in his head."

I recalled the innocent stares of the children in the emergency room as I came out. The phony ID wouldn't stand up to a check anywhere else in town but in that emergency room where the indigent were the staple of business. Once the tip line offered a reward, there'd be a swarm of sightings the cops would have to check out and somewhere on those tiny stick-it notes would be the one or two that mattered. I trusted Steve Dufresne, although we were just teammates a long time ago. Aaron would kick himself in the ass once he made the connection and realized what he could have gained from turning me in. That ratfuck would knock his mother off the sidewalk if he saw her standing on a quarter. I tried

135

not to think about my father licking his chops for the money. He'd salve his conscience by justifying it to save my life, save me from being shot by cops while I was on the run.

I wanted to drive down to the river, grab a little shuteye before I hit the road again. It was a long day since I'd swatted that fly in the car and checked out my ugly mug in the rearview. Coming down West Pike in the Hartland area of town, where I'd have a bird's-eye view of the whole lot before I reached the West Fork bridge. A white Taurus sat in the back lot, no view of the river from there; two more bland sedans in gray and silver were paired off between the single open space closest to the riverside with the best view. Cheese for the mouse—me.

I could see the pincer movement forming in my head as I kept going by the lot: the Taurus blocks the exit, the white and silver sedans jump the driver. I'd never make it to the river even if I could swim in the near-freezing water. When I was dealing with my cousin, the old Crown Vic was the car to watch out for. Ken bragged how easy he could spot an unmarked—too much kit on the dash, heavy tactical gear and equipment in the trunk causing it ride low, maybe an extra aerial, always two people in the car. Get close enough, you can see the infrared camera behind the rear license plate. Now they all have LED lights on the sides of the front license plate so the car can be seen side on. "The best way to tell," Kenny used to say, "is watch how they drive. Like assholes. Always going the speed limit, using turn signals. Who the fuck does that?"

It was in the back of my mind all along, the place where I should start my search: the trailer in Matamoras. *When you're in deep*, my instincts said, *go deeper in.*

Dusk was settling over the town. The evening air would make everyone antsy, eager to get out of the house, go places, because winter's back was finally broken.

When I reached the campground, the tournament sign had been replaced with a homemade sign with the names of the winners and blow-up photos of their catches. A dozen night fishermen were at the shoreline with their lanterns and folding chairs set up. The rods in front of the fishermen would be secured in bucket holders.

Fishing with my dad, we'd split branches shaped like witching rods. Two bass boats were visible offshore on the river running white lights at the bow and stern. I found a spot in a row of cars where I could put the preacher's car so it wouldn't stand out.

I got out and walked in the direction of the trailer, the flashlight in my hand off. I couldn't see its outlining against the scrub brush where it was parked. I kept walking, unwilling to believe the obvious until I was right on top of the spot where it had been parked. Nothing but a dirt rectangle where the weeds sprouted around the perimeter. She had it moved.

Retracing my steps at the same pace, I was lost. I didn't expect this. Now that voice in my head clamored for attention: *You're almost broke now. . . nowhere to go.*

I had to find that swine who ripped off my cash and tried to vaporize my head with a Glaser slug.

Jefferson-on-the-Lake.

It sounded crazy, even when I said it aloud. The only person who might not rat me out was up there in a biker bar. This time, no more wrecked lifeboats on the beach.

Part 2

Chapter 13
Jefferson-on-the-Lake, Ohio

Sleeping in cars. I suppose every teenaged boy has done it least one time. Come home late after a night out with friends or being with your chick. Door's locked. What the hey, sleep in the car in the driveway, especially if the beer or grass fumes will cause a parent to get in your face when all you want to do is sleep.

I must have cruised by Dwight's a hundred times the day before yesterday, another 200 yesterday. The State Lodge is just a few hundred yard around the curve on Lake Road. I found a spot where the night-shift employees parked. I had a story ready in case some eager-beaver cop on patrol decided to check out my car and found me snoozing there. "Officer, I guess I had too much to drink, see, and I didn't want to risk driving . . . that stuff in the back? Well, the old lady and me had a little spat when she went through my cell phone and found some photos of an old girlfriend, ha-ha, *wink-wink* . . ."

If he wanted to run the plates—*why sure, fine by me, I've got nothing to hide, sir*—except I'd be out the door running like a six-legged jackrabbit once he got back inside his cruiser.

Play out the string . . . I was too far committed by now. Come hell or high water, I was going all the way. Kenny Cardell was somewhere and getting to him was all that mattered. Those NASA computers on the ISS had nothing on me. I was locked in.

The warm weather reached this far north but there was still a bite in the air. I had one decent set of clothes to wear and I'd twist myself into a pretzel inside the car to get into them so the desk clerks at the lodge didn't jump out of their skin seeing me come through the revolving doors on my way to the bathroom. I'd hit the men's room and do a mini, rapid-fire version of shit, shower, and shave to get myself looking presentable.

The black eye was turning yellow and purple, healing. The swelling above my left eye was less noticeable, the side of my face less puffy, not as hot. I bought a ballcap on the Strip from a souvenir shop to hide the bald spot in back. It said I'M WITH STUPID on the front; the arrow, however, pointed straight down instead of sideways. I figured anybody wanted for a double murder in one state and a homicide in another would wear beer logos or a stitched outline of a babe on his cap. The clerks were kids in their twenties, which fact favored me as far as alerting their bosses to the weirdo in the goofy ballcap wandering past to use the pisser. Intolerance comes with aging.

Today was it. My cash was running too low. P.J. was working or long gone. Bartending isn't a job you retire on. I was going to hunt for her. I'd flash the last of my cash to the bartender inside Dwight's and see if I could talk my way into getting her phone number.

Around 10:00 I left my parking spot at the lodge and drove back up 531 to the Strip. The daytime crowd was sparse, few people on the street. Signs advertising cabins and cottages for rent were slapped everywhere ahead of the tourist season.

I found parking behind Freddie's Grill and blocked the image of the last time I was here. I wore my cap low and a black tee-shirt depicting a biker on a Fat Boy with a leggy blonde exposing massive boobs in Levi's cut off to the crotch—everybody's Daisy Mae stereotype that no guy from West Virginia actually met in person.

The tall, black street clock across from the grill stand said 10:13.

I stood in front of the double doors holding my breath the same as I had that first time a lifetime ago. I looked different now. I felt different, not as scared, although I had a lot more to be scared about.

I jiggled the latch. The dead bolts top and bottom were locked down.

"It's early, we aren't open yet," said a voice behind me.

I smiled, recognizing it: P.J.

When I turned around her expression didn't change; it matched her tone: *Just some annoying asshole trying to get in to get a load on already . . .*

"It's me, Wade Cardell."

She stared, not sure at first. "You look like you've been thrown into a wood chipper. What happened to you?"

"A lot, nothing good. OK to come in?"

I was a vampire on the doorstep, asking people for permission to enter, and I wasn't bringing anything with me that would make their lives better.

"You better. Whole town's been reading about you."

"This place hasn't changed." I was worried she had since she saw me bolt out the door and jump into a car.

"Dwight's is Dwight's," she said. "A hundred years from now, it'll be the same except they'll be flying cars outside."

She told me Angelo's family was offering a $3,000 reward for me.

"You have any idea how many junkies roam this place, Wade Cardell? They'll drop a dime on you before you can blink. We've got more meth cooks out in the woods than fuckin' deer."

"Nice to hear everywhere I go is the same."

"You're not just news here, buddy. Biker the other day told me the F.B.I.'s looking all over for you in West Virginia. He said you killed two people."

"You'd think I was the Lindbergh baby kidnapper."

"Whatever, man. You shouldn't joke. For one thing, you don't look like a comedian."

"What do I look like? Never mind. I don't want to hear it."

"I got to get the place set up. Take a booth. I'll catch up as soon as I can."

"That booth yonder?"

"Yeah, that one, shitkicker. While you're sitting there, keep your head down and give some thought to avoiding hillbilly talk. Every cop patrolling the Lake knows you're from West Virginia."

She pointed me to the one closest to the bar counter, the same one as the last time I was here. Harold would say, "Karma."

She brought me a cold can. The Bactrim and the pills I took didn't like alcohol. I needed all the wits my brain could muster. I drank anyhow. The apple didn't fall far from the tree in that respect.

Years ago, I took anything handed to me at parties—buda, ecstasy, jim jones, dirties, dust, coco puffs, eight balls—you name it, I smoked it or swallowed it. Never gave a thought to dying. I thought I was invincible. Waking up in parking lots then, too. I didn't realize I was writing out my destiny like a kid scratching words on wet sand with a stick.

She sat down, folded her hands in front of her, and looked hard at me.

"You coulda had you some cash," I said. "One phone call. It's not too late now."

"What did I say about those shitkicker expressions? I did think of it—for a minute. That bother you?"

"That makes me feel b-better. About knowing you, I mean."

"You don't know me, Wade."

"That's true."

"You always had that stutter?"

"Always. Gets worse when I'm nervous."

"My little brother had it growing up. Speech therapy didn't work. Kids at school made his life hell. He hanged himself in the closet his sophomore year."

"I'm sorry. I'm real sorry."

She checked her watch.

"We don't have much time before the esteemed clients of this establishment start coming through the door, and I have to earn my pathetic wages. You need to talk fast. Why are you here?"

For once in my life, I didn't stutter and fuck it up by justifying myself. I didn't try to convince her I was innocent. When I was done talking, I waited.

"I believe you," she said quietly. "I don't know why, but I do."

Two guys, biker types, came in talking loudly. One of them spotted her sitting in the booth and hollered, "P.J., get off that sweet ass of yourn and serve us thirsty men a couple beers!"

Yourn . . . I heard home.

I looked at her.

"Wait for me out back," she said.

I got up and left without a word. The bikers never looked at me.

* * *

"How much is half?"

I said: "Three thousand, a little over. I'd been saving for months. But who knows how much that fat bastard's spent out of it?"

"Bassett used to be pretty regular in Dwight's," she said. "Not so much lately. The regulars don't like him but they put up with him because he's got connections everywhere—dope, fencing property, trafficking runaway girls. I even heard he can get you on the dark net."

Her cabin off Route 531 was sparse but neat. Feminine touches here and there but nothing like the gals in office buildings where they have all kinds of homey shit hanging off the computer screens—smiley face buttons, teddy bears, and ceramic frogs on their desks.

"I don't live here all year," she said, catching my eyes boxing the room. "It pays good in the summer with all the tips but pre-season and post-season, the money's a little short."

"May I ask where you do live—or is that too personal?"

"So polite. A village in the Adirondacks—that's New York to you."

"A mountain girl."

"Not fucking likely."

She told me she had two sisters besides her dead brother; both had kids. "Not for me," she said.

"Why here, this place? Why Dwight's?"

"Yeah, a classy joint, huh. I don't know the answer to that question. Let's just say Saranac Lake was a nice place to grow up in but you can get bored really fast in the winter. I turned fifteen, I figured there had to be more to life than ice skating on frozen ponds in the winter."

"So you found it here."

"Don't make fun of me. I was drifting, got hooked for shoplifting. They found drugs in the car, too. Next thing I know I'm in Marysville. That's where I met Dwight's woman. She dug me and we bumped fenders. Better than some bulldyke turning me into her 'wife' or 'daughter' while I did my time."

I looked at her.

"Don't worry. You ever heard 'I'm gay for the stay.' What about you, Wade? Get tired of *tham thar* hills?"

"Now who's mocking? Growing up in a tiny town wasn't enough for me, either. You hear the same dog barking at night and you wonder, 'Will I be hearing that goddam dog when I'm fifty?'"

"Better if we swap sad tales of our youth and prison experiences later. I want to hear what you got in mind for Bassett Hound."

"You say he drinks in Dwight's. Can you get him in there, keep him there with free booze—maybe talk one of your regulars into buying the drinks so he d-doesn't get suspicious? I'll c-cover it."

My damn stutter returned out of nowhere. Looking too long into her eyes unnerved me.

"Then what?"

"Then I'll break into that f-fat jerk's cabin and look for my money. Even if he calls the cops, he'd be stupid to bring me into it. He'd have to s-say it was his."

"Which brings me to another matter altogether. Where do you plan to be all this time?"

"I'm sleeping in my car over to the state lodge on Five-Thirty-One."

"Better stay here . . . and knock that fuckin' smile off your face, dude. This is a business arrangement, pure and simple."

"Pure and simple," I agreed.

Like whatever in life was ever pure or simple?

* * *

She had me park my car near her cabin. More Harleys in one parking lot than you'd see outside the Las Vegas BikeFest. I showered while she was at work, an everyday thing until you lose it.

The spray stung on my sore parts but it felt good. She let me use her bed, which had the pleasant side effect of waking up with wood, not a bad thing, unless you lose that too—a warm bed with a woman in it. My loneliness was like a second skin.

She drove us to a family hardware store in Northtown with a list of tools I wrote down for her to pick up as well as few household items in case the place had closed-circuit cameras.

"You sure you can get in there without attracting attention?"

"Told you I used to be a thief."

"You also told me you did time for it."

"I honed my skills in prison."

"*Honed* . . . I see."

"You OK with this, P. J., I mean—"

"Shut the fuck up." She looked serious again. "Are you ready?"

I wanted to ham it up, throw in the hillbilly dialect. "Uns will be fine."

"Not *us*—*you*, paleface. Tonto's going to be back on the reservation until it blows over, you *capeesh?*"

I winced: Tony's expression from the salvage yard.

"Understood," I said. "Business, like you said."

"Nothing but, *amen.*"

Capiche—Angelo's word, too. Now I had him in my head. It made me think of him and his uncle jabbering away in the little office. Family, even if the family was crooked. Angelo's ghost glared at me over P.J.'s shoulder and fixed me with that stare from the crane the day he died.

* * *

Chapter 14

By eight o'clock, I had the hammer, chisel, flashlight, and small crowbar taped behind my belt. The steel stool with the black ribbed matting was the only heavy-duty one the store sold. I had to hope it held my weight while I worked on removing the window and that the ground was hard enough back there for the legs not sink into the ground. Folded up and carried under my arm, it looked like an attaché case for a laptop.

P.J traded shifts with another bartender, agreed to split the tips with her because daytime was "fucking ridiculous" when it came to big spenders. Bikers never seemed to have a pot to piss in, but "they know how to leave a few dollars behind for a tip when they've had a snootful."

I asked her if she had anybody lined up that night to play Big Spender for Bassett.

"Couple dudes I know—if they come in," P.J. replied. "If not, I'll play it by ear. I can guarantee you a good hour once he starts drinking free beer. I hope that's enough time."

"I'll go through that tiny cabin like a buzzsaw. I'll find it, no matter how clever he thinks he is at hiding it."

"Just get your ass out of there once you find it."

Bassett's cabin number was listed in the directory under "Bestview Cabins." P.J. would call it in an emergency: two rings and hang-up, pick up on the next ring; three rings and a hang-up meant "Get the fuck out RIGHT NOW!"

I'd call her at work once I was back in her place to let her know.

"My first time at a B and E job," P.J. said on her way out the door. "I got this."

"It's burglary, P.J., not a B and E. A class-two felony. Trust me, I know."

* * *

The first weekend on Jefferson-on-the-Lake when the weather warms up means a horde of college kids from all over the northern part of the state, many from the colleges around Erie, PA and some from Western New York, all hyped on spring break; they descend like locusts—if you don't consider the money in their pockets. The more bodies milling about, the merrier for me. The downside was that the nighttime patrols were increased along with a heavier presence of cops.

P.J. said the heat was off on me. Lake cops were never much involved and the rest assumed I was in West Virginia or on the lam somewhere.

I parked behind Freddie's during the day. P.J.'s rental contract said she couldn't have "overnight guests," probably the most frequently violated legal stipulation in the history of this resort town, which might have started out a family enterprise in the fifties but had long since abandoned any pretense that hookups, drunks, dope dealers, runaways soliciting prostitution, and all sorts of alcohol-fueled major and minor mayhem weren't the rule, not the exception. The chamber of commerce fought what the paper called "J-O-T-L's rapid-fire descent into the abyss of drug-fueled sleaze" with might and main. It was two-steps-forward, one-backward—or the reverse, P.J. told me.

I made my way down Erieview at 9:30, past a window of a tiny office with a plate-glass window I'd never noticed before. The fancy script said *Thomas Haftmann, private investigator*. A rumpled, middle-aged man seemed to be slumped over his desk with his head down—drunk? Sleeping? Heart attack? *Sorry, pal, I've got my own troubles.* I kept going.

I arrived in plenty of time to set up a position behind his cabin. P.J.'s call to Bassett was set for 8:15. The ruse was to meet a client from Youngstown who was a union boss driving up and wanted to talk to him about renting all his cabins throughout August. P.J. was to hint about a kickback to whet Bassett's appetite. She said he made a percentage off the seasonal bookings—higher occupancy, more cash in his pocket.

A damp breeze off the lake made the dark windbreaker covering the tool an advantage. Ballcap low, I walked with a purpose in case anyone happened to be peeping out a nearby window. P.J. made me take her cell to warn me if Bassett remained inside despite the lure she planned to cast his way.

"Guy's a stoner," she said; "mostly weed, but he'll turn coke whore if he can get his hands on it. He might be too stoned to leave his place."

"Yes, mother."

She grabbed my arm. "Don't fuck around with this guy, Wade!"

The fallback plan was the next night. She knew I had no cell phone, or burner, to keep from leaving footprints off the towers.

"Last phone I had got me into a world of trouble."

"Yeah, right, like you've done so well since, cowboy."

No ringing phone so far. No other lights on other than a night light. Perfect.

No need to go to the edge of that sheer bluff like last time and circle around. The last two cabins on both sides of the road were dark, either unrented yet or the renters were away celebrating on the Strip. I veered to the right behind his cabin and made for the back, hugging the side, my asshole puckered in fear of being spotted.

Setting the stool up to the window ledge, I stood on it and peered through the window. Luck was on my side. He'd left the back kitchen dark, but the cabin was so small anyone inside could be detected if you stared into it owing to the light from the front window. I could have been wearing neon and no one would see me. The ground was a little soggy, yet it did the trick. At that height, I had enough leverage to jerk the window out of its frame.

The next part was routine cat burglar gymnastics. I hoisted myself up and through the window resting my waist on the ledge. My ribs screamed in protest. I hovered there for a long moment listening to the cabin, a human plate balanced on a magician's stick. Wiggling my lower half over the kitchen sink , I gripped the edges to pull myself to a standing position on the floor. Not a skill I'm proud of—my agility from my crime days in tight places.

To business. *Now, where's my money, you fat scum?*

Upstairs to the tiny loft first. A single mattress, no sheets, a coverlet rucked up. Sour smell of sweat and dirty sheets. The slanted roof made standing straight anywhere else impossible. Clothes strewn on the floor. Muddy boots, old tennis shoes, cold-weather clothing set off to one side under the sloping roof. No chifforobe up here like we had back home, just small bookshelves minus books.

In the drawer of the tiny end table beside the bed, I found a stack of papers, a notebook of names, all female with notations about hair color and bra size, rental agreements from the company, a CCW permit made out to Theodore Malcolm Basset. A pack of rubbers, a box of jacketed Federal .9 mm rounds, and a 7-inch dildo stained at the tapered end. I pulled out the drawer to check the bottom in case he taped check the bottoms in case he taped the money there.

The other bookshelf was packed with fur magazines and an empty gun case on top. Nothing that was an obvious hiding place. I shoved the mattress around and squeezed the sides—no nifty hidey-hole to stash money.

Downstairs for the toilet and lifted the lid. I reeled back in disgust at the shit-stained bowl and rim. I lifted the tank lid. Dopers tied fishing line to their stash in waterproof baggies. Nothing there but the submerged water valve and a plug on a rusted chain.

OK, kitchen cabinets next—every can, jar, bottle of salsa, energy drink, bag of chips, on every shelf moved, touched, or shaken. Bassett was a confirmed junk food addict like Tony Bucci. Nothing but processed meats, snack foods that would put a deer lick to shame. The sweets savvy managers placed near the conveyor belts in their grocery stores as impulse buys—all jammed helter-skelter on the counter top and inside the cupboards. No cans of food other than a Maxwell House coffee container. I dug my fingers in that to be sure. No plastic bottle on the shelf or in the fridge used as a decoy to stick a wad of bills inside.

Back to the fridge. Everything in the freezer first. A bottle of Grey Goose Vodka and a stack of frozen dinners, Hungry Man Chicken and Meat Loaf. The vegetable and fruit drawers empty except for a stalk of limp celery and a moldy bar of cheese. The rest of the fridge was basically a beer cooler.

Dirty dishes, crusted remains of a dinner on two plates. A frying pan with a couple breakfast sausages drowned in grease. A blackened coffee pot. Crumbs on the counter.

Nada. Zero. Zilch-point-shit. Where, Bassett, where?

I was getting annoyed. I expected this to be easy. Nothing in the place from the stereo system to the TV looked new, expensive, or different. The La-Z-Boy near the front window was the same as before—grease-stained arms, worn to the nap behind the head. I felt every piece of furniture top, sides, and bottoms. I jerked the Ficus out of its weave planter and jabbed my fingers around in the dirt. No cash but a brick of marijuana. Poor-quality stuff—stems, seeds, and leaves all compressed together.

I used the flashlight to make sure nothing was missed. I didn't have to move much around to see into every corner downstairs. I swept my beam along the top of the cabinets in case he got creative—but the same result, no money. Bassett Hound was frugal, slovenly housekeeper, but not somebody living beyond his means.

I checked my wristwatch: 29 minutes and counting. I bragged to P.J. I'd be in and out in an hour at the most. Still time to check every wall, look for unusual grooves in floorboards, lift up the throw rug, shine the light into the vents and heating grates. So far, I hadn't ransacked the place, as if a slob like him would notice. I'd do a staged break-in once I found the money. I was tempted to break his electronics out of revenge, piss in his La-Z-Boy, crack the plasma TV screen and pull the wires out of his stereo system.

Easy, easy . . . Get the money first, then go to town on his nasty little shitbox.

Back to work: being as methodical as possible, I worked an imaginary grid. I tried not to get tunnel vision. People hid valuables in plain sight far more often than they tried to hide them. Bassett had no car so it was here somewhere—had to be. He'd never be so stupid as to pack a wad of bills to a biker bar and expect to get home in one piece.

On my hands and knees, I tapped the floorboards beneath the carpet with the bottom of the hammer when I felt metal jammed hard behind my head.

I froze. It grazed my neck, left a gash, then flicked my right ear lobe.

"Let go of the hammer," Bassett said. "Or I'll blow your fucking brains out."

I let the hammer slip out of my hands.

"Maybe we can discuss this—"

"Get up, fucker—slowly."

P.J., what the fuck . . .

"I was just looking—"

"I know what you're after, you white trash piece of shit. Shut up and turn around."

His eyes met mine: glitter of recognition, pleasure in the pain he meant to inflict.

Attack the man, not the gun—Kenny's voice back in my head now.

Three loud bangs on the door.

His head swiveled, an automatic reaction. His big mistake—

My fist connected. I aimed for his nose to stun him, blind him, but slammed the underside of his jaw instead. The result was still good; he lost his balance, gun arm flailing with his momentum.

My next move was classic Kenny Cardell. I'd seen him win fights completely drunk doing it. I butted him in the face with the top of my head. He went down hard.

Then I was on him throwing punches, one after the other, raining them down as fast as I could control my swings. He squirmed under me, dodged, batted away blows with his forearm. His fat was deceptive, I remember. He could handle himself. I'd be in trouble before much longer. My stamina was shaky at best, so I did as much damage as fast as I could with my fists, ignoring the pain in my hands and side where the ribs hurt.

Glass broke somewhere. My brain registered it, but I was unable to do more than glance to see who was coming through the door. If he had help coming—a Good Samaritan neighbor drawn to the noise—I was going to bolt for the kitchen window head-first regardless of the pain. I had too much to lose.

My eyes got as far as P.J.'s hips before he threw a short punch into my ribs. Not the sore side or I'd have fainted on top of him. I couldn't take another punch and stay in the fight. He rolled over, tossing me off like a dog shaking a flea. He was on his feet by the time I was upright. He stepped toward me. I launched a desperate, roundhouse right, putting all my strength left into it. He blocked it easily with a thick forearm.

Twice my age, bloated like a pig, yet he fights like "Two Ton" Tony Galento—

We were squared off again when he lunged. Sucking air, wheezing in pain, I stepped inside his punch and avoided it by inches. I had my right arm cocked for a punch when he did it again. He bulled into me instead, my fist bouncing off his cheek like a slap at a mosquito, and he grabbed me in a bear hug and started to squeeze. My arms were pinned. I was as helpless as muck rabbit in a cottonmouth's coils.

P.J. ended it without saying a word.

He let me go. Just dropped me before I passed out. I staggered backwards, bent double gasping for breath.

"Take this!"

P.J. shoved a Glock into my hands.

Bassett looked at the gun, then at me. I took a step toward him and threw a hard gut-punch into his belly. He doubled up, groaned, and dropped to his knees.

I swiveled to her, red-faced, angry. "Why didn't you answer the phone!"

"Is this a good time?"

So cool. I barked a short laugh, almost gagged from the effort. I sucked as much air into my lungs as I could get, keeping the gun on him.

"You . . . move . . . an inch . . . *youfatfuck* . . . I'll kill you."

His face, once twisted in a sadistic rage when he held the gun on me, was relaxed, fat jowls wagging like a big, friendly dog. P.J.'s looked drained of blood. He looked at her and nodded. "I know you, bitch. This isn't over."

I went crazy. I reversed the gun and used the butt to club him. I never said a word, I kept slamming him wherever I could strike. I was too weak to do much damage. I reared back and kicked him in the gut; he clutched his stomach, leaned over, and vomited up a yellow spume of beer onto the carpet where we'd been tussling.

A foul-smelling upchuck that included brown chunks and round bits that might have been pepperoni slices.

"Bassett, look at me," I said.

"Uh-uh-uh-uh-OH GOD, that hurts!"

"It'll hurt a lot worse if I put a bullet in you."

"What do . . . what do . . . you want from me?"

The question to both of us.

"I want my money."

"I don't have—"

More instinct than thought, I stepped toward him and kicked him in the balls.

His eyes popped the way people do when they see something unbelievable.

He dropped to his knees, placed a hand on the floor like a defensive lineman getting ready for the snap count. Then he dropped forward—straight down and slammed into the floor hard enough to rattle the room.

P.J. had me by the shirt. "Are you trying to kill him, for God's sake!"

I might have wanted to then. I still don't know. I was in a state old Harold back at Denmar would have called a fugue state. Or maybe "lucid dreaming," which he tried to explain to me once when he said I was sleeping so much I was going to get there without knowing I was there. P.J. grabbed my elbow.

"Wade, let's go!"

I didn't move. I couldn't move. I watched Bassett on the floor. His face beet-red and snot streaming from both nostrils. His mouth opened and closed soundlessly—a grouper nibbling algae on the aquarium glass—then a gob of mucous dribbled over his chin.

"Oh Jesus, look," P.J. said, backing away, pointing at him on the floor. His pants turned dark in the front and back. He'd evacuated his bowels. A godawful stench filled the room, an eye-watering odor that went rapidly from the rubbery stench of skunk to roadkill in summer.

Voices outside: male and female. Happy chatter of young people walking past the cabin. Coming home or on their way to the bars.

P.J. rushed over to the window and yanked the cord to close the drapes. Her look of astonishment at me spoke more than words.

"We need to go, Wade! God damn you! Now!"

"You go," I said. "I have to finish with this motherfucker."

"Wade . . ."

"Go! I'll meet you . . . later."

Her eyes pled with mine. "I can't do this," she whispered.

"That's fine. Get out!"

* * *

"What . . . where am I?"

"Don't be stupid," I said. "You're in your home sweet home by the lake."

"Why—"

"No more bullshit. You have my money. I want it."

He squirmed on the floor like a baby walrus, his wrists and ankles tied with strips of bed sheet. The gag I'd tied over his mouth was loose enough for him to breathe through and talk. It was sopping from whatever he coughed up; the entire cabin reeked.

I sat on a kitchen chair I'd dragged into the living room to face him to wait while he recovered his senses. The gun dangled loosely in my hand. A Glock .20. Kenny would appreciate the choice of weapon.

"Bassett, stop bawling. Listen to me . . ."

I had to get close to him because I'd put the stereo on a black radio station from Cleveland that played hip-hop and rap. Lots of thundering bass to make your breastbone vibrate.

He gargled.

I showed him the knife I held in my other hand.

"You need to listen to me, fucker. Are you listening or do you want me to take out your eyeball with this?"

The steel's touch to the skin under his bulging eye got his attention fast. He tried to scream behind the gag; his eyes watered and mores not dribbled down his cheeks.

No mercy, Wade . . . no mercy—

"I'm going to stab you up, you fat fuck. Just like prison. I seen guys get stabbed."

I turned up the radio dial. The singer's chanting, garbled dialect made violent threats to some unknown person who had offended him somehow. I was a long way from my father's favorite station playing Conway Twitty and Merle Haggard.

"Oh God, help me, I can't breathe. I'm dying—"

"Listen to me, Bassett. I am going to kill you, not hurt you, and God is not coming to save your fat ugly ass. You are mine and you are going to die on that rug. Tell me where the money is and it'll stop."

"D-don't have . . . Spent it."

I jumped up from the chair. "You're a sorry motherfucker is what you are and you are out of time. Your last chance."

I stepped over to him and sliced the gag off. I left a scimitar of cut doing it roughly and the blood poured out in a red sheet. The fat inside the cut was yellow like tiny balls of popcorn about to pop out.

He begged, cried, and argued about spending it. I leaned over and stuffed a clump of ripped bed sheet into his mouth, jamming it in his mouth against his teeth so he couldn't spit it out.

I placed the barrel of the Glock a couple inches into his rag-stuffed mouth.

"So they don't hear the gun going off, Bassett."

"Uuck . . . oooh."

"Fuck me? Fuck me? You stupid fat fuck. I can't believe you'll die for it."

I went to plan B. I'd already filled every bottle and container I could find while he lay semi-conscious on the floor. Sticking the gun behind my belt, I straddled him with a glass of water and poured it into his rag-stuffed mouth. I had one hand gripping his chin to keep him from moving his head out of the way.

"Thirsty for more? Got another glass right here."

The second glass of water followed the first with the same result: he bucked and gagged, the sensation of drowning overwhelming his brain with terror. I'd seen waterboarding on TV. Kenny said he always wanted to do it to someone. The carotid at his neck ticked like a fat worm. A forked vein in his forehead pulsed. I had to steel my nerves to keep watching his face.

His eyeballs rolled back in his head.

I used the barrel to remove the torn pieces of sheet from his mouth wary of Bassett's unusual strength. He could snap my finger off like a breadstick if he was playing possum.

"Wake-y, wake-y, motherfucker," I said. "We're not done. Bassett, my chubby friend, we have all night to do this."

"Nnnnooo, no more!"

"Tell . . . me . . . where . . . you . . . hid . . . the . . . money."

He strained his neck to look me in the face. "Don't have it. All . . . all gone," he huffed out and lay back down on the floor.

"Too bad," I whispered. "I was hoping we could end this and part as friends."

He tried to roll over on me. I slammed the barrel across his forehead, opening a gash.

The rag pieces jammed in harder and deeper this time, tripping his gag reflex. I held the pail of water over his head and let it pour down on his face. First, a trickle, then I released half the bucket.

The water shot out of his mouth in a violent reflex. His head slammed back to the floor.

"Don't faint on me, you pile of dogshit!"

I held another glass of water over his head and started to drip it into his mouth.

"What? What was that? I didn't catch that."

"Tell . . . you . . ."

That was all he said for the next twenty minutes. He was unresponsive even when I kicked him in the side of the head. I was afraid another shot in his solar plexus might actually kill him, so I waited, sitting calmly in the chair, my mind as blank and empty of thought as I had ever been in the joint. That's what it felt like, too: being back in a cell with nothing to hope for or believe in.

The digital clock said 4:08 in the morning. I didn't know if that meant morning or night.

I was in a hell of my own making. I'd crossed a bright line and cut myself loose from the earth. My Aunt Ida would have called me the Devil if she'd seen me that night. Could I come back from it? Did I even want to?

* * *

Chapter 15

The Strip was empty except for a few parked cars and some lights on in a couple of places where cleaning or preparation for the coming day was going on. It was like that time before when I staggered up from the beach, empty, drained.

It was a long thousand-yard walk down to Freddie's Grill where I'd left my car. Some criminal mastermind. The idea was to get the cash and blend in with the night crowd. Here I was alone, carrying the money, fake IDs and looking like Death eating a sandwich. The first cop that saw me would have braced me on the spot. The tools, stool, and gun went over the cliff into Lake Erie as soon as I left Bassett's cabin with the Glock tucked in my belt.

Parking in front of P.J.'s, I sat in the car observing the lot and grounds for an ambush. A light was on in her window. She opened the door before I knocked.

I lifted up the kitchen garbage bag with the money in it.

"Where did you find it?"

"His La-Z-Boy," I said. "Seat cushion had a zipper. I stuck my hand in there, felt all around, nothing but cotton batting."

I checked the chair, dumped it on its side, checked the bottom, poked a knife blade into every rip in the fabric. Looked for slits, places to secrete a wad of bills. Same thing with the foam cushion pads for the two kitchen chairs.

"I missed it first time."

"The way you missed my calls when I tried to warn you he was coming back?"

158

"I forgot to turn on the goddamned phone. I'm sorry."

"Some criminal mastermind."

"What now?"

"Sleep."

"What about cops, Wade? You expect him not to report you?"

"Stolen money, remember? I made sure he understood if he so much as looks at you on the street, he better cross to the other side. If he even looked cross-eyed at you, I'd come back and finish him. He believed me. He doesn't know who I am yet."

"I'm sure he shit himself in fear over that."

If she only knew, I thought.

"That's fucking comforting," she sneered. "My hero. I don't even know who you are? What did I bring in to my home? You were a monster back there!"

"I'm tired, P.J."

"You're tired, huh? How much did he spend out of it?"

I tossed the bag at her feet. "Count it, you want."

Heading for the shower, I left her there. There wasn't enough water in Lake Erie to wash me clean. The smell of that cabin was in my nostrils. I worked to blot out the images of the film playing: me with the gun, Bassett groveling on the floor.

Resting my forehead against the cool tiles, I let the stinging, hot water blast me until the tiny bathroom was lost in a cloud of white vapor. It was safe inside the cloud. I didn't want to leave.

The shower door stall creaked on its rail.

P.J. was coming to unload on me before throwing me out into the street. *You have it coming, shithead, for making a dog's breakfast back there . . .*

My voice? Kenny's? I wasn't sure anymore.

Maybe she'd let get in a few winks in before I had to hit the road back to West Virginia. I couldn't blame her.

Her warm, naked flesh pressing up against my backside was the last thing I expected at that moment.

"Christ, you're on fire," she said. "The water's too hot."

I turned around.

"That for me?"

I'd fucked in showers before—nothing romantic about it like TV wants us to think. It's dangerous. I slipped once and jammed a couple lower vertebrae that sent me to the hospital in Clarksburg for an MRI and a month of physical therapy. On top of my recreational drugs, I was popping Meloxicam, Tizanidine, and Gabapentine for two more months. But, then, all I was thinking about was being inside her. The horror and filth of those last hours were romped away to nothing by our bodies. My mind went somewhere else and *Good riddance*, I thought. Slippery skin slaps, mouth kisses on wet hair. Her shaved bush and the nub of clitoris made me frenzied. I hadn't had sex in so long I was beginning to wonder if I'd need a primer to figure out how to do it again.

She led me out of there dripping wet, took my hand and led me to her bed.

"This one's for me," she said. "Go slow this time."

She rolled me off and climbed on. I watched her grinding and thrusting her hips. There's nothing else so animal we do as human beings, unless it's killing, and nothing else we want to do to be more than human than this.

Lying beside her, I didn't know what to say. She spoke first: "You smoke?"

"No, I quit when I went to prison."

"I like a little pot. Fucking helps the high."

She rooted around in a drawer and came out with a joint; she lit it, inhaled, offered it to me, then blew the acrid smoke from her nostrils.

"I don't need a single thing, P.J. You can shoot me if you want. I'll die happy."

"You were just horny, that's all."

"True."

"I think there's all kinds of fucking, not just one. There's sport fucking, there's love-fucking, and there's I-got-to-get-this-white-stuff-out fucking," saying the last one in a deep male voice.

"Which one was I?"

"Little bit of all three," she said.

I leaned over and kissed her near her belly button ring.

"They say violence is an aphrodisiac," she said and sucked in more smoke.

"A what-iac?"

She slapped me on the shoulder. "You're not the dumb hillbilly you pretend to be. That violence, Wade. What you did—and I don't want to know what you did after to make him talk. It wasn't good."

"No, it wasn't. I won't even lie and say I had no choice."

"That's good anyway."

"Jesus, I'm horny again," she said and butted out the reefer in the ashtray.

"Don't let me stop you."

She hooked a leg over me and then climbed on me, pulling the sheet over herself. A quick kiss on the lips, tender, not hungry, then she slithered down my body kissing and licking her way over my stomach until she found a position on my legs. When I felt her take me in her mouth, I lay back on the pillow and closed my eyes.

The sheet bobbed with the motion of her head. She flipped the sheet off so I could watch her.

She took it out of her mouth and squeezed it. "I could bite this right off," she said.

"Please don't," I said. "I might need it again."

Whatever she replied was mumbled, urgent, lost in the noise she made after down there.

* * *

I'd been dreaming of my dead mother while she woke and got ready for work.

Same jumbled-up kinds of things that happen in dreams when you speak to dead people and they talk back to you. People from my past, bizarre changes of scenery, things said to me or I said to people that defied logic. At one point, I found myself washing out a filthy, abandoned warehouse with a power hose. All the dirt and gunk swirling down a huge drain hole in the corner. They say dreams like that only last minutes, not all night.

I leaned back on the pillow and wondered if P.J.'s morning shower infiltrated my dreams before I woke for good. I didn't believe in the supernatural, although I had family going back generations that believed in potions for love, warding off spells, curing diseases. My father's kinfolk were full of midwives, herb doctors, and granny women who mixed their babies drinks made of blue cohosh and butterfly weed or put axes under their cribs to cut off sickness and diseases.

"Twenty-one-hundred and forty-seven dollars," she said.

"Son of a bitch spent a thousand in that time," I replied from the bedroom.

"Eleven-fifty and change apiece."

"I said three-thousand, P.J. Take fifteen and whatever the math says about the rest. I just need a few hundred to get me home and get situated."

"Hey, I won't argue with that. I can use the money. I'm leaving this shithole as soon as I hear back from Dwight's lawyer. He promised me a bonus if I stayed until the start of the new season."

"Good luck."

"You, too, Wade. Make sure you lock that door on your way out, OK?"

"Will do. . . . Thanks f-for saving me . . . f-for everything."

Stuttering boy to the end, that's me.

"*De nada,*" she said before closing the door. "See you in another life."

"Another life"—didn't I wish?

* * *

I thought of saying goodbye to her before I blew town. Then thought better of it; she wouldn't like it, and I would be taking another risk hanging my face out there in public.

The preacher's car had enough gas to make it to an interstate gas station. I did need some food for the trip and thought the little grocery store was a safer bet. It was past one in the afternoon, the skies were a blue-gray and the air smelled of rain coming. I would have liked to see lightning over the lake. P.J. said it was gorgeous. But there was no sense in delaying the inevitable. I had Kenny to think about, not much money, and I needed to make time count.

"Hey, you! Serial killer!"

I was coming down the steps with a single-use bag in my hand of snack food and bottled water when I heard the voice from the sidewalk. The hair on my neck stood up. I thought about reaching behind me for the gun in my belt.

"Remember me? Niya? We gave you a ride. You were going to a job interview."

"Niya. Yes."

Her tubby friend with her, the one who mocked me. *Don't try it now, little girl.*

She wore skinny jeans and a tank top. Her Levi's were fashionably slitted up the thighs exposing flesh. No West Virginia mother would let her child leave the house to shame her like that. Even the stringy cuffs of my school pants were sewn when my father was drinking up his worker's compensation checks after the mine closed.

"Did you get it?"

For a split-second, I thought she knew about Bassett. "Get . . . what?"

"The job."

"No."

"Told you it was bullshit," Lynne said in that same stage whisper. I'd almost forgotten her name. I remembered the looks she'd given me in the car, the same as now, bobcat regarding a stupid chipmunk ready for mangling with its teeth.

"So long."

"See you."

Two girls, one nice, one not so much. People passed in and out of your life. Some of them made a difference. Some were like sticking your finger in a bucket of water and pulling it out, one of Aunt Ida's sayings. "When the last ripple is becalmed," she said, "you had the same flat surface as before."

I don't know why it's like that, men or women; it's the same way. Two dogs meet in the road. It ain't necessarily they're gonna fight or fuck every time. But sometimes you've got wonder if our DNA isn't programmed for it. Harold didn't believe in God, or so he said. "Too much evidence against it," and then he'd go into some gobbledygook about "Goldilock zones," more planets than grains of sand on all the beaches on the planet." I told him my Aunt Ida would tear him a new asshole, she heard him talking like that.

"Lumps of hydrogen and carbon, Wade," he said. "That's all we are. Our least little thought—just chemical interactions, atoms combining the same way they had since the universe began." He didn't want to take responsibility for his choices, I said. Blaming molecules for his check kiting.

So what's behind the molecules?

Strings, he said.

If that's what they taught you in college, better get your money back.

Lynne didn't know it at the time but she gave me an inspiration right there on the steps. I was going back with a couple hundred in my pocket—not much of a war chest when it came to taking on my cousin.

A plain girl like Lynne attaching herself to a pretty girl like Niya is too common to be noticeable. You see it everywhere. You even know the pretty girl is envied by her so-called friend and would like nothing better than for her to get in to an accident and wind up with facial scars. I could use that to get to Corinne: Divide and conquer.

A girl who inherited her parents' house, savings, and life insurance payouts wouldn't be short of friends no matter how unpopular she might have been. Males in her life who'd never looked at her twice would come sniffing around on the chance that girl might be vulnerable to some boning. While a sugar mama might not be as common as a sugar daddy, money's a bigger aphrodisiac than violence, and it goes both ways. If I could turn Corinne against my cousin, I had a half-chance before the circle of law enforcement tightened around my neck. I had to find out more about this girl who had blood cold enough to go on TV and say she was so "concerned" about her parents that she had to call in a welfare check. How she crossed paths with Kenny was a mystery I had to solve.

My father had a decent brain before he turned into a lush. Good common sense, a sense of order, of the kind we preferred over book learning. What's that got us anyway but a bunch of tech billionaires in Silicon Valley, a country full of nasty-minded trolls on social media and phone zombies bumping into each other on the street? We were riding home from a district track meet where I'd qualified for the state meet. He saw me surrounded by my teammates, back-slapping me and giving me the "attaboy" treatment big time. Because he was known to be a drunk all over Salem, I was embarrassed to be seen with him.

"Son, you best learn one thing in life. Nobody hates you like your friends."
It's a little late but I hear you now, Dad . . .

* * *

Chapter 16
New Zenith, Ohio

Pastor John officiated at the double funeral for Corinne's parents. The NBC affiliate channel in Columbus sent down a TV crew. Local news had photographers camped on the perimeter of St. Mark's Cemetery to snap shots of the ceremony. Across the river in West Virginia, the "senseless, brutal murders of an Ohio couple" were still a hot topic.

Tempted as I was to go, I was certain the police would have undercover officers stationed among the mourners. Only the naïve among the populace continue to believe that the most horrific crimes are the work of random killers passing through town. A child gets abducted and murdered, half the town gets obsessed with the notion some new Hannibal Lector stuck a pin in a wall map and decided to wreak horror on their little community. Ninety-nine times out of a hundred it's the custodial parent or that harmless looking nerd three houses down with no criminal record.

BCI had to be giving the daughter a hard look, even if the papers said they didn't have a clue "of the primary person-of-interest being sought for questioning." They'd wait and watch like me. If she had sense, she'd never clap eyes on my cousin again after paying him off. I hoped she was as greedy and stupid as he was. The For Sale sign planted in the yard when I drove past in a taxi told me she was already spending her loot in case I missed the new Mercedes Benz S-Class Sedan sitting in the driveway. Her parents were stiff in their caskets and she was flaunting her inheritance with a $90,000 car.

That also told me she didn't wait long to put in her claim for the insurance payout. *Greedy little Corinne*, I thought, admiring the wheels as we passed by the house. The doorbell camera was new, too.

On my way south of Columbus, I detoured to East Liverpool on the Ohio River, one of the poorest rust-belt cities in the tri-state area. A drive through downtown showed the despair in the pedestrians—so many hopeless people, losers, dopers, and scrappers all doing the backstroke in the same cesspool. Thirty years of jobs going to China—what did people think would happen? Years back, I'd dealt drugs this far north and knew where to go to find the right connections. For a few twenties, I found someone who sold me passable identification. My new ID cards included a driver's license, Social Security card, and a Red Cross blood donor's card all in the name Leon Kowalski, a name I chose from *Blade Runner*. A Replicant under a death sentence if found, he hid out as a janitor. Before his brains were blown out, he told the cop it wasn't easy living in fear every day.

I could relate.

The pastor's car was next on the agenda. It went to a chop shop in Parkersburg as soon as I crossed the state line. I should have pushed it over a cliff or run it into the river. Only the necessity of boosting my cash supply was the greater concern. Picking up a cheap car from a used car lot was essential.

Wade Cardell, gumshoe. I followed Corinne in her shiny new Beamer every chance I had. New Zenith has one intersection every resident has to pass through going in any direction. I sat in the library parking lot across the street and waited for her. I kept notes on the times of her comings and goings from the house.

I was playing the riskiest game yet; cops were bound to notice me in a town this small.

I couldn't change who I was, but I could change my appearance. If I didn't bear a strong resemblance to my old mug shot and legit driver's license, I bore even less now. I sacrificed the hair growing out to a preppie cut, high and tight on the sides. I bought three white shirts and a three pairs of grey slacks and navy-blue slacks at the Goodwill. I tossed my Timberlands and tennis shoes in the trunk for a pair of used brogans. Levi's, tee-shirts, ballcap, windbreaker went into a dumpster. I looked like a Mormon. All I lacked was the bike and the bible. In fact, I was tempted to try to find one from the used bookstore on Main. That was pushing it, however.

My tattoos stayed hidden, my scars were post-prison, including the big lightning-bolt of a scar on the top of my head where maggots had gnawed dead tissue. Over my eyebrow was a jagged scar of dead white skin from the staph infection. I tried to shed some of my accent. With the new outfit, even Kenny might not recognize me at first glance. No one would be looking for me at the scene of the worst crime in New Zenith history, although I understood the words Brion James uttered to Harrison Ford about what it was like to live in fear. It woke me up and put me down into an uneasy sleep in my new digs in Matamoras at a B & B close to the river.

The landlady thought I was a Mormon, in fact, until I told her: "No, ma'am, I'm a born-again Christian." She was afraid I was going to try to convert her and her husband in the wheelchair. I didn't want to stand out too much.

I spent the week looking for a pattern to Corinne's movements. The newspapers showed her in black and treated her with sympathy. One reporter who did an interview for the New Zenith daily three weeks after the funeral made me gag because Corrinne's responses to the questions about how she was "unable to pick up the pieces" after the tragedy left her weeping all day in her room. By then, I'd followed her to a beauty salon, an exercise club (three times a week), a shopping mall and a night club in Charleston and a dozen other places between Parkersburg and Huntington in high-end boutiques, jewelry stores, and restaurants—none of which I was sure had "family friendly" on the menu. She looked smart in her new clothes and stylish cut. It was classic how-to-fuck-up after a crime. This girl was begging the cops to investigate her. I had a crick in my neck from looking behind me to spot unmarked cars.

An unexpected source of information turned out to be the owner of the B & B. My luggage lay open on the dresser bureau. I wanted her to snoop. The Glock was hidden beneath the spare, magazine separated, along with a bottle of Old Grand-Dad.

I told myself I had to take the edge off from the shit raining down on my head—especially with the night driving Corinne put me through. I was worried about being pulled over by traffic cops in town or by troopers on the highway, who just might be bored enough or had to fill their weekly quotas. For one thing, my rattletrap Escort wouldn't keep up with the BMW's big engine, and Corinne had a lead foot. Once she hit the on-ramp, the odds were 70-30 I'd stay with her.

At least with the landlady, I hit paydirt. She was a devout Christian and liked to talk about her faith. That was easy for me. All that bible reading from my youth paid off. I couldn't match this woman quote for quote, but I could sprinkle my speech with enough holy-roller talk to make her beam. When I told her I was looking into Methodist churches in the area, she nearly orgasmed. From then on, I was invited to share dinners with the couple and even lead them at table in saying grace at the table. If she only knew my Aunt Ida's saying about "needing a long spoon if you sup with the Devil."

The killer of the New Zenith couple was "evil incarnate," "a truly godless man," "Satan's own minion"—and I forget what else she called him. As long as Kenny Cardell was alive, I didn't have to worry about being "the true spawn of the Father of Lies." He had that title all to himself.

I made an effort to smile around them when I was in the house; those comments were music to my ears. Had she ever suspected she was sitting across from the very person she condemned, she'd have dropped dead on the spot. Her hubby's faith wasn't so rock-solid compared to her fanaticism. She was the kind to hang witches from trees and burn heretics at the stake.

Funny how people have no scruples about prying into your deepest feelings when it comes to faith, but give them a half-assed story about how you make a living and they'll be content with it. I told her I was there on behalf of my uncle who owned a hunting-and-fishing store in Gallipolis; he wanted to expand to this area. I was there to scout opportunities for him. I fucked that story up when I pronounced it Guh-LIP-po-lis" like a newcomer instead of "GALL-i-po-lis." Who knew? She looked at me sideways for a moment, quiet, thinking I just put a bug in her ear and didn't realize it until later.

She didn't have a computer in the house but she had a iPad. I'd seen her open it a dozen times to check email her *Facebook* page. She was like a teenager. I'd overhear her drop remarks to her indifferent husband about what this person or that person she'd friended posted online. I would have given my eye teeth and a left testicle for that password and five minutes alone with it.

What I wanted more than anything was to find out what Corinne Barrett did or said in her own social media accounts. I could imagine the sentimental gush from friends and relatives consoling her after the murders of her parents. Poor little rich girl, an orphan in the world—thanks to Kenny—more thanks to me. My dead body in that house was supposed to put a ribbon on their plans. She obviously didn't give two shits about killing her parents but the world was out there panting for a sighting of Wade Cardell, who had fangs for incisors.

A hundred times, I'd asked myself one question: How can that girl live her life knowing I was out there somewhere? She had to figure the first thing I would do when the cops cuffed me up was to shout my innocence through the veins in my neck. Yeah, my gun and my prints and all that. But how could she be sure I wouldn't manage to convince somebody somewhere I was an innocent man? Every con I knew at Denmar except Harold claimed to be "innocent" or the "real victim." But even my brainiac of a cellmate griped about "the real criminals," the multi-national corporations who ripped off millions every day and never got prosecuted for it. One letter to those whiz kids working for the Innocence Project could have brought it all down around her ears like a house of cards under strobe lights. "Ballsy" or "stupid"—I wasn't sure, but the reckless spending under the noses of cops made me suspect she was way too confident she'd gotten away with it.

The other night I came back to my room early because I'd lost Corinne. She had a girlfriend in the car with her, somebody she was going out dancing with. I'd seen her in club clothes and foo-foo hairdo often enough to know the signs. Once she turned at the Pomeroy interchange, I was certain she was heading to Highway 33 and north to Athens, a college town full of bars. She lost me just past Pomeroy. I drove into Athens, hoping to spot the Beamer. Driving around for hours, I was giving campus cops too many chances to note my vehicle, which looked out of place among the SUVs and cute little sports cars from Daddy.

I got eyeballed by city police in New Zenith, too. A cruiser parked catty corner off Court Street near the bars. All the driving up and down felt like banging a stick in a swill bucket—just a matter of time before they decided to come running, check me out. My plates and tag were as phony as my ID cards. I thought of those busy cons in Denmar who talked, took notes during crime shows, and networked like entry-level MBAs for the day they were released; they knew where to get an illegal gun, who did first-class forgery, who fenced what and where. It was like a second America, one where people like my cousin operated within their own rules and habits. Working for a living didn't pan out for me. I never realized crime and prison's influence on me. A normal man loses a job in a junkyard, he doesn't kill the boss' nephew; he finds another job.

One thing both Americas had in common whether you tried to live off the grid or not: you better have you some money to get along in it.

I sat on my bed in the B & B in a foul mood. The couple didn't believe in leaving many lights on after ten o'clock. I'd had a couple deep swallows of Old Grandad from the trunk on my way into the house. I tripped going up the stairs to my room and went down on all fours, blurting out a cuss word without thinking. When I looked up, she was standing there looking at me with that I-smell-excrement expression on her doughy face.

"Brought you some clean towels," she said. "I put 'em on the bed. . . . You better git on in the morning."

My trips to the trunk hadn't been missed. She moved by me heading for the back stairs. From born-again Christian to radioactive demon. Her dismissal of me was pure Appalachian. She'd seen through my act or else her curiosity about me had finally deepened to suspicion—either way, I had to git.

* * *

Living out of a car again. I hadn't been past her house since that taxi ride. I was drinking more, which made me braver—and dumber. I didn't know what I expected to find: Kenny's muscle car in the driveway, I hoped, making it easy for me to get my Glock out and shoot him. I'd known him to hide his "Baby" of the moment in some friend's garage whenever the law was looking to have a chat with him. He always had some piece of shit like mine to drive around in.

Angry, fidgety, bolstered by sips of whiskey, I made another pass at her house. Corinne was locking the front door of her house when I drove by. I was halfway to parking in her driveway and banging on the door and telling her "Kenny wants his money" just to shake the tree. She was dolled up—but not in a way that I recognized for a girl going clubbing locally. White tee under a lumberjack shirt, black blazer, hair shaved on one side high and tight to the scalp. Nothing even remotely like her most recent photos in the house. There aren't too many reasons why a woman wants to look and dress like a 14-year-old boy.

She drove fast as usual and blew past several caution lights that would have left me in her dust if it hadn't been for my liquid courage. I was at the end of my mental tether and nearly all my half-share of Northtown money. I was giving this another two days and then I was giving it up and heading out West as far as the gas tank would take me. Making minimum wage for the rest of my life was easy street compared to a life sentence in a tough prison like "Misery Mountain" in Hazelton.

Highway 33 meant Athens. I'd lost her there before. This time, I had to keep up.

She bypassed the bars she'd been to before and took a left off Court closer to downtown Athens. I followed her past the city park and watched as she turned into a cement-block bar with a single neon sign blinking the name of the bar: The Pink Canoe, one word at a time.

Maybe her motive there: Mommy and Daddy weren't keen on their little girl going gay and they tried to put a stop to it like any good Christian parents of their generation. If that was the case, she beat them to the punch. I parked in the back and watched the girls enter, some dolled up in femme fashion with heavy makeup, little-girl hats, bangle bracelets on both arms and jewelry around the neck, skinny jeans tight enough to outline the notch. Some women looked big enough to eat apples off my head.

Every time the back door opened, I could hear loud dance music—thumping bass, drums, electronic deep house music.

Corrine, I thought, *I hope you wore sensible shoes tonight.*

* * *

Two-thirty a.m. and the music was still pumping through the doors, only much louder. Some girls stood outside smoking and talking. I saw the crimson tips of cigarettes create neon arcs from mouths to thighs and back again, fade, disappear like fireflies. Two girls had come out holding each other around the waist a half hour earlier. Obviously drunk, they headed for the car parked beside mine. They looked over at me, although I was slumped in the seat and stared straight ahead.

"Wrong night, asshole," the driver blurted to me, weaving to the driver's side. "Drag night was two nights ago."

Her girlfriend giggled as she climbed in and scooted over to snuggle into her.

Corinne left alone with the rest of the crowd at 3:00 when the bar closed. Some girls paired off, holding hands, while others kissed goodnight or chatted with friends on the way to their cars. Corinne's BMW was parked at the far end from mine.

She walked like someone proving to herself she wasn't drunk. A girl called out to her to "wait up!" before she got halfway there. This girl was a head shorter, wore a rainbow-colored sleeve of tattoos and black jeans, laced boots almost to her kneecaps. Corinne hadn't moved the whole time until the shorter girl practically collided into her. They held each other around the hips and kissed for a long time. Heavy kissing with lots of tongue action, pawing. Corinne's jaw bulged with the exertion. Cars gave playful honks at the public exhibition as they passed.

"Get a room, you bitches!" one shouted driving past the entwined couple.

When they broke apart, they held each other and talked for about a minute. The smaller girl stroking Corinne's cheek. The lot had emptied except for three other cars and mine. As she turned to walk away, she made a scoop of her hand and tucked it between Corinne's legs, fondling her vag in a scissoring action. I didn't hear what the girl said while stroking away. It looked as much like fighting as lovemaking.

It didn't look like Corinne's first time in a gay bar. *If only Mom and Dad could see you now*, I thought.

The long embrace over, Corinne staggered off to her car while the tattooed girl headed back inside, maybe a bartender or waiter.

Enough time, I thought. *Here's as good a place as any.*

I opened my door. No interior dome light to worry about—an old thief lesson from years back.

My fast walk covered the ground toward her, trotting to make the timing between Corinne arriving at her car, fumbling with the key fob and my approach right behind her. Once I'd made up my mind to confront her, I stopped sipping the booze during my surveillance. I was headachy from lack of food on my stomach and the whiskey I'd drunk earlier.

As soon as I heard the *beep* unlocking the car door, I was on her, one hand around her mouth, the other opening the door and shoving her inside.

"You can stop biting my hand now," I said.

She was drunker than I thought.

I punched her to make her let go, a short tap on the nose.

The human mouth is a reservoir of bacteria. *God damn it*—another round of penicillin. I was living in a petri dish these days.

"I'm not here for your money. Are you calm?"

She tried sliding out the passenger door. My hand on her collar yanked her back.

"Don't bite me again or I'll beat the shit out of you."

"Who—who the fuck are you?"

Before I could answer her question, she was fumbling in the drink holder for a keychain attached to a tube of pepper spray.

I snatched it out of her hand before she could aim it at me. I squeezed her hand hard.

"Ow-ow-ow! You fucking bastard! Let go!"

"Listen to me. Corinne, stop!"

I pulled the tube away. She scooted back, her eyes still bugged, staring at me. I couldn't penetrate the fog of confusion she was in.

"Are you calm now?"

"Who the fuck are you?"

"I'm the guy," I said, "who made all this possible."

I spread my hands out, embracing the expensive car, the hot little number she'd been kissing in the parking lot, the buzzing neon sign The Pink Canoe—all of it, like Jesus performing the miracle of five loaves and two fishes.

* * *

I didn't know if she intended to turn in at the nearest police station, floor it once we got back on the highway or do a U-turn and drive me off the road. She could have been calling the state police on her cell phone before we even left the township line. I'd lost confidence in my words to her back there in the parking lot.

She had a long drive to think about what I said and from her point of view, she'd be able to figure more options than the ones I spelled out for her. It was lucky for me she was still too drunk to do much but concentrate on her driving without getting busted for an OVI.

It had to be in her house, the only place she'd feel safe. For one thing, she brought up the notion I could be wired.

"I can't take my clothes off here," I said. "We're risking too much already. We need to go now."

The *we* a clever touch, I thought. As in: We two against them— *them* being all the cops looking into her parents' killing and my deranged cousin, who would never stop coming to her for money. I did my best to convince her that her choice of a hit man was flawed in that one major respect.

"Ken Cardell is as greedy as they come," I told her once we were inside the foyer. I had chills up my spine from the onrush of memories of my last visit to her house.

"Be quiet. Take off your clothes first."

I stripped. "See? No wires."

"Underwear too."

I hesitated.

"I've seen men's cocks before."

I did it and turned around for her to see.

"You look all beat up."

"I've had a rough month, but I'm healing."

"I'm not admitting a thing." She showed me her other hand; the tube of mace was back. "Try anything, you'll get a face full. See if you can explain running out of my house without clothes on. I'll scream 'rape' at the top of my lungs."

"OK, you have me at a disadvantage. But let me finish what I started to say back in the parking lot of your club. You don't realize how much trouble you're in. If you thought your parents being . . . gone was the end of it, you don't know what a can of snakes you opened up the day you contacted my cousin."

"I can be pretty ruthless, too. I just showed you that."

"I know. You proved it. But his ruthlessness is even greater. If he has to kill you to prove that you can't stiff him on what he thinks you owe him, he'll do it in a heartbeat."

The only thing that prevented her from fleeing out the door hollering she'd been raped was the fact I was standing right there in person without a stitch on talking in a low voice about the psychopath she linked herself to. I was just the fall guy, the patsy who was supposed to bleed out on her kitchen floor. I had to hope I convinced her by talking about the fucked-up scheme that involved my relative.

She didn't want to believe me. I understood that. It didn't change anything.

"He'll come for you," I said. "You won't know it until it's happening to you."

The fact she didn't recognize me from the newspaper photos or TV highlights worked in my favor. I could see her brain working, trying to play the best angle the whole time I gave her my pitch for cooperating with me instead of turning me in. She could claim not to know me, she could take all the polygraphs and voice-stress tests they could ask her to take—but she could never, ever explain me away once I started yapping to the cops. I'd done nothing worse than try to rob her house.

"I can do two years standing on my head," I said. "I'm not looking at death row. You are, so roll the dice if you feel like taking the chance. Your phone's in your purse. Call them."

"Maybe I will when you go," she said. "It's you they're after, not me. How will it look—my parents' killer trying to shake me down?"

"Maybe it will work—for a while. But at some point, the FBI and the BCI will get their shit together and see I'm the one telling the truth."

"What's a BCI, fucker?"

I thought: *She planned her parents' murders and didn't think the state cops would bump the local cops off the case faster than rats can fuck . . .*

"Your New Zenith cops probably never investigated anything worse than shoplifting and jaywalking. Did you actually think they were going to handle a case that got news this big?"

She didn't say anything to that. At least she wasn't screaming.

I kept my voice low, polite. Two adults having a conversation in a middle-class home.

The ringtones of her cell went off: some kind of metal music like banging garbage can lids together

"Your girlfriend? Tell her you're fine but you have a headache and can't talk right now."

It was an FBI agent named Jonathan Stettler; he wanted to know if he could stop by in the morning and discuss something "critical" with her. He apologized for the late-night phone call.

"That's fine," Corinne told him. She thumbed off the connection.

"You better get dressed and get the fuck out of here," she said. "He told me he was calling from his field office in Columbus. For all I know, he could be across the street.

I dressed in a hurry and left.

* * *

By early afternoon, I had to know. I drove to her house and parked in the driveway. I expected to see cops and FBI agents to come flying out of the shrubbery at me like you see get mustered into action for a school shooting.

When I left her in the house the night before, she was steadier on her feet, her eyes not so glazed, not even a peek from the curtains at me as I left. I hoped my talking to her was the thing that did it, not the booze. If she had second thoughts, it wouldn't take long to find out.

I knocked, three short raps.

It opened immediately.

"Smile for the camera," she said, pointing up at the lens of the Ring camera. "In case you've got any ideas."

I bit my tongue. "No, no ideas, Corinne."

Besides, I didn't kill my mother and father like you . . .

Once she cut on the lights, I looked to see if she'd moved any furniture around, changed anything to make this her place now. The drywall where Kenny's shot tore up the plaster had been patched but wasn't painted yet. I wondered if she recalled me flying down the stairs with bullets smacking the wall behind me and her command to him: *Kill them . . .* Talk about walking over someone's grave and feeling nothing. Corinne and my cousin were a good match.

"You want coffee?"

I didn't expect that. Something more like "Convince me not to call the cops in the next five minutes—"

"Sure."

The kitchen had long since been cleaned of blood and the table put back in place. I wrinkled my nose as though I'd had a whiff of coppery blood. I couldn't help staring at the floor even so. I saw the place where Kenny must have stood over me with the gun aimed at the back of my head, hesitating: *Should I do it now and take my chances?*

"You mind if I ask you something?"

"Why didn't you let him kill me right there?"

"I didn't," she said, pouring out a cup. "I told him to shoot you."

She took the mug out of the Keurig machine and brought it to me.

"He wouldn't do it. He said it would blow up my alibi."

"Oh."

Practical, common-sense Kenny. I owed my life to him, not her.

"Don't take it personal, no offense. Do you want milk or coffee creamer?"

"No, black is fine."

Then logic reared its ugly head, chimed in what I had been missing: *two down, what was one more?*

The mug she gave me had NASCAR embossed in gold on it. Her father the racing fan. I'd seen copies of *Racer* and *Grassroots Motor Sports* on the end table upstairs.

"OK," she said; "talk."

The first thing that came out of my mouth was this: "The guy you paid off to kill your parents—"

"Your cousin."

"My cousin. He's a four-star, revolving maniac. You realize this much by now, I hope. If he thinks you're a liability to him, he'll kill you. You won't see it or hear it coming."

"So you said last night. He's got more to lose than I do," she said.

"That's not true. You do, not him. You're the mastermind. If anything, he'll turn state's evidence against you and plead down. Do his all day and a night—"

"What?"

"Life Without Parole. They'll take the death penalty off the table for the first one they turn, and they'll want to deal with him, as bad as he is, to get to you."

Matricide, parricide—my former cellie and his big words reached out of my memory from some long-ago conversation about Greek tragedies. More him than me. He talked, I listened. *"The worst of crimes, according to the ancient Greeks . . ."*

I told her as much as I thought she needed to understand her situation. I wanted to put her in a tight corner with only one way out: Wade Cardell's help.

"What do you want from me?"

At last, thenk yew, Jesus.

"When he contacts you again, I want you to meet him—your Mister Black."

"Meet him? In this *house?* Are you out of your mind?"

"He'll suspect a trap here. He'll propose the place."

"How do you know he'll want to meet me?"

"Haven't you been listening to me? He's going to want everything you have starting with that car in the driveway. He'll core you like an apple by the time he's through."

I was more curious about how a middle-class girl from a good home had crossed paths with my cousin than I was about how she'd come to hate the two people who had raised her so much she wanted them dead. That I'd never understand. Never, ever.

In a roundabout way, in dribs and drabs, she told me everything . . .

Her father sold the campground and made a lot of money. He bought her a horse, an old, retired stud named Banquet 4 Two as a gift for her 4-H club project. Another girl from her 4H had a horse named Malcolm. She and this girl Kris spent every free minute together during the week and every weekend her parents allowed, although her parents didn't approve of Kris' folks because they weren't "church-going Christians." When Kris moved down to Charleston, her father got her a job as a groom at the race track because he worked for the racing commission in St. Albans.

The summer she graduated from New Zenith High, and got an email from her friend asking her to come down to visit. Her parents grudgingly allowed it.

"I didn't plan on it but it happened," Corinne said. "I went to the track every day with Kris. I helped her in the stables—mucking, brushing, feeding." Kris was allowed to walk the horses. One day she took Corinne with her to the mating stable where the stallions covered the mares. Maybe that evening, maybe a day or two later, Kris was taking a shower and walked into the bedroom with a towel on.

I knew she was teasing me. I don't remember when we kissed for the first time but it wasn't long after. She was the first and only girl I ever loved. I remember us kissing so hard our lips were bruised. I had black-and-blue marks all over, finger bruises. It was like we couldn't stop hurting ourselves while we were giving each other so much pleasure. That's true love, isn't it? That hunger—and you want it more all the time but you can never get it all, not then or later. But I knew I was gay.

She painted in the rest. I could see it coming—the bad ending, the wolf comes over to you, smiles and says: *We can run together, we're the same*—until you trip. Then you find out what running with a wolf really means. "We had that much in common," she told me. "We both ran with a wolf and we both tripped."

Kenny was a gambler who started betting in high school with money from the stuff he fenced. Kenny's dad had run off his sophomore year and my aunt doted on her only son. She never heard a bad word said about him even when the cops came to the house and threatened to put him in a juvie facility for trespassing and skipping school. After football season, Kenny was a no-show, but all his teachers were scared shitless of seeing him hulking in the back of the room, the angry look on his face, so he got passed through to the next grade. He bragged about slipping grooms at the track a few bucks for insider information—which horses came up limping, which ones had a sore fetlock, or which were sweating too hard in the receiving barn after a workout.

"So you and Kenny saw each other at the track?"

"No, not then. Kris had an older sister who liked "bad boys." She said she was seeing a boy from Clarksburg.

"When I got home, my parents found out about Kris and me. They refused to let me see her or talk to her ever again. They checked my cell phone, listened in on all my phone calls. They made me see the Lutheran minister for counseling. When I resisted and said I loved her, I was sent off to a homosexual deprogramming ministry in Indiana for a month.

"I tried to commit suicide twice. When I finally found an opportunity to call Kris months later, for five minutes that made me want to live again, I told her how miserable I was.

I added the final piece, turned over the river card: "Kris' sister told her bad boy about her miserable, lonely girlfriend up in Ohio who has these unbearable Christian parents."

"You want to hear something funny?"

"Might as well," I replied. "I know how the story ended."

"Kris isn't gay now. She's married, living in Nebraska, has a couple kids."

"That's what my English teacher from high school would call 'ironic.'"

"Yet I still go to the track in Charleston every summer," she said. "Looking for . . . whatever it was I lost. Kris' sister still lives there. She's a mess—crank bugs, missing teeth, meth mouth. Your cousin is her drug dealer, you know that? She introduced us during a race. Maybe he ordered her to. I remember the big, phony smile on his face like he's God's gift to women. Didn't tell me his name, said I could call him 'Mister Black.' He wanted to know if I still had 'a situation' I wanted changed."

"That was years ago. Yet you still—"

"—hated them. I wanted them to pay for what they did. I still hate them. I'm glad they're gone."

Gone—what a word to use.

She had that last with a sickly grin on her face, like a corpse's expression where the mortician fucked it up with the needle by sewing the jaw too tight to correct lip drift. What she said next creeped me out more.

"I have one condition," she said.

"What is it?"

"Don't kill him in New Zenith."

"Fair enough."

"Afternoon already," she said, accompanying that with a yawn revealing silver fillings. I remembered the photo of the little girl in pigtails on the wall going upstairs. What images failed to capture was stunning: her deeply hidden, black heart, the misery and sadness. I didn't want to feel pity for her. *Shoot them . . . Shoot him.*

"How much did you pay him to—for the job?"

"Ten thousand down," she said. "Another ten when the insurance paid off."

I half-turned in the chair and gestured with my thumb over my shoulder to the driveway where the BMW's polyester coating gleamed in the sunlight.

"He's been paid in full," she said. "I sold the camper in Matamoras. We arranged to meet there after—the funeral service."

I must have just missed him. Busy up north trying to get my money back.

I asked her how she could be sure he wouldn't come back for more.

She regarded me as if I'd just transformed into a winged monkey from Oz.

"That was the agreement."

I looked away from her to the light coming into window above the sink. Her father must have had the half-round windows put in after the house was built. Blue sky just minutes ago. A crimson sash seemed drawn over the tree line beyond the river.

"I'm going to bed now," Corinne said. "Finish your coffee. Make sure the door's locked on your way out."

I planted a seed. Fear of her partner in crime watered it into full bloom.

We looked like a couple having a chat in the kitchen. The loving wife who gets up to see her husband off to work, makes his coffee.

Everything in my life was a cheap, Day-Glo-painted lie.

* * *

Chapter 17

We were in a bar in Charleston once, a lowlife dive. We'd been on the road for three days scoring black tar heroin from a dealer in a motel in some Texas border town I can't remember the name of. Sandy, yellow grit blew in from every direction, got in your eyes, your nostrils, your mouth, the food you ate, your underwear.

I don't know what possessed him. We drank, too tired to talk much. He went to the jukebox in this highway joint, put in some quarters. Ernest Tubbs' "Waltz across Texas" started to play. I was exhausted from staying up two nights straight from the dope. The beer in the place tasted lousy—watered-down draft. With every swinging dick in the place looking at him, he suddenly hopped up on the bar and started to shuffle down it, like some country bumpkin doing a hoedown he made up right there, kicking over beer glasses, spilling shots of whiskey. The men drinking at the bar jumped back as if a lunatic had popped up straight through the floor. Naturally, there was a big brawl, a first-class, four-star donnybrook. Kenny held his own, though, surrounded by these rednecks. I got the hell beat out of me. One guy was a streetfighter who tried thumb me in the eyes when I was on the floor. The other one knocked me out cold with a left-right combination to my liver and face that dropped me to the floor.

It took four men to throw Kenny out the door; two guys carried me out and dumped me on the gravel in the parking lot.

"You fucking asshole," I said—only after I was able to talk.

"I fear no man born of woman's cunt!" he roared and spat blood, a chip from a broken tooth he never got fixed.

Years later, sitting in my prison cell listening to my bunkmate talk about Shakespeare's plays, I heard Harold quote that very line, although he omitted the obscenity.

Thinking of that, I knew Kenny Cardell held things back from me. Part of his *persona*—a Harold word—was to convince the world he was a larger-than-life brute and nothing more. I seized on that memory and told myself to be careful going forward.

About a month after that, I paid for the failure to remember, when he set me up for the break-in that got me sent jolted off to prison.

Getting the drop on Kenny Cardell was never going to be a cakewalk. I told Corinne you couldn't offer him money; it had to be the other way around. Kenny wouldn't be satisfied with the twenty grand. If he'd already scoped that expensive car in the driveway, he'd bide his time until he could demand a full share.

I said to Corinne: "Only one thing holds him back. That's the fear of pushing his luck with these police investigations going on. As long as their focus is on me, he's safe to move around."

Kenny didn't want to wind up getting sent to Ohio's death chamber in Lucasville farther down on the Ohio River. That would act to hold back showing his hand too soon—but it couldn't last forever. He'd watch her from a distance, patient as a vulture, and decide when to make his move. Harold loved to talk about the gods and goddesses who showed up for sport or to fuck up somebody for their own amusement on a whim.

"Why?" I asked Harold, who seemed to know everything.

"I don't know the answer to that one, Wade."

"Maybe because they could," I said.

He nodded and seemed satisfied with my answer.

Kenny looked like Greek god, and he could act like one when it came to random violence for his own amusement. But like most of the gods Harold mentioned, they had weak spots, ways to get to them. A fatal flaw, Harold called it.

Like me, Ken was a country boy. He knew pigs get fed but hogs get butchered.

* * *

186

Part 3

Chapter 18
Charleston, West Virginia

He liked nothing more than waking up in the morning with wood and looking down to see some bitch at the end of his dick. That was as much heaven as Kenny Cardell ever desired.

She was champion suck artist, all right. *Better'n a Bangkok whore.*

Kenny had to think for a moment; the booze fog hadn't lifted all the way: *Rhonda—something. Was it Jean . . . Rhonda Jean? Rae Jean? What was her goddam name anyhow?*

Bandido's Bar & Grill was his go-to bar in Charleston when he needed to lie low or get laid without a lot of hoopla involved. The place was always crammed on Friday night with ladies'-nite-out. Babes, most single but a few choice married ones mixed in. And he did like them married, less complicated that way.

This one now. Great tits, heavy and firm, and a great big ole heart-shaped ass. A clit bigger'n a baby's thumb. He remembered pumping away behind her, enjoying the view. He'd had a lot to drink and she had to work on him after she climbed aboard and his dick kept slipping out of her wet twat while she locked her fingers behind his neck and tried to pump him, grinding away in his lap with her hips, like he was a balloon that needed air.

He laughed at her. She gave him a look you get from gals that have been there before when their man goes whiskey limp. She spun around and headed south of the beltline and took him in her mouth. He grabbed both cheeks of that fine ass, making fingertip marks in the pale skin. She used her tongue on his sac, licking and pretend-biting—porn movie stuff, holding his bag tight and

188

squeezing. She traced that furrow with the tip of her hard tongue right to his asshole. Quick stabs in there—"How's that, baby? You like that? You like that, I know you do."

His dick wasn't twitchin' around now like a broke-back snake in the road. He put her on her back and jackhammered her until her moans and the headboard banging caused the people in the room next to his to pound their shoes on the wall.

She wanted to climb back on, but he liked what she was doing too much and held her head down. She didn't want that, he could tell, but, hell's-bells, he had too much going on to spend all day screwing in this no-tell motel. More stuff from *YouPorn* goin' on below now, he reckoned. Deep-throating him, turning her head to the side so he could see his cock make dents in her cheek. Doin' those twisty-type moves with her hands, playing his skin flute, like that Hollywood gal, what's-her-name? Whatever . . .

Kenny closed his eyes and helped the climax build to a crescendo by thinking of something else he liked as much as pussy: money.

Kenny always said the same thing to every broad he nailed. He figured they appreciated a little feedback for their efforts to please him. Because, when it was said and done, it was about that and nothing else.

When he opened his eyes again he heard her pissing in the toilet. Then the shower running.

Good, he thought, *get going. I got shit to do, woman. Go back to your limp-dick husband.*

He put the pillow over his head while she dressed. He wondered if she'd ask for his number. They sometimes did.

"You leavin' now?"

He didn't bother to make it sound like he cared. He wanted to be sure she wasn't coming back to his room.

"Yeah, I've got to be in Indianapolis by this afternoon."

He peeked out from the pillow and saw her hike up her panties. She had a thick swirl of tawny bush that flattened against the silk. Bald, hairy—made no never-mind to Kenny Cardell. Pussy was the greatest thing God made.

When he met her last night, she said she was a pharmaceutical rep. He laughed and told her that was his business, too. Inside of twenty minutes, he could tell what a woman wanted from him. He knew how to pop open their minds and get that little secret fantasy out. Some women came on coy as a virgin on her first date, but he'd find out what they wanted: "My husband won't do anal," "My man won't eat me," or "My fiancé won't let me give him a rimjob," or "My boyfriend doesn't want to spank me before sex." He'd heard it all, the complaints. *Just give your damn woman what she wanted, boys, what the hell . . .*

All this motherfucking fuffin' and fassin' like in books—just bullshit. Nothing complicated about it.

He liked how some women got right to it, the ones who didn't waste time playing cute. He knew how to spot a professional woman on the prowl who wasn't interested in all the bullshit. He thought it was a gift he had. Even his own mother thought so: "You ain't very smart, Kenny, but you got the looks that make women go for you." At only seventeen, he knew he had a destiny to fulfill, one that involved women, and crime, of course, but definitely one that set him apart from the rest of the bulls in the herd.

Wade, you motherfucker. I'm fixin' to think about you today. Not good for you.

He was already giving his cousin too much thought lately. Wade was the key; he understood that.

He heard the door close behind her—no *Goodbye, thanks for the orgasms, see you around*—or any of that *la-de-da* horseshit. *Why the fuck couldn't they all end like that way?*

Calls to make, people to see. He started with Buck Loudermilk in Salem.

"What's the story, morning-glory?"

"Kenny, that you, hoss?"

"I'm waitin' on you, Buck-o."

"He ain't been here."

"Never showed at Bill's?"

"With every cop in the whole god-danged state lookin' for his dumb ass? Not likely."

"Don't take nothin' for granted, it comes to Wade Cardell. I know that boy. He's shifty. Could pop up anywhere like a damn rain lily in a cloudburst."

"He comes to Salem, I be sure to let you know."

"Better."

Kenny called Daryl Sensabaugh three times, got voicemail all three. Left a message: "Call me back, shithead. I'm waitin' to hear what you got."

Sometimes he felt like a goddamned string reporter for the *Bridgeport News*. He spent an hour a day calling his contacts: *"Seen Wade? Seen Wade?"*

He knew that little prick Tommy Dufresne and his brother knew more than they was tellin' him, that's for shit sure. *So Wade got in touch with his old track buddy?*

He'd sent people into the V.F.W. to pick up gossip. Tommy always played dumb when asked. Last resort, he'd corner little brother Steve at home and find out. Drop by his house with flowers or candy for Mrs. Steve. Make sure he got the message. Had to be careful about it because them Dufresnes were a shifty clan, tight as ticks. He wasn't sure but there might could be a distant relative on his mother's side married to a Dufresne somewhere far back in the bloodline. Kenny wasn't squeamish about ruffling family feathers. After all, he planned to put an abrupt end to a first cousin—as soon as he could locate the motherfucking son of a bitch, that is.

He didn't regret not shooting him when he had Wade on the floor KO'ed back in New Zenith. Stupid girl wanted it, screamed at him to finish him off: *Kill him! Kill him! What are you fucking waiting for?*

He grabbed her by her arms and shook her like a ragdoll. *You dumb bitch, we kill him, who the fuck we got to blame for it?*

Wade, he was just a suicide waitin' to happen anyway. When she calmed down, he told her how it had to be: "He dies later, you got a real solid alibi the cops won't be able to break."

The plan was to kill him all right—but a day or two later—let the rabbit run first and before the cops revved up their manhunt. The newspapers would feature it like "Remorseful Killer of Couple in New Zenith Dies by Own Hand."

He never thought for a New York minute his cousin would outrun the police, hide so well he couldn't be found. He was a bloody mess when he last saw him. His first instinct at the time told him to do Wade right there while he had him on the floor. Let the girl take credit for killing the killer of her parents after a struggle in the kitchen. But she was so spooked by the blood he knew she wouldn't stand up to an interrogation, even by those small-town bozos. One look at her terrified face convinced him no-fuckin'-way would she stand up to a detective in an interrogation room even if he carved I WANT A LAWYER on her fuckin' forearm.

Like he always said, You can't polish a turd but you can roll it in the gutter.

"OK, Wade, you won the first round, but you ain't won the fight."

Johnny Cash ringtones: "I Walk the Line."

"'bout motherfuckin' time, Daryl, you asshole. You'll be walkin' around with a tin dick you don't start takin' my calls."

"Sorry, I was on the shitter."

"You say that ever' motherfuckin' time, you lying-ass dog."

"The old man, Wayne, he's still shacked up in the high rise all day yesterday with his 'ho. I think he's sick or somethin' but they ain't answering the buzzer."

"Maybe that cooze he's tappin' done wear his old pecker out."

"Ha-ha, maybe. I keep you posted, brother."

"You better."

One more call while he scratched his balls. Laydean Prettyman worked the bar at Bill's. She was his Momma's best friend from way back. Laydean had his cherry ticket. He was pretty sure his Momma arranged it, too—a nice birthday present when he turned fifteen and she got tired of washing the nightly goo out of his bedsheets.

She even admitted as much before she died in bed of lung cancer. *Crazy bitch smoked like a chimney right up to the day she died, got pissed if he brought over diet soda or low-cal anything. . .*

"Hey, hon."

"Kenny, how's that rope hangin'?"

"Long and strong."

"Good to hear it, baby. This goddam place is full of faggots and trannies now."

"Hell, yes, all the real men and women gone, Laydean—'cept you 'n me."

"God's own truth, baby."

"That shitass Bill still botherin' you, hon? You let old Kenny know and I be down there in a tick, put my size twelve Wellington boot right up his ass."

An old joke between them. He heard her cough, Laydean's version of a laugh. Kenny wondered if she had the same cancer as his Momma.

"Wade ain't been in, sweetie. Ain't seen him a'tall."

"You be sure let me know you see one hair of his ass.

Cough-cough.

"Yah, I be sure—"

Kenny thumbed off. *Sorry, darling, but I ain't got time to listen to you hacking and coughing in my fuckin' ear all day.*

He scratched his balls again and wondered if he had crabs. That brought a smile to his face. He wondered how his date last night would lay that news on her hubby. Could make for some interesting fireworks in the old homestead.

Fuck, where you been keepin' yourself at, Wade? Time to come back, little doggie, see what you got comin' to you.

* * *

193

Chapter 19
New Zenith, Ohio

"You little bitch," Kenny said.

Snapping to, he realized he might have offended Baby. "Not you, sweetheart," he said, tapping the rim of the dash reassuringly. "I meant that lyin' little slut whore lez of a cunt in New Zenith."

If he could have reached it through the steering wheel with his lips, he'd have kissed Baby.

Best ride under his ass he'd had since his first set of wheels at eighteen, all paid for with dope money—and a few small favors run for the boys at the Graybar Hotel. He'd been doing favors and running errands for the Aryan Brotherhood since his last bid at Lakin Correctional. They still reached out for little things from him, small stuff mostly like putting the arm on somebody or jostling somebody's memory who forgot he owed his mates in prison a little bit of loyalty. He was always happy to oblige his friends in low places. They paid well and they didn't forget their friends or their enemies. Kenny didn't plan on returning to the joint in this state or any other, but that fuck-up with his cousin was a long way from being done.

"Anything can happen, Baby," he said and doubled tapped the gear shift knob for luck.

He saw a trooper sitting in the median in front of the Pennsboro turn-off. Like a lion watching the gazelles skipping by: *Not this one, not this one—yeah, this one . . .*

"Not me, motherfucker," Kenny said, flashing a big smile at the cruiser as he drove past. He loved to twist their tails. He kept his speed at 64, though, God knows, he was tempted to let Baby run, give Smoky back there something fast to chase in his Interceptor. They used Challengers, too, maybe get to 150 on a flat-out chase. Baby could do 190, 194. He'd put her on the Bristol Speedway track in Martinsville and let her fly.

He was tempted to detour to The Charles Town Track before he was out of the city limits barely ten miles up Interstate 77. He almost turned around to get to the poker rooms in time and watch the horses on simulcast screens. He thought of his motel date, the drug rep.

He'd just come from the track and emptied his pockets inside out to show her, making a joke of it at the bar. But it was no joke. *Hellfire, fuck*—the horses, greyhounds, slots, and cards were draining him like that gal sucking out his jackjuice. Most of his second payment got pissed away in a couple weeks. His gambling was turning into a cash-devouring monster. Funny how he could handle all the poontang, drugs, and whiskey he could pack into a weekend, but put a fuckin' set of wheels on a Go-Kart and he was slavering like a toothless baby, trying to lay his down his bet.

Only thinking about Wade and what a shitload of trouble his cousin was causing him made him keep the big Redeye's nose aimed ahead. "I got me other fish to fry, bud." Getting a ticket now was tempting fate because—*well, you never know, did you?*—she might prove . . . *difficult to persuade.*

He parked behind a Costco and called from his burner.

"Hello."

"Hello, there, ya'll remember me?"

Long pause. . . . *What's going on, bitch?*

"What do you want?"

"I thought we could meet at a coffee shop. You know, catch up on old times."

"I don't think that's . . . a good idea."

"Really? I think it's a fuckin'-A-plus-plus *wonderful* idea. I'm lookin' at this sign, says McDonald's, got them big yellow arches. What say you show up here in—oh say—fifteen fuckin' minutes."

Click. Done talking.
Cunt.

* * *

At first, he didn't recognize her. *What the fuck's with the new bulldyke look?*

She spotted him and came over, obviously not happy to be there. He flashed her a big smile from the booth, took off his shades when she sat down.

"You look different," he said. "Nice 'do, that."

"Got a problem with it?"

"Me? Hell no," he laughed. "I ain't a . . . what's that fuckin' word? Bigot! I did a double this one time with a couple muffdivers from Bluefield, one of them's a tranny, and they—"

"Ménage à trois," she corrected.

"Huh, what?"

"It's called a ménage à trois when there are three of you."

He mangled the expression, trying to repeat it. She didn't crack a smile.

"I asked you on the phone what you wanted."

He shrugged his shoulders, both arms extended along the back of the booth.

"Money, what the fuck else is there?"

"You've been paid," she said.

"Now, see, that's where you're wrong, Corinne." He pronounced it *Co-reene*. "That's exactly where you're wrong."

Didn't raise his voice, held the big smile. *A grinning ape*, she thought.

"How so?"

"Say, can I get ya'll a burger? Some fries? Got some good eatin' in Mickey D's. My daddy—this was before he skipped off like a goat—he used to tell my Momma I'd a-wasted clean away if it depended on her cooking."

"I'm not interested—look, we had an agreement, Ken. We both kept our parts of the deal."

He slapped his hand on the table—too loud. People nearby swiveled their heads.

"No, and if you don't mind, don't use my name again. It might could be unhealthy for you—as I'm sure gonna remind a relative of mine when we meet up again. But the point I was about to make, Corinne, hon, is that we didn't keep our parts—leastwise, I did. You didn't. I drove by your house when I got into your lovely shitburg town and you know what I saw besides a town full of homos and cunt-faced skanks?"

Corinne waited; his act was going to go one whether she played her part or not.

"I seen this big ol' B.M.W."

He enunciated each letter.

"I also seen this sign in your yard sayin' your house is up for sale."

"So what? It's my house."

"It's your house," he said, leaning a couple inches toward her, still smiling, but letting her see what it's like to have her space invaded by him, someone his size—*just a taste of what it could be, let her mind wrap around that possibility for a while,* he thought.

"It's your house because I allowed it to be your house. Seems to me you are being very forgetful—and a little ungrateful here."

"I know . . . what you're capable of," she said.

"Good. That's good. And it's *important*," giving the word some spin like a dart he aimed at her.

Lesson learned. Now fork over some money, you bean-flicking rug-muncher before I get angry and you don't want old Kenny Cardell angry.

"But I'm not giving you a cent more."

"Now, Corinne, you disappoint me. You really do."

"You're so sure of yourself, aren't you? I'm just a—a nobody you can push around. Blackmail."

He turned his head slowly in both directions slowly, assessing the busy dining area for anyone who might have picked up that last tidbit.

"We're done here."

"No, we ain't, little girl—boy, whatever you're s'posed to be or think you are."

"How sure are you, Mister Cardell, I didn't have a miniature recorder taping in my handbag that day we spoke at the track? You know, a little insurance on my part."

He smiled at her. *Jesus H. Fucking Christ, I am going to take my sweet time with you.*

Kenny watched her go without a backward glance. He hated himself for it, but he admired her for her guts.

I'll show you guts, Corinne. Yours. It'll be fun watching you try to hold them in while they're spilling out of your belly all over the floor.

A noisy family took the booth ahead of his. The brats, a boy and girl, maybe six and four, stood up and gawked at him. He smiled and waved at the little morons. The girl stuck her tongue out at him. He stuck his tongue out at her; then the boy joined in. The mother, an overweight skank with sow teats, was busy wiping off the table with a Handi-wipe from a package she ripped open with her teeth. Both children giggled and stuck their tongues out at him in unison. The mother turned around, looked at the spectacle, and frowned at him; she snapped at her kids: "Nikki, Richard! Turn around, don't look at that man or you ain't gittin' no Happy Meals!"

Yes, Nikki, Richard, turn around before I slap your mother's homely face with Jumbo. You'll never be able to put away another Happy Meal in your life without thinkin' about it . . .

He sat there for another minute and realized he hadn't had anything in his mouth since last night's fur burger. He got up and went to the counter to order a couple Big Macs, large fries, and a large Coke for the ride back.

An old couple were walking up to the door, the man pushing a walker, as he exited the restaurant. Pivoting, he returned and held the door for them, smiling as they made their way.

The wife beamed at him. "Such a kind gentleman, Frank."

He smiled back at the old woman, her short hair crisped in delicate curls on her head; he could see the tender, pink scalp beneath.

"How my Momma raised me, ma'am." Before he left town, he left a long, very explicit, obscene-laden message on Corinne's answering machine. The crude ape used a voice scrambler.

When she played it two hours later, her face blanched to the color of a boiled potato.

* * *

Chapter 20
Salem, West Virginia

"Hey, Kenny," Laydean said, "that package youns waitin' on showed up."

The balls on that motherfucker!

"Much obliged, Laydean," Kenny said. "Be there soon's I can."

Kenny drove his big Dodge to Clarksburg like a man possessed. He did a mental check en route like a Boy Scout from ticking off necessary camping gear: knife—two, filleting and Bowie; stun gun; semiautos, the Sig (his newest acquisition, numbers filed off) and the Glock 19, a 9 x 19 mm subcompact; 2 boxes of ammo, 115 grain, copper-jacketed for greater wound channel, one for .38 and .45 ACP; (the .45s made by Kimber featuring a carry-bevel treatment for rounded edges and front-strap checkering); wading boots, tarp, rope. A Louisville slugger (an ancient Wade Boggs from his Little League days before he got kicked off the Blue Jays); two cement blocks.

That should cover it.

He was stunned to think Wade would walk into Bill's knowing half the cops in the state had him on a short list of assholes they wanted to see locked up.

"Hey, Kenny."

"Hey, Chick, hey, Zeke, what's up, you lazy old dogs."

He didn't stop to talk to anyone. Laydean had slipped down to the end of the bar as soon as she saw him come in, pause in the doorway, his bulk backlit while his eyes adjusted to the semi-dark, so she could deliver the news without everyone in the place overhearing her.

Kenny looked at her.

"He come in," Laydean said, leaning her body over the counter to whisper, her boobs mashed together. "He looks at me and sees the fellas there, says *hey, how're ya'll doin'* to a few of the men. Takes a damn stool at the bar and orders himself a beer."

"Orders a beer . . ." Kenny clucked, unlike him to repeat, not sure he was hearing this right.

"You heard me, I swear. I look right at him, like to say, 'Wade, what're you doin' in here with half the cops in creation huntin' down your lily-white ass?'"

"He goes: 'I'm having me a beer, Laydean. Just like I always do when I come in here. Tell my cousin Kenny I said hi, you see him around. Give him this.'"

Kenny took the slip of paper from her. He looked at her.

"That's right, Ken. Cool as a cucumber he was. I ain't shittin' you, neither. Them guys at the bar, all they's mouths is open like baby birds at feedin' time—"

"Laydean, he say where he's off to?" He had a little difficulty controlling his voice that time.

"Not to me," Laydean said. "He just drinks half the glass and gets up, sashays out like he's in no big hurry. He did look different in the face though, you ask me. Had a yallerish color, like, from being jaundice."

"OK, Laydean, much oblige."

He dropped five twenties on the bar top.

"Buy these old coots here a drink on me. You keep the change, darlin'."

The bills disappeared fast, all but one tucked into the bra.

"Thank ya, hon."

Going back into the light of day he had to shield his eyes. *Wade, you stupid fuck, what are you doin'? This can't be right.* He looked at the paper again. A telephone number. Nothing else. *I guess I'll just have to call the motherfucker since he gone to so much trouble for me.*

Kenny walked out into the first really hot day of mid-April. He smelled the oily, leafy green scent of cut grass. Grass in distress. *That ain't all that's gonna be in distress pretty soon,* he thought.

Like a light bulb going off in his head, Kenny knew what Wade did in Salem—visiting his mother's grave. *Can't be this fuckin' easy,* he thought. It was like one of them kiddie slates where the words were written in chalk and erased with one swipe leaving an outline you could trace. A reddish haze hovered in front of his face and disappeared like vapor.

One good thing, though: he'd grown goddamn tired of spraying cash at every man jack between here and the Ohio River to find his cousin.

* * *

Chapter 21
Clarksburg, West Virginia

"We really need to get this thing between us fixed," Kenny said.

You'd think we were talking about a broken shift cable in a transmission.

"Who broke it, Ken?"

"Water over the dam, under the bridge, whatever the fuck," he said. "What matters is *now*, Wade. You see that, right? What are we gonna do *right now*?"

"Look, I'm getting out of Dodge," I said. "Going far away and I don't want to worry about you coming up behind me some dark night. That's why I left that number with Laydean and that is the only reason we're talking right now."

"OK, Wade, I do understand, cousin. My ears work. You got all my attention. So tell me exactly what the fuck is it you want me to do."

"I've got the recording," I said.

Long pause.

"What recording would that be, Wade?"

"The one Corinne made with you at the track that day, Mister Black."

"Ain't no fuckin' tape, son. Pull the other leg, the one with the bells on it."

"I made her give it to me," I said. "She knows I can burn her whenever I want. I listened to it. It's you, your voice. The F.B.I. can match it up with all that gee-whiz technology they got now."

"Kiss my rosy-red ass, you shanty-Irish motherfucker. I said there ain't no motherucking tape."

"Got the cassette right here in my pocket. She says, 'How much do you—how much will it—' She can't bring herself to say the words, see. Then you say, 'Cost?' like you're helping her spit it out. Then you say, clear as a bell: 'Twenty. Ten now, ten after.' Just those words, no more."

"Wade, Wade, listen to me—"

"And those five words will put your ass behind bars for the rest of your life."

"Who says I can't take you down with me?"

I kept going. "—unless they give you the needle after twenty years rotting in that shithole in Lucasville. Those people in Ohio, Ken, they ain't got that formula figured out yet. Last guy said it hurt like a bitch until he croaked."

"Long fuckin' speech, Wade. Lucky I ain't payin' you by the word. I repeat what I just said. I don't believe it. Show me the goddamn tape."

"I'll do better. I'll give it to you."

"What's your asking price?"

"You to leave me be, like I said. That's all. You can have the girl. Fuck her, she's not my problem."

"Sounds reasonable, cuz. Now where do we conduct this little transaction?"

I told him I'd call again with the place and time.

* * *

"Aunt Ida, it's me."

"I can't talk to you right now. You know why, don't you?"

Innocent, God-fearing Aunt Ida. Even she knew the phone was tapped.

"I understand. Can you tell me where Dad is?"

"Probably with his new woman over to the high rise in Clarksburg."

"Thanks."

"Wade . . ."

"I know."

No, he wasn't there—damn it.

She meant I had to go looking for him. I didn't want him running around town until I had this thing with my cousin squared away.

Nothing's ever easy.

* * *

"Daryl, you spot him yet?"

"No, he wasn't where you said he was."

"I'm sending a couple guys to help you look for him."

"Who?"

"Friends of mine."

"Who?"

"Don't fuckin' worry about it!"

"I ain't riding bitch with them Morson twins again. That shitbag Dean weighs three hundred pounds and never seen a bar of soap—"

"Daryl, you—I'm gonna twist your small intestine around your fucking neck and hang you with it."

"OK, OK, fuck, Kenny."

Assholes and idiots, Kenny thought. *That's all I got to work with. No fuckin' wonder I'm poorer than a shithouse mouse.*

* * *

"I'm Miller, this here's Jody."

Miller was a couple inches taller than Jody. Both big, buffed to shit and back from pumping iron at Mount Olive. Helter-skelter tattoos from the neck down, both arms to the shoulders—weeping clowns, spiderwebs, shamrocks, and every kind of way you could ink the letters *A* and *B* on human skin. One tatt blending into another in the helter-skelter fashion of prison psychopaths.

Serious men for serious work. *OK with me,* Kenny thought.

"How's tricks these days?"

"Same old shit, different day," Miller responded. "You know."

"Been a good while since I was hangin' around Mace's old pod," Kenny said.

Mace Boatwright, one tough motherfucker. Shotcaller. You breathed only if he gave you permission. He ran more businesses at MOCC than a Wall Street broker. And did it all without a phone or a computer. His word was enough.

"'preciate you fellas swingin' by, givin' me a hand with my problem."

"Mace said you'd take care of us after."

"Oh fuck yeah, ain't nothin' free in this life, is there, boys?"

Wade, you cocksucker, I'm gonna be obliged to these AB motherfuckers until they split me open on the table for the formaldehyde tube. I'm gonna make you pay for all this aggravation so bad you'll regret the day your momma shit you out.

* * *

Chapter 22

"We should meet, talk this over, you know, like family."

"I agree, cuz. Where and when, you just name it. I'm tired of running around like a two-headed dog in a meat market."

"We can both get something out of this," I said. "I can't be looking over my shoulder the rest of my life worried about you springing out of the dark."

"What about me, Wade? What's in it for me if I agree to let you walk away? You know my ass is gonna be hanging out there in the breeze for a while."

"She's your problem, not mine. I'm a gone goose after you and I settle our business."

"You don't need me dead. Cops will need more than my word."

"That's true," Ken said. "But I'm bringin' Wade senior along with me in case you got any silly notions."

God damn motherfucking son of a bitch. I'll kill you—

My hand squeezed the receiver. My eyes started to wet, my heart thumped. *Be calm, be calm . . .*

"You still there, Wade? Don't play me for stupid, whatever you been thinkin' about doing. It won't work. You best keep in mind your Daddy's health is in my hands. You know what that means, right? Now, to business. Where you at, bro?"

I gave him directions. He thumbed off the connection.

Here we go. Time to shit or get off the pot.

* * *

Chapter 23
Clendenin, West Virginia

The motel was a good idea. Somebody's dream once upon a time. The locale ideal, really. A few miles north of the Elk, Highways 119 and 4 intersecting, Charleston another 30 miles southwest. A money-maker, you'd think. Then they finished Interstate 79 north of the city township line and that put the kibosh to the dream. You see all those abandoned stores with the busted windows, the strip malls with the plywood over the windows beside the highways everywhere you go. The graffiti. "Civic eyesores," you say, forgetting they were somebody's hopes and dreams of a path to the good life once.

The motel's fiberglass sign was busted up with so many rocks, you couldn't hardly read the name. "Parasite Motel," I thought at first, and then figured it must be "Paradise." The structure was long abandoned, the paint all flaked and blasted off by winds and weather over the years. I was in the last room farthest from the highway. My car couldn't be seen by traffic.

The Cardells were mostly Irish stock, peasants from Galway County who came over during the famine years. Aunt Ida was always saying how the Irish were prone to drink and ulcers. My stomach burned with acid sitting there on that moldy bed waiting. I focused to keep the tremors out of my hands. Practiced a few lines aloud, things I'd say when they arrived. Funny, I thought then, how the worst times of your life always come when you're feeling your lowest. Never when you're feeling good. Never when you think you can take on the world. Always when you're down on your luck. Sitting in a decrepit motel stinking of mice piss and black mold was about as down on my luck as I can get, I thought.

The sky from the window looked ugly with low-scudding clouds, their bellies looked like torn purple rags. The room I chose was more or less intact, still had some of its furniture. Somebody tried to start a fire with some of it. Spiders owned the corners, none were brown recluses, which was the only good news I could give myself just then. A generation of squatters had been replaced by winos who were replaced by dopers and taggers. A girl named Bobbi Smith was hailed in orange graffiti as The 1987 Porn Queen of Buckhannon, a long way off. The one chair in the room not smashed up was the one I sat on. I'd dragged it over from a different room. The roof had buckled years ago and water got in. The particleboard stank and swelled; the walls bloomed with huge rosettes of mold that glittered when the light fell on it.

I stayed calm until I heard the *chok-chok-thuk-thuk* rattle of a heavy-duty exhaust turning in. Then my heartbeat jumped a few beats on its own and I felt sticky under my arms.

C'mon, Wade. Pull it together . . .

I shook my head. Pep talks at this point were wasted breath, energy.

Louder, the throaty purr of a muscle car just outside the room. A couple taps of the horn.

I heard you, Kenny.

He came in alone.

"Hey, Wade."

Big smile. Not unfriendly but a dangerous vibe all the same—like he knew this was going to end right. For one of us.

"'llo, there, cuz. How's tricks?"

"How's Dad? Better yet, where is my father?"

"Uncle Wayne, he'll be here in a minute. You know how I am about people riding in Baby."

"I rode with you plenty of times," I said.

"You did, you did. But that was when we was partners. Then you took off after you got out. I thought we'd—"

"—we'd kiss and make up? After you set me up? Tried to blow my brains to smithereens with a hollow point? You know, I don't mind a broom handle shoved up my ass. It's when it gets twisted around I get pissed off. Stop fucking around, Ken. I better see my father in here in—"

I made a show of checking my wristwatch. "One minute, tops."

"Relax, Wade. He's coming, I said. This is some shithole you picked out. Why the fuck couldn't we meet up the road? I seen a Burger King, a Wendy's, and some happy-ass Dago pizza parlor 'bout a half-mile from here."

"I told you. I'm leaving West Virginia for good. Passed this place on my way west. Figured we could wrap things up here, nobody to bother us."

"You right about one thing, cousin. We are gonna wrap things up. I've had it with all the bullshit right up to my eyeballs. Now you, first things first. Empty your pockets on that bed."

He brought out a Charter Arms Bulldog and pointed it at me.

Kenny's words in my head: *Revolvers don't jam. When you ab-so-fuckin'-lutely got to get the job done right, take a revolver over a semiauto every day of the week.* I knew how far up a gelatin block a .44 slug from that bore could go.

"Knives, too, sharp pencils, whatever you brought." Another wag of the gun.

I took out a small carving knife from my boot and tossed it on the bed next to the gun.

"You take that from Aunt Ida's kitchen?"

A car pulled up beside his Challenger outside. Doors opened and shut.

Kenny called through the door. "Miller, Jody—bring him on in."

My dad came in escorted between the two big men.

It hurt to see the look on his face, so I concentrated on Kenny. "What now?"

"Gimme the motherfuckin' tape, you fuckwit."

I reached with my hand into my shirt pocket, the barrel slowly tracking it all the way in and out.

"Here."

I tossed the cassette to him. He slipped it into his pocket.

"You don't want to play it now? Prove it's real?"

"I'll play it later."

One of the men said to Kenny, "Where you want to do 'em?"

"Looks like plenty of vacancies here, fellas. My cousin picked a nice place to die in. Him and my uncle there. You pick 'em, I don't care which. Take 'em to a room."

I stood up and spat in Kenny's face.

He reacted fast with a short hard right to my jaw. He put some torque into it. I closed my eyes and leaned in the direction of the swing just enough to catch it right. A knockout punch would have ended it there.

Falling backward onto the chair I'd been sitting in, my hands reached out in time to snap off the back top rail as I fell. It was a bullnose design from a style in the seventies. The back and legs shared a tenon I'd removed while I waited. I made a prop chair basically, one meant to collapse with any amount of force.

I went to the floor with more acting than the punch deserved. Kenny's vanity wouldn't notice. I lay on top of the upholstered cushion seat and slipped my hand inside the slit I'd made. I groaned, adding a little theater for effect, twitched my legs to distract as I got my hand firmly around the butt.

"Fuckin' knocked his ass out, Kenny," one of the men said.

"Bastards!"

My father's voice.

I heard him struggling, calling my name.

"Get him the fuck out of here, boys."

I thought about my position once I moved. Then I did it.

My legs gave me a decent enough ballast as I raised the gun.

Kenny's face: his eyes popped seeing what was happening.

His gun jerked up. My father's hand swung out and batted Kenny's gun hand. It slowed him down before he could fire at me. My first round went wild, missed somewhere past his head; my second wheeled him sideways, missed his chest, a shoulder hit. My peripheral vision watched him stumble toward the open door.

The men holding my father jumped back.

I steadied my aim at the closet one. He drew back a leg to kick me, changed his mind and reached for whatever weapon he had on him. Too late. One in the belly doubled him up.

The other man shot at me from behind my father, holding him by the collar from behind to use him as a shield. A round slammed into the floor, blowing out a chunk of carpet and a puff of dust next to my face. Twisting on the floor for a better aim at him, I squeezed off two more rounds. Missed where I aimed but the result was just as good. A mouth shot through the back of his head sent blood, shards of skull, and brains onto the walls.

The man I'd gut shot slumped against a wall holding himself, cursing.

I got up on my haunches, gun up, wary of Kenny firing through the door or window.

"Moth-er-fuck-er," the groaning man said, a liquid gurgle.

I shot him in the forehead.

Three shots slammed into the wall behind me. Kenny firing from his car.

In the commotion, my father had slumped to the floor. I couldn't look at him yet.

"You're a coward, Ken! Nothing but a shitsucking coward!"

I screamed it. Silence back. Then: *Pow! Pow! Pow!*

Time that had slowed to a molasses crawl before Kenny's punch knocked me to floor accelerated to break-neck speed. My brain was trying to process everything at once. But I knew I had the advantage; it made me want to giggle and cry at the same time. He couldn't sit out there plunking away at me forever. I could wait him out.

My father moaned. I bellycrawled over to him.

O Jesus God, no, no—

He had a hand over his heart the way I'd seen a thousand times at the house whenever the *National Anthem* was played on TV or before one of my track meets. The blood leaking through his fingers was a trickle, then a flow and even with one of my hands pressed against his chest to stanch it, it became a spurt, then another, and another. My father's face was too much to bear. His eyes opened, not seeing, his mouth opening and closing; no words or sound came out.

"Don't look, Dad," I said—whatever sense that made.

I had my hand on his face, almost blubbering, rage building, when Kenny hit me from behind.

He threw himself at me like a missile. I went skidding across the floor with his weight on my back and my face plowing through the filth and debris, broken glass and raccoon shit, dirty needles, and whatever had been dropped or broken since the first vandals moved in.

"HOW'S THIS FOR COWARD . . ."

The words didn't register in my brain right away in my brain because of the surprise attack from the back room.

His fist hit me in the face so hard I thought my front teeth were broken off. I saw nothing but a red mist and felt a crushing weight on my chest. He hit me again but his fist glanced off my eyebrow tearing skin with it from his ring.

My instincts kicked in, and I turned my head before the next blow landed. Muddled gibberish streamed from his mouth along with the spittle. Like nothing I'd heard or seen before from a human being. All animal fury, no mind governing the rage. Part of my brain refocused: my cousin's right arm dangled at his side. My bullet had disabled him; he still had the strength of his left arm and the ferocity of his rage and that was plenty. Though the punches were awkward, shots that missed as often as connected, I was able to deflect any from doing more harm with my squirming and twisting. In a fight with him, with both arms to use, I'd never have lasted.

As my father's reflexes had saved me from a .44 slug, my mind saved me this time. It stopped bouncing around like a tennis ball in a room full of furniture and settled into a groove. Two words flashed into my neocortex: *boot, knife.*

The kitchen knife wasn't the only one on me just as I had that second gun under the chair.

Kenny wailed away on top of me, oblivious to anything but killing me. He didn't know what I was doing beyond trying to buck him off. So intent on murdering me with his one good arm, he reared up and threw his one-armed punches harder each time. With both hands pinned, he'd wear me down under a fusillade of blows to my face and head. I bucked harder each time, absorbing the punch, straining to move him closer to my neck so I could swing one leg closer to me.

"Mother-fuck-er!"

"—kill . . . you!"

"Wade, you fuck!"

Did it—

My hand popped free from under his bulk. Like a crab scuttling sideways over the floor, sweeping it with my fingers. Got it, dropped it. Keep going, grab it—

When Kenny punched down, gaining a better leverage, he enabled me to reach a couple inches farther. My fingertips felt the handle; then I had my thumb curled around it in a dagger grip. My eyes were puffed, closing fast. I could barely make out his face anymore. I felt more than saw his fist float over his head for the hammer blow he meant to put me out with. Before it fell, I rammed the blade in under his exposed armpit. His heavy fist stayed where it was, hovered like a ball you toss into the air before gravity can tug it back to earth. I twisted the blade with the last of my strength and fell back to the floor, exhausted, semi-conscious, my head bouncing on the floor.

He stopped swinging, jumped off me as though I'd shocked him with a live wire. He wobbled, his face reflected the knowledge of what had just happened.

Blood from the sliced artery wet his tee shirt in seconds. His left arm dropped to his side as he took in the damage. I opened my eyes as wide as I could. His face assumed a stunned, heavy look. A cow in the kill chute after the bolt from the cattle gun slammed it between the eyes.

He sagged, a big man about to totter, then his whole body sank down onto me as if he were resting there to gain his breath for another attack. My lungs were about to burst from the pressure. Tunnel vision, pain clouded my sight.

I had a final image of one of his hands twitching against his thigh in a palsy tremor. Bellowing, I summoned every last ounce remaining in my body, shut down the pain roaring in my ears, and heaved him off me.

Later, how much later, I don't recall. I crawled over to my father. I didn't get far. He seemed a long way away, sleeping against the wall, his eyes at half-mast. I crawled some more, passed out again. I don't know how long I was unconscious that time. I smelled feces when I woke again—strong, pungent, close. A large rat climbed over me and looked at me with his red eyes. I jerked fully awake, thinking I was still going to have to fight Kenny.

It's like Aunt Ida said of Hell: *It never ends, boy.*

* * *

Epilogue

My money ran out in Idaho. I was down to $55 and change. I was trying for Wyoming because I'd always wanted to hunt and fish there. My old man and I used to talk about fishing for brown trout in icy mountain streams. Bow hunting in the autumn for elk. A truck driver at a diner I was drinking coffee in, hungry but trying to conserve my cash, chatted me up. He said he was heading to the ski resort.

"Which one?"

"The one, right here, Coeur d'Alene," he said. "Right over there, buddy."

He pointed to the hills in the distance. I didn't know what state I was in, let alone the name of the city. I asked him if he thought they were hiring.

"It's May. Season's been over for a month, pal."

"Maybe they need help closing up?"

"Could be. You can try. Where you from?"

"Kentucky," I said. "A little town outside Louisville."

I couldn't think of another town fast enough.

My facial damage was healing up. Last time I looked in the mirror, I wasn't going to win any beauty prizes. I did remember tossing my guns and the knives on the floorboard, getting in the car, and driving on autopilot. I remembered a turnoff sign to Olive Hill on the 64 Interstate. I might have been babbling to myself. My hands were slippery with blood trying to grip the steering wheel. Canting my head from one side to the other like sparrow trying to see the center line of the highway. Cars passed me, semis blew by me. If any trooper had passed me on the road, checked out my face, he'd have done a pit maneuver on me right there. I know I was sobbing because I had to leave my father there in that clusterfuck of a motel. What else could I do?

The guns and knives went into the Little Sandy in Kentucky.

I spent two days in a county hospital in Mount Sterling. The long-haul trucker in his eighteen-wheeler with a load of steel coil parked next to me turned out to be a Good Samaritan. He was going to the rest room when he looked in at me. The overhead streetlight cast enough light inside my car to show me slumped over the steering wheel. He assumed I was drunk, but when he returned, he had doubts seeing me in the identical position and tapped at the window. I didn't respond. The door wasn't locked. He saw what a mess my face was in. When he jiggled my shoulder enough to wake me and ask what happened, I managed to tell him I was jumped by a hitchhiker I'd stopped to give a ride to ten miles back.

He didn't call the police or the state troopers to report me. He shoved me over to the passenger side and drove me to a hospital. I didn't tell Aaron Runyan when I returned his ID's that I made copies and that's who they thought I was.

The hospital was tiny, shaped in a pentagon in the middle of soy bean fields. The kind of hospital that has one, two doctors who work 36-hour shifts and depend on tax levies to keep it running. When my ID's failed to ring the cherries, I was cuffed to the bed rails pending an investigation. That lasted one day and the local authorities thought it was risking a lawsuit without any proof of a crime committed, so I was uncuffed the second day at the doctor's suggestion. She had a kind face, robin's-egg blue eyes, and was badly overworked. She loaded me up on antibiotics and scheduled me for a Pet scan and MRI at the big hospital in Lexington. A sheriff's deputy checked on me every five hours. Eventually they'd match up my DNA in CODIS with scrapings from Kenny's knuckles from his autopsy in Charleston—but by then I would be long gone.

While I was uncuffed, sitting in a wheelchair, waiting with a paramedic for the ambulance to take me to Lexington, I thought about confessing my identity to the doctor. She said a prayer with me. I bowed my head but my heart was empty of all feeling. A deputy was supposed to accompany the ambulance there and back. The paramedic told me they were sending another deputy because a 5-car pileup was diverting all ambulances, state troopers, and anyone else available to the site.

An old rancher who'd been gored by his bull was patched up and waiting in the lobby for his wife pick him up. We got to talking. When the paramedic stepped out to make some calls on his cell phone, I asked the old man if I could have a ride to town.

"You gonna wear that gown or your street clothes?"

"They hid my clothes. I guess this gown will have to do. Is that OK with you?"

"Long as it's split up the back, not the front," he said. "I don't mind my old woman seeing your ass but I don't want her to git any ideas."

He cracked a smile to exposed black gums.

He did better than that. He gave me some old clothes at his farmhouse, fed me, and his wife and he drove me to the Greyhound station. I bought a ticket for the next bus out, which happened to be going to Oklahoma City. From there, I bummed a ride at a truck stop with the driver of an 18-wheeler deadheading back to Colorado. Another greyhound got me to that diner in Idaho.

Seven weeks passed before I got access to a computer to check out the news. I was more concerned about people on the street or in stores looking at me too long. They news into some detail about Kenny and his past. The two Brand thugs, however, did me a favor. Reporters went looking for a story that put them at the center of it but came up empty. Criminal records up the wazoo and connections to the shotcaller; nothing to link to my father. The papers all described him as "a retired mineworker." They didn't call him a victim because they brought my name into it, thanks to the notorious double murder, which was still news but fading as there's never a shortage of atrocities to capture public attention. They stopped short of calling me a suspect. I was still "wanted for questioning" as "a person of interest."

The more time that went by, the more inaccuracies I found in the reporting. The "double homicide in the Ohio River town" was sometimes Matamoras, twice Fly, Ohio was mentioned. A *Dateline* crew went to New Zenith but no word on what they were filming or when the program would come out. The digitized Clarksburg papers consistently referred to me as a person of interest in "a suspicious death" in Northtown, Ohio and said the US Marshals were "actively pursuing leads to my whereabouts."

The same mug shot was trotted out every time with different captions: "Cardell, ex-convict," "Wade Cardell, itinerant laborer," and "Wade Eugene Cardell, former salvage yard worker."

One of the longer articles in the Cincinnati *Enquirer* did phone interviews with two college-aged women as having been "briefly acquainted with Wade Cardell, 29, of Salem, West Virginia." From the statements given by these so-called anonymous sources, both young Ohio women, I was described as an imposter, someone "posing as a student at the Northtown Community College on Lake Erie."

When interviewed, Niya declared I "seemed nice at first." The other was grumpy Lynne, without a doubt, who said she knew "in her heart" something was wrong with me by the "sneaky" way I acted and talked on the ride to Jefferson-on-the-Lake. I didn't recall saying much of anything to anyone on the way until we reached Freddie's Grill.

Not a peep on the internet buzz feeds, TV news, or papers about a bar called Dwight's or a bartender named J.P., no words about me wrecking the manager's cabin and waterboarding him, so I was spared that, which was like saying Hitler was known to pet his dog Blondie once in a while.

Unhappy Lynne. She might have sensed something about me but no one could foresee what was coming to me who wasn't a fortune teller. Even I didn't suspect all the shit I was about to step in the morning I left for work at Pick-a-Part Salvage. Or the ton of it that was about to get dropped on me the moment I threw that rebar.

Thinking about the motel was too painful and I didn't let my mind go that way for months. The only thing that coming back from meeting Kenny and his goons in that shitty motel was the chair I worked on to collapse before they showed up. You know how high-school math teachers are always telling their students to learn the Pythagorean theorem "because it might save their lives someday"—bullshit like that? Shop class might have done that for me. I helped build prop chairs for the school's theater group. They were doing *Joseph and the Technicolor Dreamcoat* and need some chairs that would collapse during the final number. Fuck if I know why as I never went to a play in my life. But I worked for weeks on making those chairs so they'd stand up to a little abuse and then fly apart at the right time with sending sharp pieces of wood into the actors or audience. Harder than you might think.

I learned that Corinne Barrett hanged herself in her parents' upstairs bedroom. It must have been right after we spoke that night in her kitchen. I couldn't work up much sympathy for her.

I've been working at this ski resort as a laborer for two months now. I like it up here where the air is clean and you see whole families of whitetail deer, lynx, and bobcat. This morning before dawn, I took a walk up Jagger's Slope above the cabin I'm renting from the resort and saw bald eagles mate and a Cooper's Hawk nesting in an alder. The other day, a Ridgway osprey was tearing a rainbow trout apart on the branch of a white pine and dropped half of it. I've seen the Aurora Borealis dip this far down after a solar burst; hundreds of white pinpricks of stars shimmered behind the gauzy, green lace.

I prefer the mountains. Flat land makes me nervous. My stutter is less obvious. I'm a combination caretaker, landscaper, gondola mechanic, and night-time security guard. Next season, the boss tells me he'll let me learn how to operate the ski lift, and if the resort expands to include X-games in summer, I'll have a year-round job. I don't mind watching people enjoy themselves. I've always been an outsider. It takes years to get to know who you are, the real person in there, I mean, which is a discovery I ought to have made a long time ago, I suppose. Better late than never, right?

I'm not unhappy with life right now. I still have bad dreams of Angelo and his bloody head. Someday I'll turn myself in, confess. I'll take my chances on the double murder in New Zenith. I'll need a good lawyer and that will cost money. I've got plenty of scars to show for it and these will go with me into my grave.

I'm not looking for more trouble. Why would I do that? It can come looking for you or me as easily as breathing air.

-END-

Thank you for reading.
Please review this book. Reviews
help others find Absolutely Amazing eBooks and
inspire us to keep providing these marvelous tales.
If you would like to be put on our email list
to receive updates on new releases,
contests, and promotions, please go to
AbsolutelyAmazingEbooks.com and sign up.

About the Author

Robb White lives in Northeastern Ohio. Many of his stories and novels feature private investigator Thomas Haftmann: *Haftmann's Rules* (2011), *Saraband for a Runaway* (2013), *Nocturne for Madness* (2015), and *Doggerel for Dead Whores* (New Pulp, 2019). *Thomas Haftmann, Private Eye* (2017) is a collection of 15 stories. In 2019, White was nominated for a Derringer. A crime novel, *The Russian Heist*, won *Thriller Magazine's* Best Novel of 2019 award, and a short story, "Inside Man," was selected for inclusion in *Best American Mystery Stories 2019*. A collection of his revenge stories was selected by the Independent Fiction Alliance as a Truly Best Independent Book of 2022.

2nd Place Winner, Whodunit competition, for novella *Burning Girl*, 2020.

For sales, editorial information, subsidiary rights information
or a catalog, please write or phone or e-mail
New Pulp Press
Manhanset House
Shelter Island Hts., New York 11965-0342, US
Tel: 212-427-7139
www.NewPulpPress.com
bricktower@aol.com
www.IngramContent.com